D1528796

Only the Brave

**Far From Home: A Scottish Time-Travel Romance, Volume
5**

Rebecca Ruger

Published by Rebecca Ruger, 2023.

This is a work of fiction.
Names, character, places, and incidents
are either a product of the author's imagination
or are used fictitiously, and any resemblance to actual persons,
living or dead, events, or locales is entirely coincidental.
Some creative license may have been taken with exact dates
and locations to better serve the plot and pacing of the novel.

ISBN: 9798391266068
Only the Brave
All Rights Reserved.
Copyright © 2023 Rebecca Ruger

Written by Rebecca Ruger

Chapter One

Megan West clomped gracelessly out of the Lodge of the Loch inn nestled between the glistening loch and the mountains beyond it. Munros, the mountains were called here, or some of them at least. There had been fifteen minutes of her life she wasn't getting back, listening to that woman on the tour bus yesterday go on and on about Munros, Donalds, and Corbetts, how hills were categorized here, based on their height.

"I'm here for the romantic castle ruins and with some vague hope to meet a rugged Highland sheep farmer who might fancy himself a nice American wife," Megan had said drolly to the self-professed *peak bagger*. "I only purchased a one-way ticket."

Though the woman had been from the States as well, she hadn't picked up on Megan's intentional sarcasm, which Megan had hoped would convey her disinterest in the subject matter, but which the woman chose to ignore because she knew everything and liked to hear herself talk.

Outside the white-washed inn, an erstwhile hunting lodge originally built almost two centuries ago, Megan helped herself to one of the rainbow of bicycles lined up as neat as bikes could be in a metal rack, which were free for guests' use. She chose the beachy blue bike over the pale lavender, mint green, and salmon colored ones and then wrestled to extract it, the bikes quartered so closely that the handle bars were tangled with others on either side of it.

With an impatient twisting of her lips, she finally yanked it free and hopped on, riding away from the quaintly situated hotel lodge, recalling the sixty-ish woman at the desk, Janet McLaren, cautioning her, "Be mindful now of the uneven roadsides. And watch, will ye, for the buses that run along the causeway."

She had a bike of her own at home, almost exactly the same as this one; hers was, she recalled specifically, *ocean turquoise*, and had been billed as a single-gear beach cruiser bike. That had intrigued her. Aside from the pretty color, she'd decided that *cruiser* sounded decidedly laid-back and that was the bike for her. She didn't intend to *bag* anything on her bike, only wanted a cost-efficient, low maintenance means of transportation around her hometown of Des Plaines, Il, just north of Chicago, home of the very first McDonald's restaurant. Mostly, the bike was utilitarian—she had no car and used it to get to and from work for nine months out of the year—though she did enjoy more scenic rides on her days off, most often along the Des Plaines river trail, which went sometimes through a forest of oaks and hickory with the meandering namesake river alongside for company.

Megan had barely pedaled out of the parking lot and she was huffing and puffing already, though she could partly blame this on pure frustration.

Her first trip overseas was so far just one disappointment and annoyance after another. And it was only Day Three. Day One had begun with her luggage going to the airport in Dublin—not even in the same country! She'd been advised with great kindness but little sympathy that she'd be lucky to see any of it during her two week stay. An hour later at the car rental place, the man behind the counter spent ten minutes detailing their contract before lifting his brows, holding up the keys, and asking which one of them—Megan or her travel buddy, Jasmine—would be driving the manual transmission, reminding them that everything was reverse in the UK, gears, pedals and which side of the road to drive on. After exchanging a stupefied glance with Jasmine—whose sole job had been to book the rental car—they had asked for an automatic transmission car. They were more than twice the cost, but it didn't matter; they had none available.

Day Two saw Megan and her travel buddy on the bus with the *peak bagger* during a wild oceanic storm so severe that nothing could be seen from the windows with the rain pelting them so hard—so much for taking in the majestic views. Simply walking out from the bus and into the lodge here near Loch Duich in Dornie had soaked them through several layers to the skin and chilled them to the bone. The fabulous dinner in the hotel restaurant had restored them somewhat and had given Megan so much hope for the rest of the trip.

Day Three—today—saw her escaping the inn on bicycle, needing a break from every one of the five thousand, four-hundred and thirty-nine crazy annoying habits and ticks of Jasmine that might see murder committed in the Highlands.

Megan gritted her teeth, wondering how she could have not known or seen any trace of Jasmine's true character, how annoying she could be. They worked together and had now for two years, having met during their orientation in the ER, the first job for both of them immediately out of nursing school and having passed the NCLEX exam to be licensed as RNs.

Megan had gravitated toward Jasmine not because of the flaming red hair and many tattoos, though she'd been intrigued by both, but because of her name. Jasmine Lane. On their first break, Megan had sought her out, introducing herself and then teasing Jasmine that she had a great stripper name if the nursing gig didn't work out.

Only weeks younger than Megan's twenty-four years, Jasmine had stared cold-stone at Megan and informed her that she had stripped her way through college to pay the bills, but that her name was real, not invented for that gig of several years. Megan's profuse apologies had been waved off with no hard feelings. The awkward beginning had proved no hindrance. Megan and Jasmine gelled instantly, quickly developing a great working relationship and what Megan had thought was a solid friendship.

She'd looked so good on paper, Megan thought as she pedaled angrily along the black paved road. Jasmine laughed at all of Megan's jokes, was a hard worker, willing to put in extra time as needed—the hospital was always short-staffed—and truly cared about her patients. At no time, either at work or the dozen times she'd been out with Jasmine to pubs and clubs after hours had Jasmine given any hint that she reveled in drama, or that she actually preferred sulking, whining, and complaining to finding anything of the positive. *Looked good on paper* referred to Megan's utter certainty that Jasmine would be such a great travel companion. In reality, here and now in Scotland, Jasmine spent more time complaining about Megan's lost luggage than Megan herself did. After the car rental fiasco—they had Uber-ed and taxied everywhere since their arrival in lieu of continuing their fruitless efforts to find any rental company with automatic cars in stock—Jasmine had sat in the Uber with her purse crunched up to her chest, arms crossed tightly, bitching the whole time that the website should have made it clear that it defaulted to stick shift as rentals.

After a while, Megan had simply stared slack-jawed at her, feeling as if she were seeing Jasmine for the first time. Megan didn't want to moan and cry about what had gone wrong; she wanted to make the best of their days here. Shit happened. They needed to move on.

But then today, Jasmine was fighting with her boyfriend over the phone and refused to leave the hotel, where the wi-fi signal was good, afraid she might miss his next call, which she was sure would come with him meaning to apologize.

Megan was simply flabbergasted. Seriously?

"Yes, seriously," Jasmine had replied when Megan had posed that question half an hour ago. "He knows he's wrong. And he will be calling. I'm not leaving this room until he does." She'd flipped her long, poker straight hair over her shoulder and had given Megan an *mm-hmm* look, her gloating satisfaction decidedly premature. "I want to hear him grovel."

Megan wasn't sure if she wanted to strangle Kyle—Dr. Kyle O'Donnell—Jasmine's long-time, on-again-off-again boyfriend and frequent verbal sparring partner or if she wanted to wrap her hand around Jasmine's neck, for seeming to go out of her way at this point to piss off Megan.

Relax, she told herself. There are still ten more days. Technically, she didn't need Jasmine to enjoy her vacation. Having grown up an orphan, shuffled from one foster family to the next over a span of eleven years, she was accustomed to solitude, to surviving by herself and making her own good time.

Lost in her own thoughts, Megan was less careful about the terrain, swerving a bit off the paved road into the gravel and storm-made mud. She wobbled and winced but corrected her path quickly enough, gaining again the smooth blacktop.

The bike was similar in style to hers back at home, but this one, despite the possibility that it might not actually be retro, but truly vintage, was sturdier than hers, but damn this road near their inn was a never-ending winding slope, constantly climbing. Though a quick glance over her shoulder showed the inn yet in sight, though distant, as in she hadn't gone that far, her legs ached already, and she was tempted to turn around.

But she glanced around, actually seeing the scenery for the first time. She was sorry that she'd just ridden along the loch for at least half a mile and hadn't spent a moment on that view. She paused now to do so, planting her feet on the ground, stopped at the stone wall on the side of the road, and dropped her shoulders in awe of the view. Even under an overcast sky, the loch's water shimmered and sparkled. Beyond, as in any direction, were more mountains—munros maybe—rich in the green of summer. The number and size of the mountains all around made her feel terribly small and insignificant but the beauty was not lost on her.

She moved on then and when the road veered right around the loch, Megan veered left, onto what looked like the bike trail, which the innkeeper had also mentioned. This snaked yet uphill, but the incline was gradual enough and the path smooth enough that she continued on. She passed a couple of walkers and a couple riding bikes in the opposite direction, nodding a greeting, assuming their pastel colored bicycles suggested they were staying at the same inn.

The trail soon leveled off and then crept slowly downhill, giving her legs a break. In the next minute, she passed a group of horseback riders, fairly confident that they were tourists as well, as implied by their very un-horseman-like gear—sneakers and fashion boots rather than riding boots—and the look of frozen terror on the face of one middle-aged woman as she white-knuckled the reins. The trail here was particularly narrow and

Megan went by them slowly and quietly, not meaning to incite the horses to match the pace of her relatively faster speed.

Accustomed to riding for long stretches and as enchanted by the wooded areas through which she rode as she was by the open parts of the path and its breathtaking scenery as it twisted through the valleys, Megan rode for quite a while. Even when she stumbled upon pavement and followed that for another few miles, the views were splendid no matter which way she faced. The terrain and the gorgeous scenery certainly invigorated her and she was loath to give up this peace to return to the lodge and Jasmine's snit. She was out in the middle of nowhere in a foreign country, not a soul around for miles now, and yet she felt oddly safe. In her familiar surroundings at home, so close to crime-ridden Chicago, Megan spent plenty of time on her bike looking over her shoulder. Just in case.

Even when there was a faint crackle in the air, what sounded like a high-pitched thunder and one spark of strange lightning—strange because it rather looked like a ball and not a streak—she wasn't concerned. She was fascinated.

And then she crested a small rise and coasted down the narrow road and spied the ruins of an ancient broch up ahead, which she'd read about in one of the numerous brochures collected during her few days of travel. Either Dun Troddan or Dun Telve, she decided this must be.

It was situated on the north side of the road, partway up the hill, a big gray ruin of a structure, some of the stones covered in green moss, the backside being more intact than the front, and having no roof over any of it. It was rather remarkable against the backdrop of the rolling gray clouds. On the hill in the forefront, just inside a haphazard wired fence, sheep lay all about the grass on the slope.

Megan applied the brakes and stopped just at the wooden gate—closed and locked with only an oversized hook-and-eye latch—and wondered if that path worn into the grass inside the gate suggested people did, or were welcome to, traipse around by themselves. A sign on the gate identified the ruin as Dun Troddan, an historic site, but there was no warning about trespassing.

On the south side of the road, directly across and sitting only a few feet off the actual road, was a long structure of old stone with a newer metal roof. It looked like a barn—maybe for those sheep—but she didn't see any house or person around to ask if she could go up the hill to the broch.

With one more glance around to be sure there was no one of whom she might ask permission, Megan unlocked the gate and walked the bike through, closing the gate behind her so that no sheep went missing because of her. She spared those docile hoofed animals one more glance, noting that though they all looked lazily at ease, to a man—er, sheep—they were all staring at the stone round house ruins.

Dismissing this as curious but not alarming, she nudged her bike along the very thin rutted path up the hill and lowered it to its side near the front of the ruins. The grass was tall up here and all around the front part of the structure where less than half of the wall remained. Megan walked around the back of it, around the aged but less ruined two story wall. Here she could walk closer to the remains and lifted her hand to run her fingers along the stone, imagining the hands that might have built this, possibly two thousand years ago according to the literature she'd read, and if the archaeologists had it right.

"Holly?"

Megan gasped, whirling around at the sound of the deep voice, decidedly male and close and clearly distressed. She saw nothing but grass and low shrubs and those idling sheep dotting the hillside.

"Where are you, lass?" was called next, the voice stronger, maybe a little angry as well. "Holly!"

Assuming the tortured voice belonged to some father searching for his lost daughter, Megan strode quickly around the ancient dwelling, looking for its owner.

Where the wall was lower, more damaged by time and possibly other factors, Megan stepped closer and leaned over the top of it, the stone meeting with her chest. Her eyes widened at the sight of a huge man sitting inside the round house.

He was...well, he was unexpected, certainly being dressed as he was and for appearing a bit woozy sitting on his ass on the ground inside the ruins. He wore a fawn colored shirt that looked as if it were made of linen and hung loosely over broad shoulders. It was made plainly with straight lines and only a little notched vee at the neckline. A plaid throw laid over one of his shoulders, crisscrossing his broad chest, the ends of it trapped inside a thick belt of brown leather. His neck was corded and thick, flesh and tendons moving as he cocked his head from side to side, as if testing his own well-being or steadiness. He had a full head of riotous hair, dark brown, and a bit longish, curling over his ears and the back of his neck.

He gave his head a shake, tossing the hair around and tried to stand.

The process was nearly painful to watch, how slow and unco-ordinated were his efforts. Having now worked in the ER in Des

Plaines for over two years, Megan had seen her share of inebriated and strung out people, but this was...this was different. He wasn't floppy but tightly wound, each movement made with an extreme rigidity that was as confusing as it was concerning.

"Sir?" She called out tentatively, wondering if he'd been here since she rode up to the gate at the bottom of the hill. Honestly, he kind of looked like he just woke up, as if he were groggy and trying to get his bearings. But again, he was so stiff, as if he forced each limb to do what he wanted.

At the sound of her voice, he whipped his head around, but even that seemed sluggish, or as if it cost him by way of dizziness. His eyes focused somewhere left of her, his gaze off the mark by about ten feet. He struck his arms out with his turn, and Megan could see veins popping in his wrist, the sleeve ridden up over his thick forearm. His hand was fisted.

Megan spied a spot further around the broch that had even less wall and where he might have entered—was he a vagrant? A homeless man sleeping here, just waking, maybe disturbed by her coming? She backed up from the wall and walked around to the opening, saying, "Sir?" once more.

He pivoted again, his dark brows creasing and crinkling dramatically.

"Cease!" He commanded, his curt tone and deep voice bringing Megan to an immediate halt. "Show yourself."

She was standing directly in front of him now, not more than twenty feet of space between them. He appeared to be looking directly at her, but he wasn't seeing her. Was he blind? Like, literally blind?

"Go on with you!" He said then, lifting his hand in a threatening manner.

He was frightening, but part of that was his size, being very tall and having a muscular build, with large arms and thighs. And yet Megan was more stunned by the overall look of him than imbued with any terror for his intimidating form and strange dress—she'd never met a man, not in costume for some reason or another, who tucked his pants into his calf-high boots. If this were a much earlier century, and with the sea being so close, she might have guessed him a pirate. Odd clothes aside, he was possibly the most ruggedly handsome man she had ever seen. Tousled hair, stubbled cheeks of golden brown, a flash of white as he bared his teeth with whatever it was that provoked him to wear so severe a face, all put together around lips shaped generously and a jaw of chiseled granite. The eyes that flashed at her but didn't truly see her were remarkably green, extraordinary even in this setting where green was all around, even as they were narrowed to ruthlessness by whatever perturbed him now. He was so...manly, so utterly masculine.

"Sir, are you all right? Should I call—an ambulance? Is it nine-one-one here like in the States?"

Surely Scotland had its own emergency number.

The question only seemed to infuriate him. His mien darkened and he fell—fell straight back onto his butt again, his knees hardly bending at all. A half second later, while Megan watched with her mouth hanging open, he flopped onto his back.

She noticed for the first time what thumped and landed at his side, what he'd held up at her, what she'd not noticed for being so engrossed in his astonishingly gorgeous face—a sword.

A sword?

He groaned.

"Oh, crap—are you okay?" There was an anxiousness in her voice, his odd behavior truly beginning to alarm her. But really— "Holy shit—why...why are you carrying a sword?"

"Cease!" He demanded for a second time. "Give me a bleeding minute, will ye?"

Megan's eyes widened again, her stomach fluttering—very untimely, very inappropriate—at the sound of his voice. If velvet mated with whiskey and their child spoke with a thick Scottish accent, it would sound like this man. *Wow.*

He didn't move for an entire minute then. Megan worried her lower lip and cautiously stepped inside the broch, having to hop down into the depressed interior where he lay. She approached with caution. Despite his lethargy, there was a vigor and vitality about him that warned she should expect that he could spring or pounce without either notice or provocation. She stepped slowly forward and then bent and grabbed at the handle of his sword, pulling it out of his reach along the ground. Geez, the thing was heavy, a very fine replica, though its presence here with this man still made no sense.

When she was out of his reach, she turned and exited the depressed interior, taking the weapon with her. Movement in her periphery caught her eye before she'd put the sword somewhere further away. She faced the interior of the ruins, being once more on the higher ground, and found him still on his back, but with his fabulous green eyes open and staring straight above while his hand patted frantically at the ground—where his sword had been but was no more.

"I'm sorry," she called out to him, her anxiety evident. *What the hell was happening here?* "I took your sword. I—I don't think you're well enough to have this."

The man sat up, exerting great energy to do so, it seemed. He closed his eyes briefly and shook his head. And when he opened his eyes again, his face hardened noticeably, his visage terrifying for how furious he looked.

"You dinna take a man's sword, lass," he growled at her, "unless you mean to eventually be skewered by it."

"Oh—okay," she said. *Okay, freak.* "I'm going to call whatever emergency number they have here." She dug into the pocket of her collared, pink sherpa sweatshirt, withdrawing her phone. She intended to Google first what Scotland's version of 911 was, but her phone did nothing, had no signal. She was able to type in the question, but nothing happened. She didn't even see any hint that the thing was scrolling or working in any way. Her phone was old and small, the icons tiny that she had to squint at them, but she was sure there was at least one bar saying she had reception. With a frequency that bordered on exasperating her phone had a mind of its own, sometimes shutting off or turning on whenever the hell it felt like it.

"Did the witch bring you as well?"

His barked question startled her away from her fruitless search to see that he'd gotten to his feet once more. He was huge, at least six-two or six-three, with impossibly wide and square shoulders. He wasn't olive complected to have been considered swarthy but he was suntanned enough that Megan silently added weathered to his description. What a shame, though, that so gorgeous a guy was nuttier than a fruitcake.

Witch? Bring her? Holy crap. Maybe this guy really was high on something. Sword-wielding tendencies aside, he was clearly unwell. Unhinged, maybe. Megan tucked her phone back into her pocket. The nurse in her wanted to help him, but this was clearly not a safe circumstance, not with him so big and brawny and they being so far out in the middle of nowhere. With that thought in mind, Megan pivoted and flung the sword far and away, well behind the tall, intact wall of the broch.

"What is this, Sidheag?" The man grumbled then. "Bluidy tricks with the mind, you scurvy witch?"

"Sir?" Megan called automatically, instantly wishing she hadn't. She should have quietly slipped away, should return to the inn and send help from there.

This time, he looked directly at her, startling her with the ferocity of his glare. Megan gulped down a breath and held it while he examined her with a curl to his lip that could not be mistaken for anything but displeasure or outright contempt.

His low but inexplicable opinion of her, having looked his fill, seemed to be confirmed when he seethed, "Bugger me."

Her eyes widened.

"I need my sword, lass," he said, his tone implacable, his green eyes penetrating to the point of distraction.

"Yes," she said, her voice wobbling a bit, "but tell me first: are you all right? Or should I call for an ambulance?"

"I'll be right as rain, lass, as soon as my sword is returned."

He certainly sounded much improved, his voice stronger, more annoyed than tortured as it had first been.

"Right," Megan said, knowing she needed to get away from the weirdo, now that he was on his feet and appeared to have complete control of himself. "Okay," she said. "I put it back there, behind that part of the wall," she said, pointing off vaguely to her left.

As soon as he moved, headed straight for her, but likely because she stood at the area where he could exit, where there was no wall, Megan moved as well. As he seemed strangely attached to his sword, more worried about that than his own perplexing condition, Megan turned and grabbed the bike and started running with it, away from the ruins and the man. Having seen one too many horror flicks where a locked door was a major set-back for the prey trying to escape the hunting madman, Megan did not run directly at the gate, but hopped on the bike and rode along the slick grass inside the gate and fence, parallel with the road. She only needed to put distance between herself and him. And while he had lastly appeared less sluggish of movement, she wasn't sure he wasn't capable of sprinting after her.

It was tough riding on the side of the slope but thankfully, the ground leveled off a bit after fifty or so yards and she was able to get going straight and with increased speed.

A nervous glance over her shoulder heightened her panic. The guy was in hot pursuit, having the inexplicable speed of any bad guy giving chase in any action movie she'd ever seen. Megan squealed with panic and pedaled harder. Dread and fright filled her lungs with each terrified intake of breath. Her chest pounded with horror—why was he chasing her!

She chanced quick looks behind her again and again, each time finding that he was gaining on her. She moaned out loud her distress and didn't need to turn anymore to know he was getting even closer; she could hear the clomp of his feet and his ridiculous sword smacking against his leg. The hair on the back of her neck stood at attention and she expected at any second for a big paw to clamp down on her arm.

There was something then to be said for her panic not having exploded, having only feared a hand coming at her. *Only*, as if that weren't terrifying enough. But she'd have shed actual tears, might have expired from heart failure if she'd ever imagined he'd have crashed bodily into her, having launched himself through the air to stop her.

He wrapped her up in his arms as he tackled her off the bike, somehow turning them so that he bore the brunt of the impact when they landed, hard and fast, on the ground. A startled and shocked "oof" escaped her, and she squirmed instantly to be free as soon as they landed. He was having none of it, his weight and strength no match for Megan's five-foot-six, slender frame. She managed to get her hands between them and started beating at his chest. To little effect; it was embarrassingly easy for him to capture her hands and shove them above her head and into the grass.

"Hold!" He growled at her, his voice not so attractive now, but dangerously menacing. "I'll nae strike you."

"But you just tackled me off my bike!" She argued against his assertion, staring up into a pair of green eyes that might be the most gorgeous she'd ever seen if they weren't attached to this monster.

"I could nae let you escape," he said, his chest heaving.

"Escape?" She whimpered and then went perfectly still, closing her eyes. *Oh, my God. How had this happened?* What *was happening?*

"Lass?"

Megan opened her eyes but refused to look into his. Instead, she focused on the veins in his neck, standing out in violent fury, and promptly let out the loudest, most earsplitting scream she could manage. Possibly the long breath she'd inhaled to enable the screech had alerted him of her intent so that he abruptly cut it short by clapping a huge paw over her mouth. Megan tried to twist and turn her face away from the clamp of his hand but once more, his strength proved far superior to hers.

After a moment, when she stopped fighting against him, when their eyes met and held, his enflamed with menace while hers surely exhibited profoundly every ounce of her fright, he growled at her, "Bluidy vixen. I've said I'd nae harm ye. Dinna shriek again or I'll be stuffing your mouth with—dinna scream!"

Megan's eyes widened. Stuffing her mouth with his fist, she'd bet he'd been meaning to threaten her.

"Will you scream?" He asked, lifting one slash of a dark brow, forcing his hand tighter against her mouth.

Left with little choice, knowing she lied—she would scream if she could, if she thought it would help—she shook her head.

"Will you murder me?" She wanted to know as soon as the hand left her face.

And she didn't know him from Adam, and wasn't certain he *wasn't* insane, but he did look briefly as if he were offended by the very question.

"I'll nae kill you. I'll keep my sword sheathed."

"You could snap my neck with your bare hands," she countered, very sure she did not exaggerate. "You could rape me—"

"I'm nae a MacHeth," he clipped, definitely taking offense at that provocation. With stiff, jerky movements, as if he realized how threatening his actions actually were, he rolled off her and stood up, surprising her by reaching down his hand to help her to her feet.

Megan ignored it, sitting up without assistance. "You're...I don't know what you are, but I think you need medical attention." He frowned anew, possibly at the use of *what* instead of *who*. But that was how he struck her—he didn't seem real, or more aptly, he seemed unreal, unearthly. There was something just...not right about him.

"I need to get back to my time," he said next, solidifying her very thoughts.

"What?" She snapped impatiently, governed by fright still. But she waved off her own question and then held up her shaking hands, her palms facing him. She didn't want to know; she just wanted to get away from him. "I don't know what that means. I can't help you, buddy."

"I'm afraid, lass, that you and I have no choice. I will require your aid."

"You can't make me help you." Why was he lumping them together? *You and I*?

"What do you fear most," he asked curtly, terrifying her all over again, "death or violation?"

"You're a monster."

"Choose," he snapped at her.

"Either. Both," she blurted.

"Verra well. Then either or both it shall be if you dinna give me aid."

Megan stood and lifted her chin to him, feeling less vulnerable on her feet, a notion that dwindled by degrees since he still towered above her and for the way his frigid green eyes raked over her, lingering upon her legs, which for some reason increased the ferocity of his severe countenance. "Help you do what?" She asked.

"Get back to my time," he said, finally returning his gaze to hers. "As I've said once already."

"I don't understand. What does that mean—your time?"

He didn't answer but asked instead. "Did you see me arrive?"

"What? No. I just rode up—on my bike, which you've now broken—and you were lying there. But I didn't realize that you were there until you called out. I thought you were injured. But I couldn't get a signal and you...I'm sorry, I can't help you." She took one step backward, overcome by a fresh line of thinking and the terror that came with it. "Please don't kill me." He was a sword-carrying serial killer, she'd just decided, feeling all the color drain from her face. The images of sad and scary posters flashed fleetingly across her brain. They were seen everywhere, all around the Highlands, on every corner, in cafes and shops, at the desk in the small office of the inn where she was staying—American girls, tourists, five of them now missing, here and then gone, not a trace of them ever found. Those five faces, seen endlessly on every news channel and on every social media outlet flittered through her brain. What hypotheses were imagined by surely many people, that those poor girls were dead, stared her in the face.

It was him, she thought. He'd taken them. He'd killed them. He and his stupid sword. Oh, but she should have kept right on going, called for help from somewhere safe.

Graeme took one step forward. "You can, lass," he insisted, referring to her assertion that she couldn't help him. "My apologies, for frightening you. But I fear I've no choice but to insist that you can and you will help me."

"You know what?" She said, crossing her arms over her chest, feigning a bravery she most definitely did not feel. But no, she wasn't going to help him in any way to affect her own kidnapping and death. He would win, surely, for being faster, stronger, filled with evil, but the coward in her didn't want to suffer. Tears gathered in her eyes. "Just kill me now. I'm well aware of all the girls missing from the Highlands over the past few years. You're the one, aren't you? You're a serial killer. You've taken them, have them imprisoned somewhere? Are they all dead now? And I'm next? Well, I won't be shoved into some ventless cellar and used for your sick, sexual gratification—"

"What is this you're bleating about?"

For a serial killer, he had a curious habit of being easily insulted.

"Cora Bennett?" Megan sneered, her eyes wide. "Kayla Forbes? Eloise? Gabrielle...um, Noble, I think her last name was—oh my god, it was you. I can tell by the look on your face."

The evil murderer stepped forward, looming over her. "How do you ken of them?" He asked, his voice containing a nasty drawl of accusation.

"How do *you*?" She returned with renewed anger, shoving her forefinger into his rock hard chest. "I don't know them. I've only heard about them in the news. What did you do to them, you monster?"

"Do I look like I bluidy murder women? For what? What did you squawk about—for carnal pleasure?"

"Well...well, Ted Bundy was pretty handsome, too. So yeah, you kind of do."

"Are you nae of sound mind?"

"Me? Me!" She squealed. "You're the one kidnapping and murdering women, running around dressed like...that." Her shoulders sagged. "But why? Why are you killing them? Please! Get help for whatever is wrong with you. Just stop."

"I did nae kill them. They're alive and well—and quite happily so."

"That's completely believable," she sneered. "Of course they are."

"I vow to you, I have done them no harm."

"Fine. And I promise you, you're going to prison for what you've done."

"You are becoming tiresome," he decided. He circled his hand firmly around her arm. "Take me to your keep. I demand to speak to your laird."

Megan slapped her hand over her mouth but was unable to hide all of her gasp. "Oh, my God." She lowered her hand and pointed her shaking finger at him. "You were screaming for Holly! That's what I heard when I first rode up. Holly Wright? Who's been missing for the last year! Jesus Christ. She got away, didn't she? She escaped and you're chasing her."

She pulled at her arm, but he did not loosen his hold so that she simply slumped to the ground, overwhelmed by the truth as she now believed it. He'd been calling for Holly.

Possibly because he did not want to lower himself to the ground as she had done, he let her arm escape his grasp. Megan flopped onto her back with resignation and stared morosely up at the sky overhead.

Stunned by how chance was their meeting and the role that something so nebulous as Fate would ultimately play in her subsequent death, Megan began to laugh. And soon it became hysterical and then she began to cry harder as well, hiccupping through gasps while tears spilled down her cheeks.

"She got away," she cried. The poor girl Holly, whom he'd been calling, who'd been missing for the last year, had gotten away. *Good for her*, Megan thought, knowing a momentary burst of joy, until fear pushed to the fore and her lip quivered. "And now I'm caught."

"God's bluid, lass, but cease with the caterwauling," commanded the butcher of innocents, sounding more aggrieved than incensed. He did now drop to his haunches beside her, managing to look yet intimidating but somehow less daunting, as if he purposefully tried to relax his expression and that was as un-severe as he could make it, still snarly and perhaps accustomed to...what? A greater fight from his victims? "Your name, lass?" He requested.

"M-Megan," she answered, already picturing it on the next missing poster.

"I am Graeme MacQuillan and I vow to you I mean you nae harm," he promised her. "I did nae lie about those lasses gone; I only met them yesterday and they were quite alive when I was...forced to leave today. Where is the nearest burgh? Settlement?"

She swallowed and answered rather automatically, inspired to agreeability by the genial tone he used. "Okay, let me think. I mean, where I'm staying is the closest, I guess. I mean, I didn't pass anything on my ride here. That's the—I'm staying in Dornie, near the Eilean Donan castle."

"Donnán?" He repeated, giving it a completely different sound and inflection with his thick accent. "The MacKenzie isle?"

"I...I don't know."

"Do you ken Thallane, the MacQuillan stronghold?"

She shook her head, eyeing him dubiously.

"Megan," he began, holding her gaze, "would you be so kind as to escort me to the inn at Dornie?"

"Are you really giving me a choice?" She asked.

"Nae, lass, I'm afraid I'm nae. But I'm offering you peace, getting on to a public inn and would I be wanting to go there if I had nefarious designs on you?"

"I don't know...anything," she said pitifully.

The killer who'd given his name as Graeme MacQuillan rose to his feet again and this time when he extended his hand to her, Megan took it and allowed him to help her to her feet. Quite honestly, she half expected at that moment, he would have made his move—drawn his sword or another weapon, pulled her into a choke hold, clamped a sedative-laced cloth over her mouth and nose.

When he did not, when he actually released her hand, Megan turned and contemplated her broken bicycle.

"Well, that's shot, I guess," she said, turning to face Graeme again, simultaneously taking a step backward. "But since it's rented, I can't leave—what are you doing?" She asked, wincing, backing away from the hand he lifted toward her.

"You have a twig in your hair," he said, still moving his hand forward, but slowly as if to cause no panic. "Leaves, as well."

She told herself to run but for the life of her, mesmerized as she was by how vividly green his eyes actually were and the husky timbre of his seductive voice, either her feet didn't obey, or she'd never truly issued the command.

"You are," she began to say, her voice halting, "you are a bit of a contradiction, brandishing a sword at me and then knocking me off my bike and now very politely plucking leaves from my hair. I don't understand you."

"I'm nae pleased to say it, lass, but that is nae going to improve anytime soon."

Megan considered him, and the very unintimidating way he'd just admitted that, the delivery almost coming with a wince, as if he were sorry he was scaring her. For a brief moment, she wondered if she only wanted to believe him harmless, not a murderer of women, because he was so incredibly handsome.

"That sounds like the first truthful thing you've said to me."

"And yet I have nae lied at all," he said and studied her with his probing gaze before asking, "Which way to Dornic?"

Absently, unnerved by his gaze which suddenly looked less menacing than it did smoldering, Megan pointed over her shoulder.

"Come, lass."

She glanced around, chewing her lip. They were completely alone up here, naught but hills and forests all around. She would have to entertain him and his pretense at innocence at least until they came upon another person or people. She would throw herself in front of an oncoming car if need be, just to get away from him.

"I swear to God," she vowed, lancing him with a mean scowl of her own, "if you are a serial killer and you kill me, I will haunt you mercilessly all the rest of your days."

"Aye, I dinna doubt you will, Megan."

Chapter Two

With his own circumstance presently weighting heavily upon him, Graeme could muster little sympathy for the lass' wheeled horse, which was in much worse shape than before he'd knocked her off it. Still, supposing the vehicle might be likened to a man's actual horse, he did not simply abandon the broken thing, but picked it up, surprised by how light it was, and tossed it over his shoulder. Within ten seconds, he was annoyed already by the many-spoked wheel spinning continuously in front of him and clamped his hand briefly upon it to stop the circling.

He then lifted the same hand to Megan, indicating their direction, that they should walk down the hill and through the gate. She rather stomped ahead of him, clearly meaning to leave him behind. To her chagrin, her shorter strides allowed him to easily keep pace with her without having to exert so much effort.

He still couldn't believe it—wouldn't actually believe it until he was shown proof—but knew a displeasing and mildly disturbing concern that he was no longer in the fourteenth century, that one of the witches who'd come to Thallane had incredibly moved him through time. Even as he'd been told of such happenings by Holly and the wives of the Thain, the Cameron, and the Mac-Clellan, he hadn't believed it possible.

But then at the bottom of the hill and across the road there stood a building that gave him pause. The stone and plaster of the sides was not uncommon but the roof covering it was something Graeme had never seen, being made of a hard substance, painted gray with lines impossibly uniform.

His brain teemed with all that was implausible and improbable. Graeme glanced to his side at the lass with the striking blue eyes and auburn hair, which bounced with liveliness around her shoulders and down her back, in reaction to her very aggressive strides.

Though he had little tolerance for the fretfulness she displayed so eagerly, Graeme decided Megan's apprehension was not misplaced. He recalled very well his first impression of Holly Wright, his cousin's wife—a time-traveler, he now knew, which he imagined he'd just unwittingly become himself. Neither he nor Duncan had been able to put their finger on exactly what had initially raised awareness about Holly, but they'd both agreed something was off about her. Only later, as in two days ago, had they learned the truth about Holly.

That was what had brought Graeme forward in time. Duncan hadn't believed Holly when she'd told him the truth, when it had been discovered that she was not, in fact, Ceri MacHeth, whom Duncan had been contracted to wed. She'd been naught but an unwitting pawn. Duncan had then thought her mad, for inventing incredulous tales of having traveled through time. He'd bade Graeme take her away, out of his sight.

Having suspected, despite the shock of her lies, that Duncan had great feeling for Holly, Graeme had not returned her to the family that had passed her off as a MacHeth, but had brought her to Cora, the wife of Lucas Thain. Graeme had been nagged by some notion that Cora, a compassionate sort who sounded uncannily similar to Holly, their speech decidedly English but then also oddly unfamiliar, might better deal with Holly, or know what might be done for the lass, if indeed she were unwell of mind.

He'd not been prepared for the truth as it had been presented by the fourteenth century husbands of other time-traveling lasses—men he'd known and had fought beside for years! But then their revelations played only a minor role in convincing Graeme of the absurd truth; the advent of witches—actual witches, floating, shimmering fey creatures—had done most of the heavy lifting of compelling him—giving him no choice!—to believe it was real.

Shunned by Duncan, who knew nothing of the absolute and outrageous reality, Holly had begged the witch who'd sent her to the year 1303 to send her back whence she came.

Even now, less than an hour from the event by his reckoning, Graeme wasn't sure if his own interfering—pleading with Holly to stay and give Duncan a chance to know and comprehend—had seen him moved through time instead of Holly, or if the witch, Sidheag, had planned all along to move him and not Holly. He recalled specifically that the witch had stared at him particularly before she'd lifted her hand to enact the magic.

Resigned to the fact that he would have few answers until he did return to his time, Graeme imagined he should presently strive more to put the lass, Megan, at ease. Unless he encountered another worthier soul who might aid him, she was all he had right now to help him navigate this unsettling business. Currently, however, she thought him guilty of murder for reasons no right-minded person would ever understand.

Mayhap he would only require her aid for a short time. He thought he might be better served by hiring out a lad as a scout. The lass was bonny, but her shrieks and tears and theatrics said clearly that she wasn't made sternly enough to weather either the truth as he understood it, or to help him navigate journeying backward through the centuries. He wondered if her beauty might also be a distraction. Despite the confusion of time-traveling, wanting nothing more than to get back to Thallane, from where the witch had moved him, Graeme found himself too often staring at the lass' toned legs in the strange black trews. Whatever the fabric was, he decided it adored her, based on the way it embraced her so fondly. Most distracting.

Move backward through the centuries? He suspected, based solely on Holly's begging the witch to return her to the twenty-first century, that he'd traveled forward to the previously unimaginable far future. But that was only a guess, and so far he had only Megan's strange togs, her tight-fitting trews and her furry tunic, curiously dyed pink, to go by. There was a sign at the gate that had given him pause, which he'd tapped his finger against, finding the shiny painted metal to be oddly precise, smooth and ridiculously thin, shaped so perfectly with rounded corners, unlike anything he'd ever seen before.

She already thought harshly ill of him, so that Graeme believed he hadn't anything to lose by clarifying this now with the lass. "I'm nae daft nae mad, lass," he prefaced, "but I'm a wee turned around in my journey so I'll need to ask ye, what year do I find myself in?"

Having ignored his presence at her side for the last few minutes as they walked along the unerringly smooth black road, which was not only darkened muck or mud but a solid surface, she whipped her face around to him, pinning him with a pair of snappy blue eyes.

"What kind of question is that? It's 2022. Did you hit your head? Is that what made you all woozy and groggy when I found you?" Her eyes widened, showing more of the startling clear blue. "You talked nonsense like this earlier, about needing to get back to your time. Are you injured? Did you fall?"

Graeme heard little of anything that followed her pronouncement of the year. Twenty-twenty-two? More than seven hundred years away from where he lived—when he lived, he corrected internally. Bluidy hell, but would that make it more difficult to return, being so far removed?

To distract her from her present concern—she appeared to be surveying his head and hair quite critically, slowing her pace and tipping her face up to do so—Graeme asked, "Under whose banner do ye live, lass?"

"I don't...what does that mean?"

"Who is your laird?"

"Laird?"

"Sire? Husband? Brother? Who defends ye and yer house?"

"Uh...no one defends me. I...defend myself." She lifted her chin with this proclamation, harkening back to her supposition that he slayed women for sport, advising him she could protect herself.

Of course, she could not. Not against him, if he had evil designs on her. Her black trews begged attention and consideration but no thoughts conjured by her body-hugging trews were evil by any means.

"From where do ye hail?" He asked instead, supposing she did not in fact live at an inn, at which she only mentioned she was staying.

"I'm from the States," she said. "Near Chicago."

Graeme frowned at the unknown place. "England?" He asked, but only a moment later he recalled Holly and Cora and the other time-traveling lasses had mentioned this place, the States.

"Chicago, Illinois," she clarified, frowning sideways at him, measuring her steps so that more distance was put between them. "America?"

"I dinna ken it," he said and then thought to warn her, "Ye canna outrun me, lass, so dinna engage in a flight that will only see us winded and me annoyed and dragging ye onward with my hand clamped on ye."

Her slim shoulders sank in such a way as to suggest defeat, as if she been thinking exactly that and was sorry to know it would be a fruitless endeavor.

"I've said, have I nae, I have no plan to harm ye? I just need some guidance until I get my bearings."

She nodded, keeping her chin low now, her gaze on the ground. Her hands were unseen, tucked into the sides of her furry tunic. She glanced up after a moment, at the long stretch of winding road ahead of them.

"I was trying to think how long I'd been riding before I discovered the ruins," she said. "I'm certain it was more than an hour. And now on foot—since you've ruined the bike—will take us twice as long if not more to reach the inn."

Graeme nudged the vehicle she mentioned, the machine on his shoulder.

"This is a bike?" He asked, repeating the new word carefully.

Another frown answered him before she rolled her eyes. "Yes, it's a bike. Bicycle," she said, mountains of impatience detected in her tone. "What? You've never seen a bike before?"

"I have nae."

"What are you, like a hermit?" She asked. "Or a mountain man who only comes to town once a decade or something?"

"I dinna ken hermit."

"Hermit," she said, "like a loner, someone who lives off the grid."

"Lives off the grid?" He questioned next.

"Are you doing this on purpose? Acting like you were just born yesterday?"

Nae. I was born seven hundred years ago, did not seem like a proper response at this particular moment.

"We would progress quicker on your bike?" He asked next.

"Well, we would have," she said, her head bobbing left and right with her continued or returned annoyance, "if you hadn't crashed into me and it and bent the tire rim there. This is only good now if we plan on going in circles."

She flashed her blue eyes fleetingly over the bike and then up and down Graeme.

"I don't think both of us could ride it, though. You're...pretty...big."

Though the statement intrigued him, Graeme knew he had things of greater import to be mulling on at this moment, not whether he detected awe or dread in her tone as she'd uttered that opinion.

And then, wanting to speed along their trek to this inn, which hopefully would hurry his return home, Graeme brought the bike off his shoulder and considered the front wheel, which had borne the brunt of his assault and was indeed bent to use-lessness. He laid it on the ground and planted his booted feet on either side of the oddly soft but firm outer edge of the wheel and proceeded to stomp upon it until it straightened a wee bit.

Stepping off, Graeme surveyed the results. Good, but not great. One of the curves still had a divot of a dent in it. He lifted that end of the bike so that the wheel was against his chest and used two hands and all his might to push here and pull there, straightening the wheel yet further. The circle was closer to perfectly round.

He might have had her test out the vehicle now but feared she would only ride away from him, which he surely would attempt if he were in her position.

"How does this work?" He asked instead, assuming he would drive the machine but not sure yet where she might fit. The blue leather saddle was shaped peculiarly; there was no way both of them would fit on there.

Megan's mouth gaped as she stared at him, bringing his gaze to her lips, which were formed generously, seductively, apparently no matter what expression she wore.

"Of course," she said, shaking her head. "You didn't know what a bike *was*, so it follows that you wouldn't know how to ride it." She laid her fingers over her lips briefly before saying, "We can't both fit on there. But you seem to run quite well. Maybe you should jog beside me while I ride?"

Said with too much hope, and possibly supposing his lack of knowledge about certain twenty-first century items and places suggested he was an idiot in general, she could not hide her joyous expectation, obviously planning to speed away from him.

"Nae, lass," he said. "If it's usable, we'll use it together."

Once more her shoulders dropped, her disappointment evident. Actually, it looked more like confusion, this confirmed by her next halting statement.

"You...certainly don't act like a serial killer."

"Aye, and for guid reason," he clipped, wearied by this line of accusation. "I am nae."

Holding the bike by the bar that crossed over the top front, Graeme put one leg over the middle of it until he straddled the seat, as she had done when she'd used it.

"Two hands on the handle bars," Megan advised, stepping closer, mayhap warming to the idea of the truth, that he had never seen, touched, or ridden a bike before this day. She pointed down at the metal arms sticking out from the cross bar near his shins. "Those are the pedals. You turn them, er, propel them with your feet, which moves the tires. Obviously."

"Tires?"

"The wheel," she explained, touching that firm but flexible black tube that surrounded each wheel. "Well, the wheel is this whole thing, I guess. But the tire is the black rubber part."

Graeme tested out the mechanics of her instruction, applying his feet to the wee pedals and stamping hard and repeatedly.

"Oh, geez, no!" Megan cried. "Softly, softly. You're not trying to kill it. You're just trying to make them move in a circle." She reached down and put her hand on top of his left boot, forcing it around and forward.

Or she tried to. Graeme held himself stiffly, presented with a view of the top and back of her head, her hair falling riotously around her shoulders, shimmering with golden glints created by the sun trying to make its presence known.

"Okay, forget it," she said when she could barely move his foot. "Either let me show you or we'll just walk the whole way." Her thin and neat brows drew together. "Actually, I'm not walking that whole way and since you don't know how to ride a bike,

I don't trust that you won't crash us again." She slapped lightly at his left hand upon the handle bars. "Let me in," she said.

Graeme opened up his arm, completely shocked when she lifted her leg over the middle bar, essentially standing directly in front of him, only inches between them, and impatiently kicked at his foot on the right pedal.

"I'll pedal," she said. "You just sit there and keep your feet from dragging on the ground." She dug both her feet into the pedals and started turning them, the motion slow as if she faced great resistance. "Hang on," she said when the bike began to roll forward slowly.

Graeme supposed his weight did not make the going easy. Like shoving a bìrlinn off from the banks, he did kick his feet against the ground for several steps until she had the bike in motion.

She was petite enough that he was able to bracket her with his arms and hang onto the cross bar, just inside where her own hands gripped. But then he felt he was interfering with her steering and moved his hands, boldly placing them on the tops of her hips, holding her firmly around her waist.

"Take it easy, buddy," she said over her shoulder.

Graeme loosened his grip and then removed one hand altogether, using it to hold his sword away from the back wheel as they rode.

He didn't look directly in front of him for quite a while, having to grit his teeth to avoid doing so, but tried to keep his attention on the scenery that rolled slowly past them. Aside from the odd black road, and seeing so far no other structures or buildings, the mountains and trees and sky all looked the same as it did in his time.

But he couldn't avoid it forever—no man could, he told himself—and let his gaze finally land on her. On her bottom specifically, which was almost level with his chest for how she stood upon the pedals, her tight cheeks moving up and down with each revolution. Her hips lifted and fell, her bottom moved left and right and up and down, the fabric leaving little to the imagination in regard to her shape. Fairly quickly, Graeme decided he adored those black trews for the way they adored her.

But bluidy hell, what torture was this?

Only their route, which took them off the smooth black tar and onto a narrow and bumpy trail through a thinly wooded vale, removed his attention from her sweet bottom. The rougher path forced him to grip her side tightly again but only for a moment before the trail climbed higher and their progress slowed. Megan rode the wheeled horse well but struggled now to move the vehicle, with Graeme's added weight making the trek more difficult.

He clenched at her hip and dragged his feet. "Cease," he commanded when they hardly moved at all.

"This wouldn't be so hard," she said over her shoulder as she stopped, sounding breathless, "if you weren't so big. The bike is meant for one person." She placed her feet on the ground as well.

"Aye, I understand," he said, and removed his sword and its sheath from his belt. "It will be easier for me to do the work. Here, hold this." He extended his arm around her, handing her his sword.

She wouldn't take it. "I can't ride and hold this—"

"Nae. I'll move the bike. Sit up on the bar," he said, tapping his hand against the two foot crossbar that she used to steer the bike.

"What? I can't. There's no fender over the tire, nowhere to put my feet. We should just walk, I think."

"Megan, turn around and sit on the bar," he instructed patiently.

With movements suggesting a wee annoyance, Megan pulled one leg over the center pipe and dismounted completely. She placed her hands on her hips, exactly where Graeme's had been a moment ago, and frowned at him.

"There's nowhere to put my feet," she argued again. "I'll fall right off."

"I will nae let ye fall, lass. C'mon, get up there." He patted the bar again. "Face me. Put your feet on this support," he suggested, pointing to the bar between his legs on which the saddle was perched.

She looked about to argue yet more but Graeme wouldn't allow it, taking her hand and drawing her near.

"It will work, I vow," he said to her.

"It's...awkward," she argued still, though she allowed herself to be pulled close.

Her cheeks were painted a becoming pink, but Graeme could not say if her most recent labors or her perception of *awkward* were to blame for this. When she hesitated though, her free hand fisting near her chest, Graeme pulled her closer and effortlessly lifted her with hands at her waist again, settling her onto the crossbar.

She went rigid of course, and a fleeting panic saw her clutching at his shoulders before she removed her hands from him and accused, "You are very manhandle-ly."

Ignoring her wee outrage, Graeme persisted with his manhandling, lifting her foot by the ankle to set it against the bar between his legs. Her eyes widened but she did not protest and even set her other foot atop the first.

Next, he handed her his sword again. "Now you can hold this, lass."

She did, clutching it with one arm against her side, leaning over to make sure it didn't touch the ground.

Graeme set his hands on the handles on either side of her and pushed off with his feet. At the first bit of motion, Megan clutched at Graeme's upper arm.

"Aye, hold tight," he said with some intent to relieve her of the noticeable embarrassment she suffered for having touched him so freely and eagerly.

It took several tries to get the hang of it, to get the bike moving as smoothly as was possible on the rough incline, and once Megan was pitched forward nearly off the bar, but he did eventually catch on to the use of the pedals, which worked in conjunction and better when he kept the crossbar stiff and straight. He discovered fairly soon that greater speed meant a smoother ride; it was more difficult to keep the bike straight when moving too slowly.

Within a few minutes, they were rolling along steadily, Graeme quite pleased to have conquered the challenge so swiftly. They crested the incline and rode on level ground for quite a way before they began to sail downhill. Megan's trim frame allowed him to see beyond her, but he did have to keep his head tilted to one side. He was accustomed to constant motion and often hard labor, but after a short while his thighs protested mightily the continuous motion.

"My ass is not liking this," she grumbled with a grimace after one particularly harsh bump.

"Your arse is fine," he contended, allowing her to dissect that statement as she wished. Possibly his inflection, his emphasis on *fine*, might have been what wrought the greater frown from her. "Och, the trail splits," he said, noting two paths ahead.

Megan turned her head, her fingers inadvertently clutching more tightly at his arm as she did so.

"Take the left trail," she said. "Wait, no. The right one."

"'Tis as riding a horse," he observed mildly, "save that man nae beast is forced to do all the work."

She laughed at this, facing him again, showing him a brilliant wide smile and a flash of white teeth.

Jesu, but she was only more lovely when she smiled.

"So maybe now you can imagine how the horse feels," she suggested. "Do you ride? Horses, that is?"

Graeme's brows knitted at this curious query. "Do ye nae?"

"Me? No. I've never ridden a horse."

"Because ye have the bike?"

"Um, no. Because—well, I'm not sure why. I guess the opportunity never presented itself. I don't think I know even one person who owns a horse."

Ah, so she was not as wealthy as her garb would suggest. He couldn't imagine a person laying out more coin for this bike than they would for a good steed.

They rode in silence for a while, Megan sometimes turning her head to watch the trail and the route. On several more occasions, the uneven terrain saw her holding him more securely. Twice, her feet slipped off the shiny pipe between his legs and she pitched forward a bit, compelling Graeme to release his hold on one side of the crossbar and assure her seat was not lost. Once, she nearly dropped his sword and showed him a wince for her near carelessness. Eventually they found again the smooth black tarred road, making their trek less dangerous. Graeme wondered how swiftly a horse could run on so smooth a track; 'twas even better maintained than the ground of the lists.

And while he mostly kept his regard trained on the path ahead of them, Graeme could not help but steal glances at her, more often when she was not facing him. He'd be lying to himself if he pretended he wasn't captivated by how bonny she was. Her cheeks were flushed pink, giving her a charming radiance; her hair was slightly mussed from the ride or the sometimes swift breeze, blowing over her shoulders toward Graeme. She smelled like heaven, some soft and sweet scent that was not cloying but intriguing, making him almost wish she'd fall further off her perch, crashing into him with her fresh scent and supple body.

Graeme gave himself a mental shake, warding off any further deliberation about Megan and what he'd like to do with her. He needed her help, but had neither the time nor inclination to get involved with her in any other capacity.

When she seemed to be facing him for a longer stretch of time while he watched the road beyond her, he did abandon his steady regard briefly to meet her gaze, so easy to do when she sat so close to him. He'd caught her staring, said the heightened blush creeping up her neck and cheeks, the redder flush somehow making her eyes appear even brighter blue.

Megan bit her bottom lip with embarrassment and then rushed out a distracting question.

"Where is it you're trying to get to?" She asked. "And please recall that saying you need to return to your time tells me nothing."

"The MacQuillan stronghold, Thallane." A thought struck him. Like as not, he should first return to where he left Holly—or rather where he'd been dragged away from his cousin's wife. "Unless ye ken a place called Newburn, the Thain fortress."

She shook her head. "But when we reach the inn, the woman at the desk might," she offered hopefully. "Or I'll have service then for my phone and we can Google it." Her brows drew together slightly. "Are you...not from around here that you don't seem to know where you are?"

Dismissing her second sentence, of which he could make neither heads nor tails, Graeme focused on her query.

"I've nae been around these parts for a long while," he said, which wasn't specifically a lie since he hadn't been to Dornie in a few years.

She flipped her head around when they rounded a curve in the road. Graeme didn't know what to make of the white marks running along the road but avoided questioning Megan, thereby increasing her unease or suspicions about him.

"You should stay to one side of the road," Megan said as they rolled down the middle of it.

"Nae," he said but didn't explain that with the jagged cliffs flanking each side of the road, which was depressed into the earth, anyone might appear upon the rises on either side, and he needed to be in the middle, affording him even a split second more for his reaction should they be accosted. The very thought of brigands and thieves and angry clan wars of his own time had him scowling, belatedly, over the fact that Megan had been travelling all this distance without accompaniment, no escort at all, not even a small dagger as far as he knew. Surely, she'd have drawn it on him by now had she any weapon in her possession.

"What manner of lass are ye," he asked, "that ye ride about unaccompanied, and with nae weapon? Ye said ye defend yerself, but how? And what of yer male kin, allowing ye to do so? What goes on in this cent—?" He caught himself, barely, clamping his lips and jaw, peeved with himself for being sloppy with the truth.

Megan's frown returned. Her lips parted as she stared at him, her gaze and countenance stiffening with wariness.

"I—I have my phone," she said, her voice smaller than it had been. "I didn't think I needed to carry—"

Her reply was cut short as Graeme swerved violently to the right, his reaction instinctive, stunned by the white metallic monster heading straight at them at a vicious speed. A loud blaring noise filled the air as the demon machine whipped by. Graeme was wild-eyed, having a darting impression of a man inside the monster, hollering behind a glass window. It had wheels as did the bike—black tires but of a grotesque size.

So startled was he, so frenzied was his reaction that he sent the bike off the road, rumbling bumpily into a ditch. He reached intuitively for Megan as they were both lifted and thrown from the bike but didn't get a good enough hold on her, latching onto only a fistful of her furry tunic before they both went crashing a second time to the ground.

His left side rammed hard against the unforgiving ground, and he grunted upon impact, the force of the blow not so different than being thrown from his horse. Immediately, he scrambled to his knees, detecting only aches but no broken parts, and crawled the few feet to where Megan had landed on her back. Without thinking, he crawled nearly on top of her, his elbows on either side of her shoulders.

"*Jesu*, lass, are ye—?" He stopped, pushing the cloak of hair away from her face, breathing again when he found two stunned but very angry blue eyes upon him. Her eyes appeared now as sapphires, the blue brilliant under a fringe of long curling lashes and knitted brows two shades darker than her auburn hair.

"What the hell is wrong with you?" She cried, and then coughed. Her hand, crunched between them, flopped onto her chest.

Graeme combed his gaze over her entire face, flinching when he found blood at her temple, just at her hair line. "Ah, Christ, I'm sorry, lass," he said. He moved his finger over the dribbling blood, determining 'twas naught but a bad scrape, the skin abraded but not deeply enough to require attention. Still, he was responsible and felt awful to have caused any damage to her pristine skin.

Megan shoved brusquely at his hand, possibly angrier at him for being thrown again from the bike than she was terrorized by the speeding demon machine. Reluctantly, Graeme rolled off her and to his feet. Once more, she ignored the hand he extended, rising as well with snappy movements.

He surveyed the roadside brush and the road in both directions, but perceived no further danger.

"Why do you keep—why did you do that?" She bit out at him, making a show of brushing off her tunic and trews with jerky motions.

"I saw the..." he began, looking back out at the smooth pavement, where no trace of the rolling monster remained. "What was that?"

"What was what?" Megan asked tersely. "The car? Okay, Graeme, no offense but you're really starting to scare me. Or frighten me more, I guess is more apt. Please tell me you know what a car is."

There was no way he could lie to her. He could not quickly enough erase the confusion and alarm from his mien to convince her. *Car*—whatever it was—was too easy, too clean a word to describe that...that monstrosity that had just roared by them. His chest heaved with a wee fright, such as he'd not known since he was a lad. He stared at Megan, unable to verbalize so rare an occurrence: fear.

"Graeme?" She stepped closer, lifting her hand, her own annoyance forgotten. "Are you all right? You look as if...Christ, you're as white as a ghost. Please tell me what's going on."

Graeme focused on Megan. Megan, who was unafraid of the car, was more worried about his reaction. She was a tender heart, he decided, so easily swayed from terror and confusion by her own compassion, presently her concern for him.

"Graeme?" She laid her hand on his forearm and smiled consolingly. "It's okay."

He did need her help. If she didn't believe or couldn't comprehend, he would simply move on to someone who could. For some reason though, he had an inkling he could and must trust Megan with the improbable truth.

"We dinna have anything like that where I come from," he said purposefully.

"Geez, where *do* you come from?"

"Nae *where*, lass, but *when*." At her unfathomable but unmoving expression, he said, "I come from the year of our Lord, thirteen hundred and three."

Chapter Three

Megan stared blankly at him. The part of her that understood his words waited for him to smile, to reveal—confirm—he was joking.

Graeme MacQuillan did not smile.

But still—obviously—he was joking. He must be.

Megan burst out laughing. "You looked so serious when you said that," she said. "But I guess that would explain why—or how—you don't know what a bike or car is...or...or why you're dressed like that and are carrying a sword." Her smile faded and his, the one that should have come to finally give it up that he was kidding, never came. But no, that was—well, that was simply not possible. She laughed again, more nervously now. "Seriously, though. Where are you from?"

"I've just said," he answered evenly. "I ken it's hard to comprehend—or, in Cora Bennett's words, *hard to wrap your brain around.*"

"That's not funny," she said, disliking his form of humor immensely. "That poor girl is missing, probably dead, and you're using her to further a joke? That's...that's pretty low."

"I dinna jest, lass," he said, seeming almost sad to reveal this, what he pretended was the truth. "They're nae dead, nae Cora or Holly, and nae Kayla or Eloise or Gabby. They're alive and well. Holly is wed to my kinsman, Duncan—"

"Stop," she cried, childishly covering her ears. "Enough. You've had your fun, weirdo." She bent and grabbed the handle bars, bringing the bike to a standing position, and faced Graeme MacQuillan—obviously a seriously deranged person—and flashed an unamused glare at him. "Have a nice life," she said and started walking away, pushing the bike along with her. She struggled up from the small ditch at the side of the road, having to dig her feet in and push off hard until a larger, stronger hand clamped down on the middle of the handle bars and maneuvered the bike with ease up onto the pavement. "Stop! Leave it," Megan yelled at him, scrambling to catch up to him, slapping at his hand when she did. "I don't know what your game is, but it's been played—wasn't fun and now it's done." With her hand once more on the bike, she pointed her other hand over her shoulder, toward the next tight curve in the road. "The inn is right there and that's where we part company. Likely, they would hear me scream if you thought to try anything now." She pointed sharply at him. "And don't think I won't call the police on you if you hang around there—"

"Megan, if ye would—"

"I will not," she assured him testily, marching away from him, meaning to get back on the bike. "I'm done. My first trip to Scotland already sucked. Amazingly, you've managed to make it worse. So thanks for that. Good day." She climbed onto the seat.

Graeme jogged ahead of her and stopped what little progress she'd made along the side of the road, standing with the front tire between his huge thighs and gripping the handlebars. His left hand landed on the edge of hers.

"I dinna mean to alarm ye with daft tales of rubbish, lass," he said tightly. "I had the same reaction as ye—a scoffing disbelief. I ken it's impossible, but it remains true. Those lasses, they're alive—happy, I vow to ye. But I need to get back and I need ye to—"

"I can't help you," she argued. "I told you that." Megan tried to shake him off, tried to propel the bike forward against the size and strength of him, fruitlessly, which was not unexpected. "Let go," she growled through her teeth, more annoyed now than fearful.

He sighed, his broad chest expanding with his own misplaced frustration but did release the bike, his big hands sliding away from the handle bars as he stepped back.

Megan darted a glance at him, deciding his disappointment was well-played. He certainly looked it; his frown subsided, resignation overtaking his handsome features. A part of her did feel bad for denying him, even as she knew she shouldn't since he was clearly unhinged. "I'm sorry," she said. "Maybe...I don't know. Maybe you need to check into a hospital."

He nodded. "Aye, I'll do that." And he backed away a bit more.

Wanting one more look at the ridiculously handsome nutjob, taking a moment to memorize the exact shade of his magnetic light green eyes, Megan rolled the bike slowly forward, but kept her gaze trained on him.

His eyes truly were a remarkable shade of green, light with flecks of darker brown in the centers, though not enough to call them hazel. Fine lines splayed away from the outside corners of his eyes, the creases untouched by the sun. Two thicker lines rose away from the inside of his brows, up into his forehead, born of those scowls which she had already met. His face was divided into light and dark. The bare light of a hazy sun shone on his left side, giving a brightness to the nearly black and silver stubble and the beautiful texture of his rugged skin. The right side of him was cast in shadows, the hollow of his sharp cheekbone pronounced by a darker shadow, his right eye blurred by shade.

Megan's study of Graeme sharpened to alarm once more as all the color drained from his rugged face as he stared beyond her. Her own awareness heightened, Megan glanced behind her to see another little sedan speeding around the bend. What was his thing with cars?

She turned back around just as Graeme crashed into her again. This time he didn't topple her off the bike, but wrapped both his arms around her while she still straddled the bike. He twisted them in such a way that his back faced the oncoming vehicle. Megan wasn't overwhelmed with as much terror as confusion, able to see little, her face buried against his chest. His arms were powerful, his hold tight but not crushing, not entirely unpleasant except that it was so startling, how he'd pounced on her. She pushed against his chest as the car whizzed by them.

And that's when she felt it, the dangerously fast beat of his heart and the heat of him, as if he were suddenly awash in fear. Graeme MacQuillan? Afraid?

Recalling the way he'd blanched a moment ago, remembering his odd and overdone reaction to the first car they'd seen, Megan was tempted to believe him—at least the part that claimed he'd never seen a car before today.

"It's gone," she said against his chest, meaning to assure him, the caretaker in her at work. "All gone." She lowered her hands between them and wrapped them around his lean waist, patting lightly at his back. "It's gone."

Slowly, stiffly, Graeme released her, pushing himself backward. He appeared modestly sheepish for his overreaction, maybe for having exhibited fear when she had not. He was large and virile and very masculine, was probably used to being in control of himself, possibly encountered little if anything that frightened him.

"Why do they thunder as they do with such menace but then only pass right by?" He asked, staring at the road, only his profile visible to her, while he ran a hand over the back of his neck.

Megan opened and closed her mouth twice, trying to understand what he was asking. "Because they are only trying to get from Point A to Point B," she said finally. "They're not out to get us—not that you can't be hit by a car," she clarified quickly. "But that would be an accident...unless of course you have really evil enemies."

"Every man has enemies, lass," he stated. "Mine dinna happen to have cars."

She hadn't moved since he'd released her, remained as she'd been only with her hands returned to the handle bars.

"Graeme?"

His shoulders rose and fell with the big breath he'd inhaled and exhaled before he turned and faced her. He was no more afraid, but what she perceived as his embarrassment for having been so was still evident. He faced her but did not meet her eye.

"Are you hungry?" She asked. She didn't know what possessed her, but then she had no sense that she wanted to rescind the question or withhold the inevitable follow-up invitation. Frankly, she didn't know what to make of him. Outside of his masculinity and beauty, he fit into no category or type of man that she knew. And yet she believed, somehow, despite their short and unsettling acquaintance where he'd twice tackled her to the ground, that she was in no danger.

He met her gaze now, displaying what she imagined was some hope that she believed him and would help him—which was not the case, certainly.

"Aye, I've a hunger-rot," he acknowledged.

Regardless of everything that was wrong and awful and unfixable about him and their meeting, Megan smiled at this. "A hunger-rot. Yes, me too. Would you like to have supper at the inn with me?"

He patted his linen shirt near the left side of his waist before answering. "Aye, I would."

Megan nodded, her smile suddenly less genuine, an instant remorse tingling inside her. How would she explain him to Jasmine? How would he behave in a public place? Clearing her throat, she stepped off the bike again and walked it up the road. "It's not far now," she said, not sure she could endure another ride on the handlebars with the odd stranger who professed to be from the fourteenth century. She hadn't hated it, the ride, but she certainly hadn't loved it. Too close, too chummy a circumstance, one she'd rather not repeat, having struggled so hard to keep from gawking at him, having not missed his frequent probing examinations of her. "I might suggest leaving the sword outside when we go inside the inn," she said as he fell into step beside her. They kept to the side of the road and Megan did not know what to make of him when he purposefully stepped around her to walk on her left side, between her and any oncoming car. Despite the fear he'd been unable to hide of automobiles, he was trying to protect her.

"A hostile territory, then?" He supposed. "All weapons left outside?"

"Um, well, I'm not sure about that," she said, striving again to understand all the things he *didn't* understand, not to mention the why or how of that. "It's just that your sword looks authentic, and people might frown upon dining next to a man of your stature, wielding a broadsword in the inn's restaurant." She gave a transitory thought to wonder if he was laughing inside at her, for every time she'd explained something to him that obviously he should know—bikes, cars, proper sword etiquette. She wouldn't be surprised if he was simply harassing her with his caveman bit, if it was all just one big prank, even as she still wasn't sure anyone could have successfully faked the terror in his gaze at the sight of the car coming round the bend moments ago.

"I will nae relinquish my sword, lass," he vowed. "Ye did nae give a surname, lass. Who are your kin?"

Though she was pretty certain he'd changed the subject because he had no intention of giving up his sword or even arguing about it—clearly, that wasn't debatable, but maybe the no-nonsense woman, Janet McLaren, behind the small desk of the family run business would have better luck divesting him of what Megan was sure was only an unusual affectation—she answered his question anyway.

"Well, I have no family here," she said. Here, or anywhere, she thought. "I'm from the States, as I mentioned, and just vacationing here."

"What is that, va-ca-tion-ing?" He asked, repeating the word as if he'd never heard it before.

Oh, but this was the UK. "I'm on holiday," she said instead. "And my surname is West."

"'Tis a direction," was his response to this.

"Yes, but it's also a last name."

They walked on in silence then for the next few hundred yards, Megan not unaware of his constant head-swiveling or the way his right hand sat at the ready upon the handle of his sword, as if he would—was accustomed to—unsheathing the thing when any perceived danger loomed.

The road was narrow—relatively, considering her American standards—and fringed on either side by jagged low cliffs topped with lush greenery and a variety of trees, all equally green in the height of summer. The cliffs lowered gradually as they walked on and soon the loch and the driveway of the Lodge of the Loch came into view on their right.

The inn was as unimpressive on the outside as it was cozy and charming on the inside. The exterior was oddly shaped, the roof of the sprawling, two story, white clapboard building not having a peak but rather being inverted, its profile looking like a V. There was a large barn-type structure very close to the hotel, its blue paint weather beaten, chipped and peeling. The parking lot was wide and spacious, but sloped far greater than the road and was more gravel than pavement. A large dumpster sat at one end of the driveway, suggesting that work was being done on the place though Megan had seen no evidence of this. Megan counted six cars in the parking lot and groaned inwardly when she spied Jasmine pacing back and forth in front of the entrance near the small, covered porch.

"This is where I'm staying," she said to Graeme as they turned into the yard of the inn.

His current frown—he seemed to have few other facial expressions—appeared to be one of confusion as he surveyed the entire property, particularly the cars parked there so benignly. As she removed her gaze from Graeme, Jasmine spotted her, her eyes and mouth opening wide. She raced forward to meet them before they'd gotten too far into the driveway.

"Oh, my God, Megan!" She shouted when she was yet twenty feet away. "Where have you been? You've been gone for hours!" She smacked the back of her hand lightly against Megan's shoulder when she reached her. "You scared the shit out of me!"

"Sorry about that. I um, had a little trouble with the bike," she pointed to the bike, with its not perfectly round tire and which still carried clumps of dirt about several areas of the frame, while grass and more dirt clung to some of the spokes. Did Kyle call?" She asked, in an effort to distract her.

"No," Jasmine whined, pursing her lips. "But he will. And I'm going to give him hell when he—Megan, who is this guy?"

"Oh, sorry," she murmured, turning toward Graeme, who was staring rather ferociously at Jasmine, particularly at her dyed red, pony-tailed hair and the sleeve of tattoos, visible since she was wearing only a tank top with her joggers. "This is Graeme MacQuillan. He ah...he helped me with the bike. Graeme, this is my friend, Jasmine." He inclined his head in acknowledgement and narrowed his eyes as he exposed Jasmine to one of his meticulous perusals. To Jasmine, Megan said, "I thought I'd repay him by having him join us for dinner. I hope you don't mind—or are you not going down to the restaurant but still waiting for Kyle to call?"

Jasmine, whom Megan sometimes believed thought herself irresistible, treated Graeme to a very thorough and very unsubtle perusal of her own, looking him slowly up and down.

"Yeah, I don't think I want to miss this, so yes, I'll be dining with you." She tilted her head and gave Graeme her best smile, which was quite stunning—Jasmine *was* gorgeous—but it seemed to have little effect on Graeme.

Megan chewed her lip, knowing some worry about some of the strange things Graeme said, or questions he asked, hoping he said or asked nothing too bizarre in front of Jasmine. Too late now though, the idea of dinner looming, seeming now not one of her better ideas, having invited Graeme.

She rolled the bike further to where the rack awaited its return, knowing she would have to confess the several mishaps with it to the woman behind the desk, as she was the owner of the hotel lodge—or rather the matron, as she'd introduced herself. The front door opened and Megan whipped her head around, for some reason worried that Janet McLaren had spied the nearly ruined bike from the front window and had come to give her grief. But it was only four guys, obviously guests, exiting, possibly on their way out for the night. Her worry abated, Megan marched on, tucking the bike into the rack.

"I need to wash up a bit," she said, though she didn't think she would have time for a shower, or rather she wasn't sure she could or should leave Graeme alone that long. She was about to ask Jasmine to keep him company out here, but then supposed it might be considered rude not to invite him in to use the bathroom. "Do you need to use the facilities?" She asked, which effectively pulled his snarled gaze away from those four guys who were now getting into a four door sedan. At Graeme's blank look, she decided for him. "This way," she said, inviting him inside with a wave of her hand.

"You go on up," Jasmine said, walking along with them. "You and your...friend. I'll stop at the desk and inform them we'll be three for dinner, not two."

"Thank you," Megan said and then addressed Graeme again. "You and I can head straight upstairs." And hopefully no one would remark upon the strangely dressed man carrying a sword. There was less chance, she suspected, that his presence would go completely unnoticed. Graeme MacQuillan would turn heads anywhere at any time and not only because of his odd outfit and huge weapon.

The front desk was actually not directly in front, not the first thing a person encountered entering the building but was through a door on the left. The stairs to the second floor were immediately inside the entryway and Megan climbed them straight away, turning only once to make sure Graeme was following. He still wore that puzzled scowl of his, his gaze darting all around the foyer and possibly into that front office where Jasmine had gone, the door always open. Megan continued to climb, guessing she didn't have to worry about him staring at her ass as she walked ahead of him. Not that he hadn't already had a front row seat while she'd ridden the bike for them.

From inside her cell phone case, she retrieved the key card for the small suite she shared with Jasmine and used that to unlock the door, which she pushed open and then stood near, inviting Graeme to enter. He entered cautiously, she would have said, his green eyes puzzled as they looked at the door's lock and then the interior, his seeming befuddlement only increasing when he paused just inside, where the bathroom door was.

Fearful that Jasmine had left a mess and knowing her own toiletries took up a good portion of the small vanity top, Megan shut the suite's door and stood beside Graeme, peering inside the bathroom as well. Nothing looked drastically or awkwardly out of place; there were no panties or towels strewn about the floor and the toilet showed only clear water.

His expression was so credible as total befuddlement that Megan was momentarily speechless. She stared hard at him, not immune to the effect the bright lights of the bathroom had on his green eyes.

"What...what have ye?" He asked haltingly.

"It's...it's a bathroom," she said, stepping inside the room, whipping back the shower curtain before she went to the sink and turned on the faucet. "A pretty normal one, with all the basic necessities—toilet, shower, sink." She lifted and lowered the toilet seat and then turned and shrugged at him.

Possibly he didn't hear her, being as he was—or appeared—stunned by the running water. He stepped inside and closed in on the vanity and sink, his scowl sharpening to a fierce mien of deep suspicion. His hand tightened around the hilt of his sword.

In an effort to lessen his inexplicable unease, Megan stood next to him at the sink and ran her hand back and forth under the water.

"Just water," she said. "A little too hot." She moved the faucet handle to the right and tested it again. Better.

She glanced up at Graeme, finding his intense scrutiny occupied by the mirror now, a small two-by-three-ish rustically framed thing. His gaze was on her in the mirror, his astonishment both hard to ignore and more difficult to comprehend.

She inspected their reflections, and wondered if he were actually taller than her earlier estimate of six-two or six-three. She was five foot six, maybe half an inch more in her running shoes, and he appeared more than half a foot taller than her. And while all of her fit in the mirror from her vantage point, only half of him did, his impossibly wide shoulders and the drape of his plaid blanket unable to be seen in full from this view.

While he gaped at her—or the mirror itself—Megan gave greater consideration to his startled countenance, deeming it both baffling but to her mind, an honest reaction, which begged the question: "Have you never seen a bathroom before?"

He shook his head and turned around.

"What is that?" He asked pointing to the shower.

Megan demonstrated the faucet there as well, igniting a rain-fall of water from the overhead shower head. "It's a shower. You know, where you take off your clothes and wash yourself."

"I dinna ken," he said, his voice quiet. "And that?" He point-ed again.

"The toilet," she informed him, apparently the first time any-one ever had.

"What do ye do in there?"

Megan smiled. "Not in, of course, but on. You sit there. Or stand. Guys stand, obviously."

It was not obvious, said his expression. He tilted his head and leaned over it, inspecting it dubiously.

"But what purpose does it serve?"

"Well, you...um, you use it," she said, most unhelpfully. "You ah, relieve yourself." Her cheeks turned thirty shades of pink, she was sure, when he straightened and regarded her. "Take a leak?" She said, wondering if that were familiar to him. "Or more...oth-er....um business. Oh, my God. I can't believe I'm having this con-versation."

She couldn't tell if he still didn't understand what it was used for or if he only doubted the truth as he stared hard again into the clear water in the bowl.

"Okay," Megan said stiffly. "Let's move on." She paused outside the bathroom door. "Sorry. Unless you need to use it?"

He shook his head slowly, as if he weren't quite sure.

"Anyway," Megan said, continuing into the room, which included two queen beds and a little sitting area of a table and two chairs near the windows, which overlooked the loch. "You can—do you mind just hanging out here while I wash my face and change? Jasmine should be back any moment."

"She is a warrior, your friend?" He asked.

"What? Jasmine? Why would you—oh you mean like a bad ass? I guess. She pretends to be, at least." Between her well-toned bare arms, her bright dyed hair, and the tattoos, people probably regularly mistook her for a tough woman, when in reality she was a bit of a pushover and, as learned in the last few days, a whiny one at that.

"The paintings on her mark her as a warrior."

"Um," Megan said and smacked her lips. "No, she's not a warrior like that. She doesn't own a sword if that's what you're thinking." At least, she didn't think she did.

He nodded and then immediately approached the big picture window and stared out there.

Megan would have preferred, and certainly felt as if she needed, a good long power nap but knew that would not be feasible now. Just as she neared the bathroom again, Jasmine reappeared, the sound of the lock mechanism being activated alerting Megan of her return.

Jasmine's eyes nearly overlooked Megan completely, going first beyond her to the broad figure silhouetted at the window. When she did face Megan, she made a face with wide eyes and lifted both her hands, silently asking—if Megan knew Jasmine, and she did—*What the hell? Who is this guy, really?*

Megan mouthed *I'll tell you later* but didn't wait for Jasmine's response before asking plaintively, hating to be such a pain, "Can I borrow yet another outfit for dinner?" The only saving grace of the trip, or more specifically of Jasmine as her travel buddy, was that the woman had packed as if she were moving to Scotland permanently and she and Megan both wore a size six.

"Of course. I was going to wear a sundress," said Jasmine, whose petite curvy frame and shapely legs were the envy of many. "You want one, too?"

"Sure. Thanks. Just toss it in here," Megan said before she entered the bathroom and closed the door. She stood briefly with her back against the door, her hands behind her, closing her eyes and tipping her head back.

What the hell, indeed.

But then she heard Jasmine's muffled voice, surely attempting to engage the decidedly un-chatty Graeme MacQuillan in conversation and Megan pushed herself away from the door, considering it unwise to leave Graeme unattended for long. She washed her face, brushed her teeth, and applied fresh deodorant, having stripped down to her bra and panties. Just as she was running a brush through her hair, Jasmine returned, knocking quietly, saying she had the dress.

Megan only cracked the door, being that she was undressed, and gave a quiet thank you before closing the door just as quickly as she'd pulled it open, not wanting to engage in whispered conversation here and now.

The dress, once donned, proved to fit everywhere but in the chest. Megan was not well endowed by any means. Whereas Jasmine was tiny and curvy and could likely fill out this bodice superbly, Megan was willowy and lean and only wishful of possessing a C cup. The turquoise and red paisley fabric was blousy all around her sparse cleavage. *Ugh.* She tied the matching braided fabric belt, knowing there was little to be done about it now. She then took five more minutes to use her curling wand on her hair and apply bronzer, mascara, and lip gloss.

She spent only thirty seconds more to tidy up before exiting the bathroom.

"My turn," Jasmine said, looking almost relieved to see Megan. She wore an expression similar to the one she'd used ten minutes ago, but this time as she passed Megan, there seemed to be more negative attached to it, as if she might have asked the more grave and/or outraged, *What the eff?*

Graeme was still stationed near the window, his feet braced apart, his arms crossed over his chest now, looking somewhat relaxed. He turned as Megan approached, any hint of leisure gone the second his green eyes landed on her—and then proceeded to scrutinize her from head to toe, his censure glaringly obvious and vast.

"Bluidy hell—what are ye...? Bluidy hell, Megan," he seethed again.

This, by far, was his fiercest scowl yet. Megan felt every inch of her flesh heat with shame. More ridiculous, her nose flared and warmed, tears threatening to present themselves. Honest to God, she hadn't dressed or groomed herself with any hopeful intention of turning his head. She did the basics, what she'd always done—*same old, same old*, Jasmine had teased her more than once. Mortified, she splayed her fingers over her chest, covering the vee of the wrap dress.

Stunned, Megan looked down at the flutter sleeve, v-neck, ruffled hem dress. Nothing seemed amiss. Granted, she would never be considered a raving beauty, but she knew she wasn't unattractive, certainly not to have garnered this intense reaction.

Lifting her chin, swallowing any possibility of tears, revived by fury, Megan announced, "Well you have officially become the rudest person I have ever met." She turned toward the door, meaning to show him out. "I feel I went above and beyond any kindness that might have been expected of me today," she said hotly, her ire risen to epic proportions, "more so since you've done nothing but act like a caveman, assaulting me, knocking me not once but twice off the bike, talking like a madman the entire time and now...now this." She pulled open the door and turned to him. "So I'm done. But I do thank you—your unprovoked and unforgiveable rudeness likely just saved me an even bigger headache. Have a nice day."

"Megan," he began, looking not nearly as remorseful as he should, looking still pissed about something, "ye canna go...anywhere garbed as such." His long strides carried him quickly across the hotel room. "Why do ye bare your flesh to hungry eyes? Why—?"

His next question was interrupted by the bathroom door opening, almost directly beside him.

Jasmine appeared, more scantily clad than Megan by a great measure, wearing a clingy, sleeveless, deeply veed and seriously short dress of bright fuchsia.

Graeme gaped and then darted a look back and forth between Jasmine and Megan.

"Och, shite," he said then, smacking his palm against his forehead. "'Tis a stew, aye?" He supposed, swinging his arm and turning his head back toward the interior of the room, where sat two beds.

"A stew?" Jasmine questioned.

Graeme frowned. "Eh, brothel, I ken is the word."

Megan's mouth yawned large and long with her astonishment. Jasmine's reaction was not much different.

Jasmine recovered first. Less appropriately outraged than she was amused, Jasmine put a hand on Graeme's thick bicep, using him to leverage herself while she put on her strappy high heel sandals. "Dude," she laughed, "seriously? You're not scoring any points here, trust me. And the sword has to go. I mean I'm all for it, the eyes it will bring our way in the restaurant, but no, it's not cool to bring weapons to dinner." With her sandals attached properly to her feet, she stood straight and leaned sideways toward Graeme, holding up her hand near her mouth as if she was about to share a secret, though she didn't lower her voice at all when she said, "Much cooler than calling us whores, but still not cool." With that she turned toward Megan and sailed through the door, calling out as she went, "I'll go get our table. You two straighten out your squabble before dinner, please and thank you."

Megan swallowed a lump in her throat, really hating that she was more hurt than anything else by Graeme's reaction to her once she'd changed. Christ, *had* she wanted him to find her attractive? She blinked and turned back from the corridor, where Jasmine had disappeared.

Graeme was staring at her with a still-displeased ferocity, his brows drawn down. Megan was pretty sure his teeth were clenched. She cleared her throat. "I don't think we need to bother with clearing up any squabble. Let's just...call it even and part ways."

"Nae," he said, shaking his head, taking one step closer to her. "I still need ye."

"That is not," she said, lowering her gaze from him, "and never was my problem."

"I apologize for my outburst, for having offended ye, lass."

She lifted her gaze just in time to see his green eyes rake over her again from head to toe. She thought she recognized now what his swift rage had concealed before—frank male appreciation—and an answering tingle quivered up her spine. But she held her breath while Graeme's chest seemed to heave a bit. His jaw was still clamped, though, she wasn't sure yet what to make of that.

"They—the lasses—in my time a lass dinna dress to...provoke as ye do."

The fleeting spell under which she'd been held, produced by the momentarily seen admiration of his gaze, dispersed quickly at his words.

A brittle laugh escaped. "Oh, that's right. Your time. The fourteenth century." It was ridiculous, the very idea, but then it also made for a perfect justification for his continued shock and awe over so many modern things, big and small.

"I ken it's implausible," he said, "but it remains the truth."

"I do not dress to provoke—male attention I assume you mean," she said, meaning to sound stern but failing spectacularly, her voice small. "I dress to feel pretty. And this week, I am forced to dress in Jasmine's clothes since the airport lost my luggage." She clamped her lips then, angry at herself for what she'd just done. She'd done it on purpose, had changed the subject from his time-traveling baloney, not wanting him to incriminate himself as insane by going on about it. He was still somewhat intimidating, still unexplained for the most part, but he was also terribly magnetic, and Megan felt a little like a piece of metal in close proximity, unable to escape the pull of him.

Graeme held her gaze with his startling green eyes when he said, "I ken ye dinna need gowns, even ones such as this, to be bonny. Ye just are."

"For a prostitute, you mean?"

He winced accordingly and showed his first-ever grin to her. It was as lazy as it was boyish, much less of it appearing rueful. It was also gorgeous, seductively so, as was everything else about him.

"I am normally nae so obtuse," he said. "Or so clumsy with my words. I do apologize, Megan. Will ye allow me to escort ye to supper?"

The part of her that was a bit seduced by his smile, and his apology, and his casually-stated opinion that he thought her pretty, eagerly nodded. Megan offered a fledgling smile of her own.

"Again, I ken it makes nae sense," he said, "but would ye humor me, and employ some pretense, as if ye do believe me, that I'm nae from this time?"

Megan nodded tightly.

"Very well. Then please show me how this...these things work here inside this chamber—the bathroom, ye said it was."

Her eyes widened. "Um, I will *tell* you how they work. I most certainly will not show you."

"Fair enough, lass."

Chapter Four

Ten minutes later, Graeme and Megan descended the stairs, her peculiar footwear—not unlike her friend's for its curious sole with a long stem attached to it—tapping consistently against the wooden floorboards.

Like as not, he appeared in control of his emotions, a man without a concern in the world. 'Twas not the case. Few were the battles that had not caused him strife and varying degrees of disharmony, but never had he experienced so constant and unnerving a sense of doom, knowing a certain dread that while the situation was not unchangeable, he was at a loss as how to right the wrong done to him. And presently his head pounded, the cause of which could certainly be traced to his irritability over his own lack of control, over how little he understood about life in this time. Loss of control was the most vexing element of this circumstance; control was vitally important.

He willed nerves and muscles to relax as he followed Megan into the dining hall.

Despite his uneasiness, he was still in awe of the garderobe where he'd washed up, by the water that appeared so magically and the soap that he'd used, which was pumped out of a jar, its consistency akin to honey. He didn't even mind that his hands and face now smelled of some sweet floral concoction, so mysterious was the entire experience, the cloths offered by the inn being the finest, softest he'd ever touched to his skin.

He only left his sword in her chamber after Megan had vowed he would have no need of it, that in fact it might cause more trouble than it could ever prevent. Having spent a good few minutes tidying the pleats and lay of his plaid had given him a wee sense of normalcy.

He'd balked at the very idea—what was a man without his sword?—but had deferred to her greater knowledge of what was acceptable and what was not.

"I promise you, Graeme," she'd said, using her mesmerizing blue eyes to skillful effect as she'd stared up at him, "you won't have need of it—of any weapon for that matter."

Her assurance, coupled with the slight distraction that was her garb, had managed to persuade him. Fine, 'twas not slight, how diverting was her shapely figure in the immodestly short gown, which showed so much of her warm, sand colored flesh. Her skin could not possibly be as soft as the finest velvet, but damn if it didn't look as if it were. The shift was peculiar, being so busy with a pattern, but Graeme hadn't been looking at the dress when first she'd appeared before him. He'd known from the start that she was bonny, but her loveliness was different in the shift. It was as if suddenly he'd felt how fine-looking she was, as if something wakened to awareness in his head and heart and gut. Plenty of beautiful women he'd seen and touched in his time, but never had he suffered a reaction as he had with Megan. He was forced then to remind himself that he was going home to his time. He could not—should not!—delay simply to be near her, so close to her soft skin and luminous eyes and her oh-so-tempting lips.

She was, as she'd pointed out, more gracious than she'd needed to be, regarding everything he'd put her through, not least of which was briefly assuming she and her friend were whores.

'Twas too soon for him to have grown accustomed to the inn's interior, the square boxes that served as chambers, the bathroom as Megan had called it and all its intrigue, the perfectly smooth walls, some of which were decorated with what looked to be an embossed vellum with a repeating pattern of poorly depicted flowers. He felt as if his head were on a pike, swiveling left and right to take in everything that intrigued and bewildered him: the expert craftmanship of the wood mouldings; windows with very clear glass; and the candles of this time, which Megan had showed him were lit or doused by only lifting or lowering what she called a *switch*, among so many other things.

Megan approached a woman standing behind an odd wooden box, which was equipped with one of those peculiar candles, which was hunched over the pulpit and covered by a half-cylinder made of gold. The woman, whose arms were also bare, arched a brow at Megan before slanting a critical glance over Graeme. He was no more impressed with her and her eyebrows that appeared to have been painted on, making her appear perpetually surprised, than she was with him, and he let her know just that with the narrowing of his eyes, which widened hers.

"We're here to meet Jasmine Lane," Megan said. "We have Room 203."

"Yes," said the woman." "Right this way."

Megan smiled briefly up at Graeme and then proceeded to trail the woman through a square entryway and into a cavernous dining hall.

Following in their wake, Graeme's steps faltered a bit. The size of the room astonished him as much as what it contained. There were numerous tables, more than twenty perhaps, though they were square and not long, mostly occupied, each one covered with precious white cloth. Just to his right was a framed structure of gleaming wood that had a golden pipe running along the bottom of it. In front of this curiosity were a dozen four-legged stools but taller than any he'd ever seen. Behind that wooden structure stood a woman pouring out drinks from glass bottles—there were hundreds of them lined on the wall, shimmering and glistening under the dim candles that appeared to have been inserted into the ceiling there.

"Graeme?"

He snapped his gaping mouth shut and looked at Megan, once more unnerved by everything that was unfamiliar to him. What little ease he knew was only because of Megan, her presence, and her complete *lack* of astonishment over everything that was inundating him with wonder and shock.

Mayhap she sensed the current upheaval within him. She'd paused and faced him but now closed the distance between them, no longer following the eternally startled woman.

"C'mon," she said. "Jasmine is back there."

She lifted her hand as if she would grab his though she didn't go that far, did not reach toward him.

Graeme tightened his hand into a fist and nodded stiffly. "Aye."

His reward was another flash of her captivating smile.

They joined Jasmine at a cloth covered table at the back of the hall.

"I thought you guys skipped out on me," The red-haired lass said.

The table sat near a column between two windows of amazing size. Megan made to sit with her back to the window as Jasmine was.

"Nae, lass," he said. "I'll take that seat."

"Oh," said Megan, seeming surprised by not irked. "All right."

He waited until she was seated before occupying the padded, metal-backed chair between the two lasses. Jasmine beamed at him, her smile made by one side of her mouth lifting. Graeme gave his attention to the hall and not her. He was born in the thirteenth century, not yesterday, and understood straight away that Jasmine might believe he'd begged the seat from Megan simply to be near her.

"Are you a whiskey drinker, Graeme?" Jasmine asked. "You're Scottish, you must be," she divined. "Please don't disappoint me by ordering some fru-fru drink."

"Aye, I once recovered from a sword thrust to my shoulder at Lindores Abbey with the Tironensian monks. They had a fair distillery—"

"Wait," Jasmine commanded, shaking her head, laying her hand on the table. "A sword thrust to the shoulder?"

Graeme nodded. "Aye. 'Twas in truth nae come upon inside any worthy battle but in a wee skirmish with—"

"Very amusing," Jasmine cut him off. "I thought you were serious for a moment. But we have established you're a whiskey drinker. I was going to try either a Glendronach or a Glenfarclas." She consulted closely in the dim light a stiff piece of parchment. "They describe that second one as a citrusy, chocolatey libation. Sounds like my kind of alcohol. Which do you recommend?"

She stared hopefully at him and then was distracted by a small black device sitting on the table near her elbow that sprang to life, humming a wee bit while the black front was lit up with an image of her face very close to a lad with drowsy eyes. Jasmine picked up the device and said to Megan, "I told you he'd call." She then stuck her tongue out and stood from her chair. "I'll take it up in the room." And she dashed away, putting the device to her ear as she went, saying in a less enthusiastic voice as she moved away from them, "I'm on vacation. I told you we'd discuss it when I got home."

Graeme glanced at Megan who shrugged and murmured, "Guy trouble."

Just then a black clad lad approached the table, smiling profusely.

"Hi, I'm Adam," he said, clapping his hands together. "I'll be your server tonight." Though his hair was short around his collar it swept down low over his forehead, nearly covering his eyes. He flipped his head, tossing the locks up and away and asked, "Can I get you something from the bar?" His smile remained in place but seemed to falter momentarily as he laid his gaze upon Graeme's tunic.

Megan passed a fleeting glance at Graeme, possibly deciding he didn't understand what the lad was actually offering, and smiled openly at the server, announcing, "Yes, I'll have the Drunken Berry cocktail." She faced Graeme again. "Just a whiskey, right?" When he nodded, she informed the server, "My friend will have a Macallan 18, neat. Thank you."

"Very good," said the server, clasping his hands firmly. "I'll get those right away."

"'Tis nae a banquet," Graeme remarked.

"A banquet? Oh, no, they don't have a buffet. We order individually, each table. They have breakfast buffet daily, I know that much, but I don't see anything here on the menu about it." She paused from perusing said item and lifted her blue eyes at Graeme. "You haven't even looked at the menu."

"Do I need to?"

"Well...how will you decide what to order if you don't look at the menu?" She chewed the inside of her cheek and considered his disinterest in the subject. "Would you like me to order for you?' Megan offered. "Tell the server what you want for dinner? You look like a meat and potatoes kind of guy."

Graeme nodded, his gaze distracted briefly by the other people in the crowded hall. Several of them were giving hearty attention to devices similar to the one that had called Jasmine away. Most tables were sat with only two people. He'd yet to understand their manner of dress. Men wore short breeches that showed half their legs. Some women wore shifts similar to Megan's in form, revealing too much skin; others wore short breeches as well or ones that were more modest and at least covered their legs almost to their ankles. A woman directly across the room and facing Graeme had her face painted so ludicrously that he imagined it was akin to what William Wallace had once observed about the painted ladies of France, of the cosmetics used in both brothels and by those in regular attendance at the French court.

"You certainly look the part," Megan said, a hint of nervousness in her voice, drawing his gaze back to her. "I mean, considering the way you are dressed and the very fact that you carry a sword, taken with how in awe you seem of everything around you—I can't tell yet if that's genuine or not—one might actually guess you were really from an earlier time."

She'd emphasized *might* as if she were still loath to even consider the possibility that it might be real.

Graeme leaned his elbows on the table and clasped his hands in front of him inside an elaborately set table, replete with bright silver utensils and cloth napkins of forest green. He angled his head toward Megan.

"Unless ye witness it firsthand, I ken there is no way to truly believe. But what reason should I have to tell fibs? It does nae serve me. I was delivering Holly—ye said ye ken her as Holly Wright—to Newburn under orders from her husband, Duncan MacQuillan. I ken Lucas Thain of Newburn already and his wife, Cora—she wears..." he paused, lifting one hand to his face, "some strange accoutrement about her eyes. I ken Michael MacClellan from our time with Wallace years ago, but only just the other day was introduced to his wife, Kayla. There was another laird present, Aedan Cameron, who had in his company his wife, Gabby."

She tilted her head and showed him a face that said she did not at all appreciate being served what she supposed were more lies.

"I ken, it is implausible," Graeme acknowledged. "But there they were. And Holly kent straight away what Cora wore on her face, such as like we've nae seen in our time. And they—the lady wives—said they hailed from places I'd never heard said—Kansas, Pen—Penn-cil...I canna recall that one exactly. But they spoke as ye did, of *the States*. And Holly wept, her relief palpable, ye ken, to have found that she was nae alone in her journey."

There was something oddly charming about the way she bit her lip then, a wee bit of havering going on, as if she wanted to believe him but found it as improbable as it actually was.

"You said Holly had married your cousin—Duncan? Then why were you bringing her to that place? Newburn?"

Graeme sighed, reminded of the tragedy of it. "Holly wed Duncan under false pretenses. 'Tis my understanding that when she arrived in our time, she was absorbed by the MacHeths, our closest neighbor and most bothersome enemy. To endorse peace, Duncan had arranged to wed the MacHeth daughter, Ceri. As it was—and as we learned soon after—Ceri had died a fortnight before the nuptials and the MacHeths bade Holly take her place. When Duncan learned this—after he'd wed her and brought her to Thallane—he banished her from Thallane and charged me with delivering her to the MacHeths. I kent that was nae a safe circumstance for Holly and decided entrusting her instead into the hands of Cora Thain was a finer choice."

He paused when the lad named Adam returned, setting a tall crystal glass filled with a reddish-pink colored liquid before Holly and placing a squat glass before Graeme, its contents of a warm honey hue.

"Have you decided yet?" He asked.

Just as Graeme wondered what decisions were expected, Megan advised the lad, "We'll need a few more minutes." She then returned her attention to Graeme and asked, "What made you think that? That taking Holly to Cora was a good idea?"

"'Twas nonsense, I've since decided, my reasoning," he confessed. "From the first day we met Holly—at the wedding itself—Duncan and I were a wee disturbed by all the very English sounds she uttered. 'Twas English as I'd never heard another speak save for Cora Thain. And now ye. I..." he continued, pausing to shrug, "I ken after only one meeting weeks before that Cora was possessed of a soft heart. She would aid Holly, with whatever ailed her."

"Your cousin sent her away—banished her—because she wasn't Ceri MacHeth?"

"Aye, that was the heart of it, the betrayal, the deceit," he answered, knowing Megan would need the full story if there was any chance that she would wholly believe him. "And mayhap all would have been saved, mended, what have ye, but that Holly explained to Duncan that she came from another time—this time, I've since reckoned—and Duncan could nae be wed to a madwoman. He had deep feeling for her, I was certain, but he had nae choice."

"Okay," Megan said, wanting to understand one aspect of this narrative, "either you are Duncan's muscle, like you do all his heavy lifting, or he trusts you more than anyone else. In either case, I suppose you and Duncan are very close?"

"Aye, as brothers would be," Graeme told her. "Born but weeks apart, having nae brothers born of our mothers, we were brought up as such. I ken nae one save Duncan who I trust without reservation. Nae one person. I would give my life for freedom, or for any of my kin, but for Duncan I would give it gladly if need be."

She both envied him having someone with whom he shared such a bond, and then was decidedly warmed, albeit surprised that he revealed the depth of his closeness to his cousin so vehemently. She couldn't imagine herself giving up her life for anyone, definitely not with any gladness.

"So you took Holly to Cora and then what happened? " Megan prompted, her attention only briefly diverted by taking a sip of her drink. Her brows shot up and she gave a second glance at her drink, looking pleasantly surprised.

"Why is your ale pink?" He asked.

"It's not ale, actually, but a mixed drink. It has raspberry puree in it," she said, and then grinned. "Along with a healthy dose of gin."

Gin must be a good thing, Graeme decided.

"Okay, go on," she encouraged, putting her elbows on the table and her hands around the crystal glass.

The skin of her bare arms looked as velvet would feel, soft and luxurious, inviting touch. Her blue eyes glistened, reflecting the table's candlelight. Her hair hung in loose and graceful waves over her slender shoulders. In that moment while she stared so expectantly at him, exquisite and appearing as if she were open to at least consider the truth if she only had all the specifics, Graeme lost his focus. He cleared his throat and approached his own drink, taking a cautious sip. 'Twas smooth and yet robust, the flavor, causing Graeme to consider the liquid in the glass as he lowered it from his mouth.

"Good?" Megan asked.

"Verra."

"Great. Now what happened after you took Holly to New-burn?"

"Aye, so the Thain and Aedan and Michael acted swiftly to separate me from Holly, which I dinna favor at all. They attempt-ed to describe to me the time-travel," he said, bringing in the meat of the epic as casually as he could. "Naturally, as ye do, I re-buffed their tales and began to fear that Holly was in true dan-ger from these people I ken were friends and nae foes. I want-ed to get her out of there. Aye, Duncan had banished her, but he'd've had my head on a pike if a hair on her head had been harmed, I still believed. And then we're standing inside New-burn's hall and a...an old hag is what she was, kent from the wedding as Holly's aunt, appeared." He paused, recalling the moment and all the ensuing madness. He stared at Megan and searched for the words to describe it all. "She was so...ordinary. Just an old crone. But Holly began hollering at her straight away, accusing her of trifling with person's lives. I dinna want Holly near her and meant to intervene and the hag looked me directly in the eye and said—I'll nae forget the words—*Ye will go while we stay here. Ye are promised to another*. Had me fair peeved, the perceived threat of it."

"And she just...what? Waved a magic wand or something and poof—you were sent here?"

"Nae exactly," he replied. "She appeared as any mortal would, flesh and bones and solid, standing before me as ye sit beside me now."

Adam appeared once more, looking hopeful that some decision had been made.

"Oh, right," said Megan and perused the stiff parchment that she'd called a menu, running her finger over the paper. "Um, I'll have the Menu Two, with Spiced Cauliflower to start, the grilled sea bass as my entrée, and the dark chocolate delice—am I saying that right? Delice?—as my dessert. And my friend will have the Menu Four. Let's do the pan seared scallops and the roast sirloin of beef as his starter and entrée, but instead of the assortment of cheeses for dessert, can he substitute the sticky toffee pudding?" The server nodded while Megan asked of Graeme, "You don't want cheese as dessert, do you?"—posed in such a way as to suggest that no, he did not.

"Pudding is fine," he allowed, wondering what was wrong with cheese.

Adam then collected the parchment from Megan and the one that had sat near Graeme but had not been touched.

"Will you keep an eye out for my other friend to return? She should be back any minute." She smiled at Adam's agreeable assurance that he would, watched him walk away but a moment and returned her attention to her drink and to Graeme. "Where were we?"

He'd return to the tale, of course, but asked first, "Am I your friend, Megan?"

Though the lighting was neither so favorable as outdoors nor as glaring as that of the chamber she'd let abovestairs, the stain of her instant blush did not go unnoticed.

"Well, I mean," she began, giving her gaze to her drink, moving a little stick inside it round and round, "we are *friendly*, or have been—bike mishaps and bad beginning notwithstanding. But no, obviously having only met you today, we are not friends. I guess it served as a better descriptor than, *Yeah, this guy from the fourteenth century would like a dram of whiskey*."

"Ye do believe me then?" He pursued, charmed by both the way she'd navigated the friend query and her answer— that was not really an answer at all, save that it revealed she didn't know what he was.

"Believe you about being from another time?" She asked, lifting her blue eyes from her drink to meet his. "No," she said unapologetically. "But you tell a fine story, so points for that. You're certainly entertaining."

Another sigh erupted from him. He sat back in the chair, pulling the glass of whiskey backward as he went. 'Twas pointless then, keeping company with her. He needed to move on, to find someone who first, believed, and second, might be able to help him. He lifted the whiskey and drained it in one gulp.

"If that be the case, I canna linger, lass," he informed her, beginning to rise from the chair. "I need to find—"

Her hand at his forearm gave him pause.

"Wait. You're just going to get up and walk out? But I want to hear the rest of the story, about—"

"'Tis nae a barmy tale, lass," he growled at her. "'Tis the truth as it happened."

"Okay, okay. Geez, I'm sorry." She inhaled and exhaled and thinned her lips. "Fine. Actually, it's probably for the best. As you just made a point of it, we are *not* friends and owe each other nothing." She sat back herself now, bringing her glass of raspberry and gin with her, taking a long drink. "Good luck with your search and...and all your shady business. Nice knowing you."

It was the disappointment that he sensed in her that clawed most severely at him. She'd just disclosed that she didn't believe a word he said, but was loath to give up his company?

"Megan," he said, "I canna waste time—" her widening eyes alerted him of this most recent blunder of words. "*Jesu*, I dinna intend to imply...I dinna feel ye are wasting my time or that I...shite. Again, I apologize," he said, more on this day alone than he had in all his three decades of life combined, he was beginning to suspect. He swiped his hand over the stubble on his jaw. "Forgive me."

Megan did not respond to his request for forgiveness, and then could not if she didn't wish the server, Adam, to hear it, as that lad arrived now bearing two ceramic trenchers, placing one before Megan and one in front of Graeme.

Graeme's brow raised at the fare, his nostrils pleasantly aroused by the aroma, as he stared at three colossal sea scallops set on a bed of greenery. Steam rose from the aromatic mollusks divested of their shells, watering Graeme's mouth.

"Sorry, it just dawned on me that I should have asked if you're allergic to seafood," she said mildly, having yet to sit forward to address the food laid before her.

"What is allergic?"

He held back a grin when her answer was preceded by a long-suffering sigh, as if she were weary of answering what surely might be considered continually foolish questions.

"Allergic," she repeated, with only a shadow of annoyance shading her tone, "like having an allergy. Certain foods don't agree with you? And consuming them can have adverse effects, some potentially fatal."

"I've nae ever had any difficulty with anything harvested from the sea."

"Then likely you are not allergic. Carry on."

They stared at each other, both unmoving. He *had* just said he needed to leave.

Before the scallops arrived.

Before he'd hurt her. Like so many things about Megan West, little escaped his notice, certainly not the flash of pain at his impolite misstep of words.

Her steady blue-eyed gaze nearly challenged him and then she did aloud. "You were all set to take off a moment ago—didn't want to be wasting your time, you said. I take it you're reconsidering that, given that the scallops look and no doubt smell amazing?" She lifted her brows at him, but otherwise held herself rigidly.

He was well aware that he was not a man gifted with finesse, certainly not for soothing the hurt sensibilities of a tender-hearted lass. He was equally as sure, despite their relatively short acquaintance, that the last thing he wanted to do was injure Megan's feelings.

Or leave her.

Yet.

He reached forward and took the glass from her stiff hand, placing it near her small trencher—he wasn't sure what *spiced cauliflower* was, but would ask after the injury was addressed—and then took her hand in his, pulling it away from her chest.

"Will ye pardon me, lass? I'll nae even use the truth of where and when I come from to excuse my boorish behavior. We might merely agree that I am an eejit."

The hard look about her bonny face melted. A softer, serene expression transformed her, brought back Megan as he knew her.

Still, she questioned, "Is this about the scallops, though? Is that why you're suddenly in no hurry to depart?"

Even as he discerned a pardon, and her returned lightness, he answered evenly, "Nae, lass. I am nae ready to say farewell to ye."

She'd given him plenty of reason to believe she might be of the same mind.

Chapter Five

Refusing to address internally the relief she felt that he stayed, that like her, he didn't want to say goodbye just yet, and carefully avoiding looking too critically at the unkind things he'd said—a long-held habit of ignoring red-flags in people; a symptom of being an orphan, one social worker had tartly informed her, adding that she was looking for love in all the wrong places—Megan picked up her fork and gently stabbed a piece of the roasted spiced cauliflower.

She wasn't sure what to make of the way Graeme stared so dubiously at her fork and then at the one included in his place setting. He picked up the utensil and tapped his forefinger to the tines before repeating what Megan had done, spearing his scallop with it. And somehow she was not at all surprised when he shoveled the whole huge thing into his mouth.

"Let me guess," she said, aiming for a non-judgmental tone, "you've never seen a fork before either." She waved hers at him.

He shook his head. "I ken the knife and the spoon, but nae, I've never seen the like." He sent his glance around the restaurant. "They simply lay them about, the knives? Weapons for any man to arm himself?"

Megan grinned and picked up her butter knife. "Ah, yes, so much damage could I do with this." She eyed it speculatively. "With its softly rounded end and barely serrated good side."

"You mock me?"

He sounded more impressed than put out.

"Yes, I do. A little bit, anyway." She sent him a sideways glance and a grin before digging into another bite of her cauliflower, which was phenomenal. She detected hints of garlic and cumin but could not identify all the herbs employed. But then it was of little matter since it was so delicious.

"And what have ye there?" He asked.

"Spiced cauliflower. Yummy."

He favored her with yet another blank look.

As it was becoming a habit, she explained without him having to ask. "Cauliflower is a vegetable, kind of bland but not without its own appeal. But they've seasoned and roasted it, and this is fabulous. *Yummy*, if you were wondering," she continued, "is like saying, *this tastes really good*. And how are your scallops—or how were they?" All three colossal sea scallops had disappeared quickly.

"Yummy," he said, showing her one of his rare grins. "And why do ye hide the cloth under the table?" He asked next.

"Hide the...?" It took her a second to understand. "Oh, my napkin." She shrugged. "I guess it's habit. One of the families that raised me was, well they were pretty fussy about etiquette and proper this and that." Actually, they believed themselves descendants of old money and an old name and acted the part. Truth was, they were too old to be fostering pre-teens and the old money had been gone a few generations before them.

Their server returned then, removing their empty plates and asking if they'd like another drink each. Pretty sure at this point that there wasn't enough gin in the world to make Graeme's story any more believable, Megan consented anyway, and Adam left them again.

"Will you," she asked Graeme then, "please return to the stor—to what happened at Thallane? After the old hag threatened you."

"Let us give it a rest for a while, lass," was Graeme's response. "Let me ken about ye."

She didn't utter the immediate thought in her head: *That's a short and boring tale.*

Instead, she asked, "What would you like to *ken*?"

"What are ye willing to share?"

Megan gave him a self-deprecating smile. "There's not much worth hiding. And fine, I'll babble away about myself but keep in mind, the conversation about the hag and you and all those people at Newburn should probably take place while Jasmine is gone."

"We've time for that, lass."

"Okay, but promise you won't leave me hanging," she qualified, to which Graeme gave what appeared to be a solemn nod. She took the last sip of her drink, which was quite nice despite being a little too strong for her tastes. "Um, let's see." She was not at all comfortable talking about herself, certainly not when her life was as hum-drum as she'd said, with many more lows than highs. Because of this, she rather rushed out a bunch of very generic information. "I told you I'm from the States—which you probably realized because of my very American accent. I'm twenty-four years old. I have no brothers or sisters, no family at all as a matter of fact. I'm a nurse in Chicago, or just outside of Chicago, in a smaller hospital. I like being a nurse. I mean, school was hard for me, always has been, but I like the job. I like helping people. During Covid, it was so hard, not just the long hours and wearing all the gear and the masks in the beginning, but watching people die all alone, with no family around them. That really bothered me."

She paused when Adam brought their second round of drinks, advising their dinners should be out shortly, backing away as he did so.

When Graeme looked yet as if he wanted more information—or expected still to be entertained by her sorry little life—she added with a shrug, "I live in a small one bedroom apartment, have no pets—I mean, I would but I work too much—and have no car but a bike, which is very similar to the one you crashed twice today."

He grinned at this small slur against him and observed, "Ye dinna care to speak of yourself."

"Not so much." And she wanted neither to appear pitiful nor to garner sympathy and so then did not repeat that there wasn't much worth talking about.

"I dinna ken *nurse* as ye've used it, but might assume from context that ye are a healer of some renown if, as ye state, ye work too much."

Megan laughed outright at this and then quickly waved her hand in front of her, telling him, "Sorry. I'm not laughing at you but myself. I am a person of little import, not renowned for anything. But yes, you are correct, a nurse is a healer." She drank from her glass once more and watched Graeme take a sip as well, aware of his green eyes watching her over the rim. Still, she blamed the ensuing blush on the alcohol in her drink.

It wasn't frustrating, having to explain such basic things to him, but she had some suspicion still that he was amusing himself greatly at her expense. Of course he knew what all these things were—nurses, forks, toilets, cars—but was having a good laugh inside for how ridiculous she was to bother to instruct him on each word or thing he pretended not to know.

Wanting very much to remove the spotlight from herself, she asked again if he would continue with his story.

Graeme nodded but before he might have resumed the narrative, a loud crash was heard from the other side of the restaurant. He leapt to his feet, so swiftly Megan leaned back, startled, her hand at her chest, mumbling, "Christ."

Almost as soon as she heard the noise, she recognized it for what it was, some hapless server dropping possibly an entire big oval tray of dishes. Plates and utensils clattered on the tiled floor, said the clamor, the former likely shattering all over the place.

Graeme did not realize what most likely had happened, but had risen so swiftly that he'd nearly sent the chair onto its back. His right hand went immediately to his hip, where he might have expected his sword to be. His lip curled when he was reminded that it was not on his person but in Megan's hotel room.

"Graeme," she called to him, her voice seeming to lessen the severity of his ferocious frown. "It's all good. A server probably dropped a bunch of dishes." At his lack of immediate submission to the probable truth, she added cheekily, "Seriously, it's fine. There are no marauding clansmen on the move."

He did sit back down but his jaw remained hardened for a few more seconds, his eyes scanning the entire open dining room, as if he expected she had it wrong and some danger was imminent.

Adam appeared then, wearing an almost tolerant grin. "That was the new guy," he said as he presented their entrees. "I don't see a future for him in the restaurant business." Having delivered their food, he clapped his hands together and asked if they needed anything else.

"I think we're all set," she told him. "Thanks, Adam."

Her mouth watered at the grilled sea bass laid over polenta paired with a vegetable medley of eggplant, beets, and fennel hearts. She lifted her gaze from her plate to watch Graeme consider his roast sirloin as a condemned man might drool over his last meal.

"The menu said it was served pink, meaning medium rare, I would guess," Megan said. "I hope that's okay."

"Aye," he said, without removing his gaze from the plate. "I dinna imagine I will find fault here."

Megan took her first bite of the sea bass and watched Graham dive into his roast.

He smiled broadly, didn't seem to care that it briefly showed some of the food in his mouth, and caught her staring at him.

"Dinna fash, lass, if I weep like a bairn," he said, a new lightness unveiled in his tone. "I've never tasted anything like this. Beef, is it? From a Highland herd?"

"Presumably," agreed Megan, tickled by his delight. "Now do you think you can manage two things at once? Salivating with glee over the divine roast *and* telling me what happened at Newburn? At the same time?"

Graeme finished chewing and swallowing his second bite before he answered. "I can manage more than one thing at a time," he told her, his gaze turning to a smolder that wasn't directed at his dinner. "Ye might be surprised, lass, what I am capable of."

Did she imagine it? Or had he just directed that statement strictly to her mouth?

Gulping down a sudden prickle of awareness, Megan followed that with a swig of her drink.

"So aye, the crone—Sidheag, she was—came to the Thain's fortress, looking for Holly. The lass gives Sidheag a blistered ear and then—"

He paused, having loaded a forkful of his potatoes into his mouth, closing his eyes to savor his first taste.

"What is this I've just swallowed?" He asked, tapping his fork against what remained of the potatoes on his plate.

Grand master of lying or not, Megan was certainly enjoying his reactions. "Horseradish cream, smashed potatoes," she said with a smile, "or at least, that's what the menu said you were getting with your roast."

"Potatoes?"

"Yes, a root vegetable, very starchy. Yummy in the tummy but bad for the hips," she said flippantly. "I take it they're yummy?"

"Verra. Will ye try? Is that allowed? Or forbidden?" He asked, holding up a forkful between them.

Megan filled her fork with a bit of polenta and a chunk of a sea bass. "It is not only allowed but encouraged, but there are rules. You have to trade bites," she invented, moving her loaded fork next to his. "Tit for tat, or the offering can be withdrawn."

One corner of his mouth lifted but he did move forward to claim what filled her fork. Megan moved at the same time, drawing the lumpy but gorgeous potatoes into her mouth. For one, two, three seconds they were only inches apart, eyes locked and lips parting. The forks empty, they remained close, each tasting the other's fare.

Megan chewed slowly and swallowed—the potatoes were amazing. "That was polenta with the fish," she told him, "which is a cornmeal based dough. I think they baked it to make it poufy." She'd lowered her voice since they were so close but certainly hadn't intended that it sounded as husky as it did.

Their forks empty, the food sent down to their stomachs, they remained as they were, Megan held prisoner by the sudden burning intensity of his green eyes. Her breathing became fitful, unaccustomed to being eaten alive by a gaze. Her lips parted and she blinked. Swallowing only her saliva now, she straightened and smiled awkwardly at him.

"I believe you're stalling with this story, sir," attempting to give a certain firmness to her light reprimand.

"I am nae. I want to get it out ere your friend returns. Your Jasmine seems less inclined to believe—which dinna mean it is nae true," he promptly qualified, "but I ken she leans toward theatric and 'twould take all evening to get to the heart of the event."

"I love Jasmine, but you're not wrong," Megan said, adding a wince for being a disloyal friend, even though she was only speaking the truth. "Still, it makes me feel like you consider me the more gullible one."

"Ye are nae gullible. But I beg ye to borrow, if ye dinna own already, an open mind."

Charmed by his phrasing, she nodded. "I will try."

"Lo and behold," he continued, "another witch appears, but this one is nae an old crone, but mayhap in her fourth or fifth decade, not unsightly, but then I recall little else but the fact that she dinna walk into the hall at Newburn, but simply...appeared—and Sidheag ken she was there ere the rest of us saw her. Most amazing was her...aura. She floated, lass, a full foot above the ground, and glowed. Dinna glow like she were on fire, but as if she carried with her a wee sun of her own to illuminate her. In any case, she and Sidheag start going at it, arguing about what games they've played with mortals, shifting them around in time. And then the glowing witch—och, she was Samara, it just returned to me—waves her hand and Sidheag is transformed, is nae a hag but looks like the other one—clearly a fae creature of some design." He paused and waved his hand back and forth while he chewed and swallowed more of his roast. "Holly begs Sidheag again to send her home. She asked the lasses—Kayla, Cora, And Gabby—if they wanted to send messages with her. They refused her favor, stating they'd had conversation about the very idea, how to tell their kin they were nae dead. I could see how it tore them up, but they ken what you've proven, that it is too impossible to be believed. They dinna want their kin addled with either hope or more fright."

He stopped again but not to eat. He was reliving it, Megan guessed, determined by the way he stared blindly ahead of him, away from their table. His jaw clamped and briefly his nostrils flared.

He caught himself and stiffened his spine, sitting even straighter than he had been, and busied himself a bit more with his dinner before continuing.

"Next, Holly begs Sidheag once more: *send me home*. I implored her stay, knowing Dunc would behave differently if he but ken the odd truth about her." He paused here to glance sideways at Megan. "He would deny it, but he loves her fiercely."

Megan sighed internally at the very idea.

"Next, Sidheag lifts her glowing hand. She looks at Holly and then at me...and that's the last I recall. I awoke inside the broch. I canna say how long I lay there until you stumbled upon me."

Her fork hadn't moved since he'd picked up the story, and it didn't move now. Megan studied him openly, chewing the inside of her cheek. It—the entire tale—sounded no more believable than the result of it, that he'd traveled through time. But what kind of idiot was she that she wanted so desperately to believe him? Red flags, indeed. This one was bright and glaring, possibly on fire.

She drew in a lungful of air and exhaled through her teeth. "Okay, let's assume I do believe the very outlandish tale—I do not yet. But if I did, how could I possibly help you?"

"I fear, lass—and greatly—that Holly might have actually gotten her wish. She may have come back here with me, mayhap was...dropped in a different location—I dinna ken how it works. If she's here, I need to bring her back with me. I ken Duncan would want that. If she's nae here, I only need to find Newburn and hope the witches are still there. I ken it's seven hundred years later, but I might guess they travel easily through time as well, though to be fair, I'm nae sure. Aside from that, I imagine returning to the broch and waiting is my next best choice."

"I feel as if I don't watch or read enough sci-fi to be of any help to you," was Megan's overall conclusion about the entire affair. Of course, this made no sense to Graeme and his expression said as much. Megan sighed.

"I suppose if Holly has returned, it would be on the news—*all over* the news and social media, once she makes her presence in this time known. That's easy enough to discover. But if she has come back—assuming all this baloney is true—who's to say she's not suffering her own trauma and wanting to steer clear of the press?"

"Ye are talking to yourself, are ye nae? I dinna understand...half of what ye've just said."

"Sorry, yes. I guess I am." Of course, it would be easy to discover if Holly had returned. She needn't be here more than a day before she realized the uproar that had been caused by her disappearance—the fourth American girl in a few years. If she had even half a brain in her head, she'd go straight to the police and alert them of her...return. What she might tell the authorities, Megan could have no idea. But it would definitely make the social media rounds, soon if it hadn't already.

"Would you be able to find Newburn—where it *had* been—from here?" She asked Graeme, who had just cleaned his plate and pushed it aside.

"It might take a bit of searching—do ye ken where I might command a steed?"

"Assuming by command a steed you mean find a horse, the answer is no. But I do have the Uber app, so we should be fine once you get your bearings, or more specifically, once you know exactly where it is." She would help him—crazy as it sounded—but she wasn't paying a hired car to roam hither and yon looking for the ruins of a seven hundred year old fortress.

Graeme picked up his glass of whiskey, only half full now, and sat back in his chair, studying her as intently, if only with half as much smolder, as he had a moment ago when they'd traded food.

"We?" He questioned, one dark brow arched.

***

Several things had become perfectly clear to Graeme over the course of their meal.

First, though not foremost, was that twenty-first century foodstuffs—and possibly the cooking methods—were far different from what he was accustomed to. That beef could have been cut with the barely serrated, rounded blade Megan had teased him with earlier. Before this evening in this dining hall, potatoes were unknown to him; he wasn't sure he wouldn't bemoan the unavailability of them in his time when he returned, imagining the flavor would be long remembered. Next, having a clear view of most of the dining hall, he was a wee perplexed by the habits and behaviors of all the persons present, guessing there to be more than two score filling the tables of the hall. No one left their table, though; no one mingled with others or moved seats to start different conversations. And the lad who served them, Adam, addressed only this table and a few others, the inn seeming to have a surplus of kitchen servers and other servants, some who did little more than pour water from clear glass pitchers or remove emptied plates. All very curious.

Most revealing during the last hour was Megan herself.

He didn't want to be but could not help it—he was captivated.

An untimely but seemingly inescapable circumstance.

Jesu, but he wanted to know more about her, wanted to crack open the shell she'd wrapped around herself. She was, by his own estimation, which might be subject to change based on the short duration of their acquaintance, nearly perfect.

Aye, she didn't believe his truth but she sat here still, hadn't dismissed him out of hand for his outrageous tale—or hadn't been able to, try as she had several times. Soft-hearted she was, he believed, clinging to an earlier assumption about her. And instilled with either a need or merely a want to help.

And he'd never believe otherwise, not in ten more centuries of travel, that she didn't feel some connection, some pull toward him as he did her. 'Twas not only because she was the first person he'd met upon waking. There was something visceral and significant in every touch, some powerful exchange with every meeting of their eyes. He'd never experienced such an intuitive draw toward a person, had never before sensed that this moment or hour, or this day was all they would know, and grieved already a wee bit over this.

You will go while we stay here. You are promised to another.

Sidheag's divinatory words returned to him.

Could it be…?

He didn't know if that were possible, if a person could be promised—by witches? fate? providence?—to another. But he did know the more time he spent in Megan's company, the less was the urgency attached to his yearning to return to his time.

"Okay," Megan said, "yes, *we*. I've decided it will cost me little but a bit of time to help you with those few things, finding out if Holly has returned and maybe, somehow, finding that place, Newburn. I can give up that much of my vacation. Obviously, all this…business will have to include Jasmine since I came on vacation with her and cannot just dump her. You understand, right?"

"Aye," he said and inclined his head toward the entryway, where Jasmine herself was seen, finally returning.

Megan saw her as well and quickly leaned forward toward Graeme, laying her hand over his where it sat on the edge of the table. Instantly, he felt the heat of her touch, but how was it that already it was so familiar?

"I'm sorry, but if she balks—as she has a right to do and which I kind of expect she might—I have to, for lack of a better phrase, side with my friend and, um, well, you would be on your own."

Her wince was small but heartfelt, Graeme judged.

Jasmine with her glaring red hair and painted arms wound her way between tables, saying well before she was upon them, "Guess what? Kyle is taking the next flight from O'Hare and meeting me here!" She clenched her fists and joined her hands together at her chest and hopped up and down in place, her exuberant joy aimed at Megan, possibly awaiting a responding clamor.

"Great," Megan drawled, a wee stunned by this, mayhap a wee irked by this addition to what she called her *vacation*.

"Isn't it?" Jasmine asked, sliding into one of the two empty chairs at the table.

Graeme's gaze stayed with Megan, watching the play of emotions across her face. He deemed she wasn't so much annoyed or angry as she was wounded by the insensibility.

But people saw what they wanted to see. He'd known Megan but hours but easily detected the wee hesitation before she forced herself to smile. Jasmine pretended she was aware of none of Megan's consternation.

"That is—that's great news. Awesome. I'm very happy for you, Jas."

"Me, too." She scrunched her shoulders upward and tilted her head. "It's romantic, don't you think? He's dropping everything to fly over here to spend the next week with me. He'll be here in the morning."

"Very romantic," Megan said, her false smile yet intact.

Blithely oblivious, Jasmine went on, flapping a hand out first at Megan and then Graeme. "I figured you two might want some time alone, so it's perfect."

"Perfect," Megan said, doing an admirable job now, with the shock of it fading, of showing Jasmine what she wanted to see and hear.

"Awesome," said Jasmine, smacking her palms down lightly on the table. "I'll leave you guys—"

"Where are you going?" Megan interrupted, clearly upset at this point. "You just got here. You didn't eat."

"I'll order room service," she said as she stood. She winked broadly at Megan. "I have a little maintenance to take care of, if you know what I mean. Don't expect the bathroom to be free for at least the next hour." And with an airy wave, she was off again.

Megan sat, shoulders slumped and lips parted, watching Jasmine weave her way once more through the hall. After a moment, she either recalled Graeme's presence or felt his close scrutiny and turned toward him, wearing a fresh smile.

"She is wonderful, honest to God, but sometimes she...." A sigh was breathed out. "Sometimes she isn't."

"And here now, lass, ye learn one"—he sat forward and raised his forefinger to emphasize *one*—"benefit of meeting a man from another time. I dinna ken what to make of half the interactions I've been witness to. Ye are given spectacular leave to be yer honest self. I have nae ability to judge anyone or anything at this moment."

Her smile improved, genuine now. "Brothel accusations aside, of course," she teased.

"Naturally—yet that was nae a judgment, merely a conclusion, now kent to be in error. But dinna pretend ye are nae irked if ye are with all this that Jasmine just thrust at ye."

Megan sat forward, placing her elbows on the table and dropping her head into her hands, briefly still until she straightened, her hands pushing back, moving the wealth of chestnut hair away from her face and shoulders.

"Perfect timing," she said next, her attention fixed not on Graeme.

Adam approached again, bearing with him the next course.

"Just what I needed, thank you Adam. Would you also bring us a cup of coffee each, the Americano blend? Thanks."

Graeme's brow knitted. The fare was beyond satisfactory in taste and presentation, but he'd be lying if he said he weren't a wee disturbed by how tiny were the offerings.

"Is it not what you were expecting?" Megan asked, her brow drawn, her fork already hovering near her rich brown cake.

"I expect to find nae fault with it, lass," he said, "save that there is nae enough of it."

She relaxed. "I agree. Come the dessert, they should bring it in wheelbarrows."

Because her eyes had been reignited by the coming of the brown cake, Graeme watched her as she tasted it.

She used the side of her fork to cleave away a small bit of one corner and slid that between her lips. In the next instant her shoulders sank, liquid with pleasure. Her eyes closed and she tilted her head back, exposing the fabulous arch of her neck, her skin creamy and pale, an irresistible invitation, which Graeme decided he was bound to ignore at least until they left this dining hall. The wee moan of pleasure that followed could not so easily be ignored.

Graeme shifted in his chair and moved his gaze to her hand, the one holding the fork. As was the skin of her face and arms and the distracting triangle of skin at her chest, her hands appeared to have been formed flawlessly, without blemish. Her fingers were not particularly long but were slender, each movement graceful, inciting a tantalizing image of her small hands laid against his bare skin.

"You haven't tried your pudding," she said, wringing his attention from her hands.

"Aye, but I will," he said and reached for a fork left unused on the table, before deciding the recognizable spoon would serve him better if the consistency of the pudding agreed with its appearance. He availed himself to three hearty spoonfuls before he nodded at Megan, advising of his satisfaction.

"Now I don't normally share my dessert," she said, lifting a forkful toward him as she had earlier, her bare elbow returned to the tabletop, "and certainly not when it's a decadent chocolate cake, but I might make an exception this time if you are wondering if this is as close to heaven as you might ever get."

Grinning at her charming articulation, Graeme began to prepare a spoonful of his pudding for her.

"No thanks," she said, waylaying him. "I'm not a big fan of toffee flavor. Or more importantly, I don't want it to interfere with all the yummy chocolatey goodness happening inside my mouth and belly."

His grin stayed in place as he leaned forward to claim the offering.

"Dark chocolate delice," she reminded him. "I'm not sure what delice means but I'm guessing it's located in the dictionary somewhere near delight or divine."

'Twas indeed a cake, moist and dense, with a sweet brown paste woven through it and covering the top of it. It was, undeniably, heavenly.

But Graeme's eyes were on Megan. Megan with her bonny blue eyes and great expectations, her anticipatory smile a thing of beauty.

"Perfect," he said, referring to her and not the cake.

Hoping to expand her satisfied grin, wanting to see one of her larger, brilliant smiles, he said, "I will give to you all the gold and coin I possess to take ownership of what remains." He pointed to her plate.

He was richly rewarded, her smile dazzling.

"No deal," she said, moving the plate to her far side. "Not for sale. And FYI, I am instantly suspicious of any man who tries to come between my chocolate and me."

A chuckle burst from him, the first he'd known in a long while. It felt good.

"Fair enough, lass."

Chapter Six

They remained at their table only long enough to finish their respective desserts and drink half a cup of coffee each, Graeme marveling yet again over another supposedly new flavor.

Graeme had, she was pretty sure, offered to pay for their meals.

"To whom do I give the coin for the fare?" He'd asked.

"Do you mean, how do we pay the bill?" Megan asked. "It's all set. They have my credit card on file, will charge it to the room." Along with Jasmine's room service, no doubt, she thought irritably.

She'd saved plenty for her vacation, had more than sufficient funds in her bank account and had cleared the entire balance off her credit card months ago in preparation. It was the principle, or Jasmine's lack thereof, that irked her.

"Are you expected somewhere?" She asked as they left the dining room. "Or simply wanting to get away by now? And we should say goodnight here?"

"I canna leave ye," he said.

The words sent an unexpected thrill down her spine, one she was happy to encounter. It had been a while since any guy had given her the time of day. And frankly, none of them had intrigued her as much as Graeme MacQuillan. And that, despite the persistent and troubling notion that he might actually be certifiable.

But maybe he didn't know of the tumult he caused inside her with only those words. He tamped the thrill quite easily with his next statement.

"Ye said ye'd assist me in locating Holly—if she might have come—and to find Newburn."

"Oh. Right."

Graeme took her elbow in his hand and steered her around a group of people walking into the restaurant.

"Supposing we really can't get much done until tomorrow, being that it's late now," she said, assuming it must be past nine since dusk had fallen, "shall we walk around the loch?"

"To look for Holly?" He asked as they paused near the front door of the inn.

"Um, no. Just to...walk. You know, aid digestion? Stretch our legs? Engage in a leisurely activity?"

He did not know, said his blank look. Apparently, fourteenth century knights did not partake in relaxing walks that served little purpose. But he sent a glance through the glass in the window of the front door, considering the descending gloom and then turned back to Megan, before inclining his head toward the stairs to their right.

"Aye, but nae without my sword, lass," he told her.

"Naturally," she said.

They climbed the stairs once more and she knocked sharply on the door to the small suite she shared with Jasmine, not wanting to catch her running around in a towel. The answer that came from within was muffled enough that Megan guessed she was still in the bathroom. She slid the key card into the lock and entered, calling out near the bathroom door. "We're headed out for a walk. We shouldn't be too long."

"Don't do anything I wouldn't do!" Jasmine called merrily from behind the bathroom door.

Megan made a face at the door, uncharitably wondering how small was the list of things Jasmine wouldn't do and then promptly feeling poorly for being such a bitch—even secretly—toward her friend.

Graeme collected his sword from where Megan had tucked it earlier inside the closet and they stepped back out into the corridor and headed back downstairs, Graeme attaching his belt once more to his lean hips.

Graeme held the door for her—clearly, chivalry had been born at least by 1303—and they stepped out in the twilight and proceeded across the driveway. Their first view of the loch, which sat right behind the inn, had to wait until they'd cleared the drive and gained the road.

Megan guessed she should caution Graeme, "Just so you know, we might see more cars whizzing by, but at this time of day they'll have bright headlights. I just don't want you to be alarmed or me to be tackled again."

"Ye say they mean nae harm?"

"None at all," she answered. "We only need to stay out of their way, so along the side of the road like this is good."

Graeme fell into step beside her, once again taking the inside track so that he would be closer to any oncoming traffic. Loony or not, he was at least courteous.

"Do you feel better, or more yourself, when your sword is attached to your hip?" Megan asked.

"Aye. Any warrior worth his weight will tell ye he feels undressed without it."

She had to admit, if he were lying, if this were merely—and cruelly—just a game he was playing, he never faltered. All his answers came swiftly and easily, seemingly without any pre-planned orchestration to fit them into his woven web of lies—if that be the case.

"You speak English very well. If you're from the Highlands of the 14th century, shouldn't you be speaking Scots' Gaelic?"

"*'S urrainn dhomh bruidhinn ann an cànan sam bith a thogras tu*," he said, presumably in Scottish Gaelic. "I was fostered in '88 and '89 to Gilbert de Clare, the Earl of Gloucester," he furthered, "and taught primary English beforehand simply to get by, learning more during those years with the earl and the other squires and pages."

"You are...you are a knight then—er, now? Or at this point?"

"I have that honor," he acknowledged, "bestowed upon me by King John." His lips compressed briefly before he continued. "'Twas just before the debacle at Dunbar, ere the abdication of the king."

"You fight then—or have fought—in all those battles that I've read about, during the First War of Scottish Independence?"

He slanted a slight frown at her, possibly over the title she'd used for those bloody years.

"*I* didn't name it," she said. "I just read about it."

"Aye, I fight," he answered then, "along with every able-bodied true patriot. Ye say *first*?"

Megan grimaced. "Yes, but don't worry about the second set of wars. I don't think they begin in your time for like thirty years or something like that."

"Ye want to believe me," he guessed, after they'd walked a dozen steps or more in silence. "What prevents ye from committing to belief? Ye are nae without a strength of yer own; is it that ye fear my greater strength? How swiftly and easily I could subdue or kill ye?"

"Those are my options, if it came to it?" She asked, not without a grin. "Be subdued or be slain?"

"Were ye an enemy, aye, those would be the only options available to ye."

"You are merciless?"

"When it serves, aye, I am."

"All right, for the sake of argument, let's pretend it is all real, every incredible, unfathomable, improbable thing you've told me. You had to have suffered your own disbelief, when first you heard of it, right? When Holly told you where she was from?"

"Aye, but then I witnessed the witches—"

"Okay, but there's the difference, Graeme," she interrupted. "I *haven't* seen anything, certainly not witches. So on the chart of 'willingness to believe', I'm where you were at when you were only told about it but had no solid evidence of it, hadn't seen anything to convince you."

"I understand," he said, his tone dull.

"And I hate to say it," Megan continued, "but whatever questions and thoughts you had about Holly when first she mentioned she'd traveled through time, whatever you thought about her—that she might be crazy, that possibly she'd imbibed too freely, whatever—that's what's going on in my head about you." Because he was staring at her when she revealed this status, she shrugged a bit. "Sorry."

"And yet ye keep company with me," he challenged, "walk with me in darkness now."

"Well, you haven't hurt me, and you have shown some tendencies toward protectiveness—"

"Could all be a ruse," he suggested mildly.

"Then I've misread you, wouldn't be the first time," she allowed. "I have rather of poor history of character judgment so take it for what it's worth."

"Ye judge from yer heart and nae yer head, would be my guess."

"Hm, I'm not sure you know me well enough to make assumptions about me," she deflected, even as she thought he might be right. She wasn't ever eager to see or assume the worst of people.

The moon hung low over the loch, brightening the gray water to silver. A very small pebble beach ringed most of the loch and there the softly rolling water broke almost soundlessly. Beyond, the mountains were brightened modestly by the yellow moon, their silhouettes hazy against the backdrop of a sky that seemed it could not ever be too black for all the stars that shone. Graeme had barely given any attention to the majestic scenery.

"Does familiarity breed contempt?" Megan asked him. "I find my breath stolen almost hourly here in the Highlands and yet you've hardly shown any appreciation for all the grand vistas and smaller but still spectacular views we've seen today. Please tell me it doesn't grow old."

At her words, meant only to invite conversation and not as a rebuke, he did lift his gaze to the loch and mountains beyond, staring for several long seconds before he answered. "It does nae grow old. And I imagine I should nae be puzzled to find the vista so similar to what it is in my time, save for there being so fewer forests—time should nae change something so grand as the beinns nae so mysterious as the moon."

She tipped her head back, but only for a second, needing to keep her eyes occasionally on the side of the road, where the gravel was loose and sometimes she was forced to step around larger brush. She should have changed out of her heeled sandals.

Should have.

Sadly, most of her life was seen through her reflective *should have* lens.

She wondered if that might prove true with this circumstance, all of it, her dream vacation to Scotland and meeting Graeme MacQuillan. Would she at some later hour or day see any of her Scotland trip through the *should have* lens?

I should have traveled alone and not with Jasmine.

I should have ignored the confused man found inside the broch.

I should have heeded those bright red flags.

I should have not invited him to dinner.

I should have....

"And what has yer brow wrinkled as such just now?" He wondered.

"Just...everything," she said dejectedly. "But what's rolling around in my head now was most recently provoked by you, just now saying you might only be feigning all this...everything, that it might only be a ruse. I was thinking I'm ninety percent sure you're not a serial killer of women, and maybe fifty percent certain you're not a raving lunatic, but...those exclusions don't tell me what you really are."

He paused on the side of the road, essentially forcing Megan to do the same. He closed the distance between them to little more than a foot and was no less handsome in the pale moonlight, his green eyes glistening more like onyx. Though she wore heels, she was still compelled to tip her face upward at him.

"I am Graeme MacQuillan," he stated proudly, "son of John, kin to the laird of Thallane, captain of the MacQuillan army, descended from Maol Chaluim mac Choinnich, son of Kenneth. My màthair was Margaret, granddaughter of Gille Brigte, mormaer of Strathearn. My wife and child are dead and buried, but my kin abound at Thallane. I am nae a liar."

My wife and child are dead.

"Graeme, I'm so sorry. What...what happened to your wife and child?"

He shook his head, his face impassive, hard to read in the shadows. "'Tis in the past. And there it will remain. We were but bairns ourselves when we wed."

Megan nodded promptly, allowing him his wish of privacy, but was unable to wipe the sympathy completely from her face.

"I dinna say that to invoke pity, lass," he said, reading either her mind or her countenance, "but to give ye a sense of who I am. Ye should nae fear me. I would nae sooner harm ye than I would desecrate my bairn's grave."

Megan nodded, having little choice but to accept it—and him—at face value. If it walked like a duck....

They'd come to the place where the road turned left around a bend and the loch curved right.

Megan turned, still able to see the lights of the inn maybe an eighth of a mile away.

"I should probably head back in—not that I think Jasmine will worry about me, but you never know...and it is late."

"Aye."

They walked in silence, appropriate conversation hard to invent or imagine after what he'd just revealed, not least of which was the fact—dependent upon his definition of bairns—that he'd married very young.

At the edge of the drive, just before they would have turned into the parking lot, Graeme paused.

"I'll say guid night and watch ye go in, lass."

Megan considered the door to the inn and the window there, the lighted interior showing no one moving about inside, the inn settling down for the night.

"How will I get in touch with you?" She wondered.

"I'll find ye, lass, on the morrow."

"Oh, okay. Kind of vague." Which, quite frankly, was her way of hinting that she didn't actually trust that she would ever see him again. "Are you intending to be a man of mystery?"

His gorgeous mouth twitched. "That would have required keeping the truth of traveling through time from ye."

Megan's answering grin agreed. "Yeah, I guess so."

"Sleep well, Megan West."

Her mouth curved into a smile, amused by his semi-formality, not yet accustomed to what the sound of her name rolling off his sensual lips did to her insides. Each time, it felt as if butterflies had taken flight in her stomach.

"Good night, Graeme MacQuillan," she said, trying, mostly unsuccessfully, to imitate the rich, velvety sound of his accent.

She waited only for his grin to come and was not disappointed, and then happily committed it to memory before she turned and walked across the drive toward the door.

I should have kissed him in the moonlight.

"Megan."

Footsteps crunched on the gravel of the driveway. Megan turned just as he reached her.

He looked as if he wanted to say something but then tightened his jaw, holding the words inside.

Megan's lips parted—why had he stopped her?

And then he kissed her.

He took one more step and without a word cupped her cheeks in his hands, molding his beautiful mouth over hers. There was no soft and slow teasing or tasting, getting a feel for her. The kiss was deep from the get-go, his fingers threading into her hair. With an expertise both unexpected and previously unknown by Megan, he stroked his tongue inside her mouth, tasting of good whiskey and toffee, which tasted good on him. Megan clung to him, her hands on his thick and solid biceps. She opened herself immediately, her response as eager as had been the start to the kiss, taking what she needed, offering what he seemed to want, her full participation, an answering, robust passion.

God, he was amazing.

It lasted forever, Megan enthusiastically leaning into him and all the sensations evoked, his kiss as powerful as was the man. And yet, as formidable as was the man, as fierce as was his kiss, there was also a softness to it, a reverence that awed her.

He ended the kiss and the abruptness of that, the way he wrenched his mouth from hers, the way he shoved her backward with his hands at her arms while he moved a step back himself, the way his mouth twisted with so much displeasure was ten times more unsettling than the probability that she'd just willingly and eagerly kissed either a genuine time-traveler or a real-life lunatic.

"What—Graeme?"

"Go," he said—growled actually, looking distinctly...annoyed.

But it was he who left, turning and walking down the drive and out into the road, fading into shadows while Megan stared, puzzled and open-mouthed and yearning for more.

***

A still bewildered and titillated Megan returned to the inn, having to use her keycard at the front door since it was locked after a certain hour. Why had he kissed her and then looked so pissed about it? She couldn't know for sure, but no one had ever told her so, but she didn't think she sucked at kissing. Was he angry with himself for having done it, for being unable to resist the...what? Temptation? Curiosity? Had he only wanted to determine if kissing was the same in two vastly different centuries?

The kiss could not be forgotten, would not ever be, but damn if Jasmine didn't unwittingly do her best to ruin all Megan's fun with reliving it as soon as she entered their suite.

Megan found her packing her suitcases, which lay open upon the bed that she'd claimed.

Because Megan's gaze focused there, on the suitcases being filled, Jasmine gave no greeting, but explained the reason straight away.

"I hope you don't mind, but since Kyle's coming now, he thought it best if we found our own place."

Honestly, the sheepishness shown in her scrunched shoulders and hesitant voice wasn't enough to appease Megan.

"It would be awkward, right, you sharing a room with us?" Jasmine asked when Megan said nothing, being too shocked to even think of a response.

This was what pulled Megan once and for all out of the happy stupor created by Graeme's kiss. And that kind of pissed her off, that her little romantic, sensual bubble was not burst by cold shower water or some distraction on social media, not by a romantic view or even by any beginning attempts to sketch out what a day spent with Graeme tomorrow might have looked like, but by Jasmine's fake remorse and her misclassification of the truth as it was. Sharing a room with *them*? No. Everything was booked on Megan's credit card, for which Jasmine had yet to pay her half. *They* would be sharing Megan's room, essentially.

"Kyle doesn't want to be so far out in the boonies," Jasmine said, having at least enough shame to wince a bit more now. "I think he booked us a place in Glasgow."

She would lie to Jasmine, but she could not to herself. It hurt. But having grown up as an orphan, she'd learned first and foremost to hide all the negative emotions. It had been a long time since she'd cried when leaving one foster home for another, leaving what little security she'd known. She hadn't cried in school, when she'd been bullied for essentially being an orphan, for having no family. She hadn't cried at failing grades or mean teachers or over any guy who'd broken up with her—there had been a few, mostly related to the fact that she wouldn't sleep with them quickly enough to suit them.

She cried, to be sure, but rarely—at sappy movies of whole-some families; every time she read a romance book that *didn't* have a happily ever after; seeing images of abused animals, dogs in particular; when she was beyond terrified, as evidenced just today—but she didn't cry in front of people if she could help it, did not let them see her pain, not ever.

"When will you be leaving?" Megan asked, her voice flat, which she was sure Jasmine would fail to notice or possibly, she might choose simply to ignore.

Another wince came but there was a grin hidden behind it, so pleased she was getting her way without any drama from Megan. "First thing in the morning. That woman, Janet, in the office, said there's a shuttle that leaves here at seven sharp that will take me down to where I can catch a bus to Glasgow."

Megan refused to even entertain the idea that this might have been pre-planned, and she was only now just hearing about it, but she did not dismiss it completely from the realm of possibilities. Had the phone fight been staged—or faked?—to garner sympathy, make her more amenable to Kyle coming over to Scotland?

"Great. That worked out perfectly, didn't it?"

Taking Megan's feigned delight as a positive, Jasmine gushed, "It did, didn't it? Are you sure you don't mind? I mean, you can come down to Glasgow with us...if you want. But I know you've paid for four days here and the excursions to Skye and...those other tours. You probably wouldn't be refunded if you cancelled any of them now."

Megan laughed outright now, knowing when she was being manipulated. "It'll be fine. I'll carry on and meet you for the final three days in Glasgow. How's that?" She had a hotel booked there—for her and Jasmine—for the end of their trip.

"Um, yeah, sure. I'll see what Kyle says."

Or, I'm guessing I'll just see you at the airport, Megan thought, though managed to refrain from grinding her teeth.

"Oh," said Jasmine next, before Megan might have closeted herself in the bathroom, "I know you still don't have your suitcase, but do you mind if I just leave you one more outfit? Would those periwinkle shorts work? You have your t-shirt still and your pink sherpa if it gets cold—though the weather app said it would be sunny and mild, warm-ish, tomorrow."

"Actually, I'll be fine. I'll wear my leggings," Megan said, waving a dismissive hand from the bathroom doorway, cutting all vacation-y ties, wanting to owe her nothing. "You can pack all your stuff." After a quick, completely bogus smile, she stepped into the bathroom and closed the door.

Chapter Seven

As predicted, the morning dawned with bright sunshine shimmering in through the windows, which encompassed one entire wall. It was warm on Megan's face, which was angled toward that side of the room.

Megan had been briefly wakened by Jasmine, not too long ago, she thought. Jasmine had merely announced that she was leaving. The goodbye was short and sweet, Jasmine not quite able to conceal her giddiness. Megan had rolled over, having told herself late last night that it was all fine. Maybe Jasmine hadn't relished feeling like a third wheel with Megan and Graeme. No harm, no foul.

Curiously, she hadn't mooned over Graeme MacQuillan's kiss last night, certainly not to the extent she might have expected of herself, and as was warranted by so knee-knocking a kiss. Honestly, she was still leery of him, part of her unable to believe he was real, while the rest of her still clung to all the obvious suspicions, one of which supposed she shouldn't be surprised if she never saw him again. Sadly, she knew that she'd be more than only a little upset if he did not show this morning. Which, of course, begged the question: *how hard up am I to have a guy's attention—and his kiss; don't forget the kiss—that I happily ignore so, so many warnings signs?*

I'll find ye, lass, she'd heard repeated again and again in her mind before she'd fallen asleep. Good Lord, but a four-letter, one-syllable word shouldn't be able to curl her toes so wonderfully as *lass* did from his lips did.

She showered quickly and then sang along to the music playing from her playlist as she bounced around in front of the mirror, blowing out her hair, occasionally singing into her microphone brush. This was more an attempt to be and feel unencumbered, and light and happy, and less a reflection of her actual mood.

Having washed out her panties in the sink last night, as she had every night of this trip, Megan donned those and then her black leggings and her graphic tee, which announced in bold letters that *The Dude Abides*, around a screen print of Jeff bridges in those made-famous sunglasses, from one of her favorite movies, *The Big Lebowski*.

She grabbed her phone and her pink sherpa, brushed clean of all evidence that it had met harshly with the ground several times yesterday, threw her small purse over her shoulder, shoved her feet into her sneakers, and headed downstairs just after eight. She checked her phone, which had sat on the charger all night, rolling her eyes, not surprised that the battery bar showed only half full. Having no idea where she might find Graeme, if at all, she quickly scanned the restaurant, which in the mornings was set up for a breakfast buffet. He wasn't there. She poked her head outside the front door—not there—and decided she would or should carry on with her day as if she expected to spend it alone, which should start with breakfast. She walked past the staircase again and the office on her left and then only happened to glance inside the open lounge, as it was termed by the inn's brochure, but which looked as if it were original to the house, when it had been built as a hunting lodge. The walls were outfitted in wood from floor to ceiling, the rustic mouldings dark with age, and with heavy, outdated draperies covering too much of the large windows, which like almost every other one in this sprawling building, offered a fine view of the loch and the munros beyond. Different arrangements of leather furniture and traditional tables sat around the perimeter of the oversized room, the middle of which was occupied by a grand billiards table, possibly old and valuable, equipped with several signs advising that children should not touch it.

At the far side of that pool table, standing in silhouette in front of one of the windows, was a man. Graeme, she knew immediately, the shape and size of his impressive figure already known to her.

Her sneakers were nearly silent upon the parquet tile wood floor but he turned before she was halfway across the room, hearing or sensing her presence.

"Good morning," she said, her smile spontaneous, her heart skipping a beat simply because he was here. Neither her constant recollecting nor the crazy dream she'd had where she and Graeme were trapped in a dungeon, tethered to a wall with heavy chains had done her wrong—he was as handsome today as yesterday. Her gaze flitted over his mouth, recalling the seduction of his kiss, and Megan understood she was now doubly vulnerable around him.

"And to ye, lass," he said, uncrossing his arms from his chest.

"Oh, you're wearing the same—" she stopped and tilted her head at him, her brow knitting. "Graeme, where did you sleep?" His beautiful dark hair was mussed, as if he'd raked his fingers repeatedly through it.

"Close."

"Ooh, cryptic," she remarked, hints of impatience in her tone for his ambiguity, for the very fact that he didn't look entirely pleased to see her, which brought a lump to her throat. She didn't ask about his sword, which was curiously—but blessedly—not worn at his hip today. "You know, if you had told me you had no place to stay, I would have seen if another room were available. Or... I don't know, you could have stayed with us. Jasmine and I could have shared a bed." An uncharitable thought occurred to her, that he was merely a homeless person, oddly in possession of an old sword and medieval garb, intending only to swindle a bed or room out of her for a few nights.

No. Impossible, she decided.

But then, so was time-travel.

She caught him staring at her tee with an expression she judged as puzzled. Glancing down at Jeff Bridges and then back up at Graeme, she told him, "Don't ask. In ten centuries time, I could not explain this shirt to you."

"'Tis verra...I dinna ken what to make of it actually."

"No, I guess you wouldn't," she allowed. "Well, Jasmine left already so—"

"Aye, I saw her."

"How did—never mind, I don't want to know. She and Kyle wanted to be near a bigger, bustling city. But breakfast is included in my stay, and I've paid for two. Would you care to join me once more in the restaurant?" The question came loaded with confidence, presuming a positive response since he was, in fact, here.

Graeme nodded.

They approached the same podium they had yesterday at the entry to the restaurant, where Megan announced her name and room number, and they were promptly shown to a table not far from where they'd sat last night. She'd chosen the 8 a.m. time slot with that exact hope in mind, that the room wouldn't fill up for a while yet, and she'd have a nicely situated table and view.

As he had last night, Graeme directed Megan to a certain chair, which was fine since it allowed her a better view, choosing one for himself next to her, but which put his back to the wall between the windows, persuading her to ask, "Why are you so particular about what chairs we sit in?"

He gave her a look that implied the question was obtuse. "How can I protect ye if I have my back to the room?"

It dawned on her that he hadn't smiled at her today. Well, okay, he rarely smiled, so far as she'd been able to tell. But while she knew her heart had been a wee giddy to see him this morning, she wasn't sure he felt the same.

A bit disconcerted by the possibility, Megan scanned the single sheet of card stock paper that was the menu, which was actually just optional add-ons to the breakfast buffet and then was nearly relieved when a server approached. It was a young girl, she couldn't have been more than sixteen or seventeen, her cheeks ruddy with a blush, her gaze mostly trained on Megan, and only darting occasionally—and nervously, Megan guessed—at Graeme.

Megan saved her the trauma of being too long at their table, ordering coffee and orange juice for both of them, before the girl, Kirsten by name, advised that they could head to the buffet whenever they were ready, the plates waited them there.

"Do I need to explain the buffet line to you?" She asked, a hint of skepticism in her tone.

"Like as nae ye do," was his response.

Stilted, she judged it, and wondered if today's coolness was attached or related to what had happened after he'd kissed her, how perturbed he'd looked then.

"Actually," she said, standing from her chair, unable to hide her own pique, "it's all pretty self-explanatory. Follow me and fill your own plate. That's a buffet."

There were little cards set in front of each item, but Megan didn't need them to identify the individual eggs benedict—called Eggs Royale here—with pink salmon peeking out from underneath the eggs and hollandaise, or the smoked bacon or black pudding, the blistered cherry tomatoes, or the small haphazardly cut thick waffles. Only the one that named the dish as potato scones might have surprised her, at least the potato part of it. There was fresh fruit, Cumberland sausage, a station to build your own porridge bowl, and even an entire selection of hummus—hard pass for Megan; the sometimes grainy, pasty texture freaked her out.

She kept half an eye on Graeme, who did indeed follow her and apparently needed little guidance after watching Megan begin to fill her plate, moving down in front of the cloth draped table. Several other patrons walked along in front of them and on the opposite side, yet another example to follow, so that Graeme's plate quickly began to fill. Megan was not surprised in the least when she saw that meat made up the majority of his overfilled plate.

"You can come back up as many times as you like," she informed him. "The server will take away your used plate and you start fresh with another."

There! The first hint of something outside a general frostiness, his brow lifting and his eyes lighting at the very pleasant idea. Proof, she supposed, that the old adage about a way to a man's heart had some truth to it.

They returned to the table and dug in, little conversation exchanged save for commentary on the breakfast food.

Megan's mind began to tilt and whir. She'd said she would help him with his bizarre requests—find out if a missing girl had returned from where she'd been for the past year, the fourteenth century, and try to discover the location of a more than seven-hundred year old fortress, where he might or might not encounter a witch who possibly would be able to return him to that same century. As wild and implausible as that sounded, she was game, but she'd drag her feet quite a bit—possibly pout as well—if he intended to maintain his present aloofness.

In all probability their endeavors would not come cheaply, certainly not with a few extra things she had in mind, one of which was buying herself enough wardrobe to last the remainder of her trip. Thus, before she committed to spending money on him and the precious time of her vacation, she had to know one thing.

She took a sip of her orange juice, eyeing Graeme over the top of the tiny glass, hardly able to prevent herself from enjoying his delight in the food once more. So that was sad, that he hadn't looked so happy to see her as he had breakfast. Why had he kissed her? Why did he come back today? Was he just taking advantage of her kindness?

Megan set down her glass though did not pick up her fork again, but continued to stare at him, waiting for him to realize her regard.

When he did, leveling her with a question in his striking green eyes, she screwed up the courage to ask, "Why did you leave me so abruptly—so angrily—last night after you kissed me?"

***

"Do ye ask why I left or why I was angry?"

"Either. Well, both now that you mention it." She held herself perfectly still then, was possibly holding her breath as well.

"Same answer will serve either query," he told her, meaning to expound but finishing off his juice first. He was indebted to her for numerous reasons, not least of which was her willingness to assist him in his journey, but also because she had thus far permitted quite a bit of incidental abuse from him and of course, hadn't shunned him outright after he'd revealed his story. "I should nae have kissed ye lass," he said, repeating the refrain that had sounded harshly in his head all the rest of last night after he'd taken leave of her. But how to explain it to her, her mildly forlorn expression cautioning him to tread very carefully. He did not wish to hurt her in any way.

Save that it would reveal more than he either needed or wanted to share, the truth was his best shot of explaining himself without causing her pain. He'd longed throughout all of yesterday to kiss her, often and with great detail in his mind even before he'd taken the liberty. Having met her kiss and tasted her succulent lips, he wasn't sure he'd be able to last as many hours today without stealing another. And damn, if it hadn't irked him beyond measure last night, that her kiss had been as perfect as she. Leaving, returning to his time—God's bones, even this now, all the time he would spend with her attempting to do so—was only made all the more difficult because he'd been unable to resist the temptation of her lips.

He started again. "I should nae have kissed ye. I apologize to ye for that even as I can nae exactly find it inside to regret it as I should. But Megan," he said, turning his palm over as he spoke, his hand slightly extended toward her, "ye must ken ye provoke a fierce craving in me. Your lips taunted me all the day long, with every word uttered and on every occasion ye bit the lower one. Charitable character and all ye've done for me aside, 'twas only a matter of time, I reckoned, 'fore I had to ken if all of it were true. Nae, I told myself, she canna be so bonny and so generous of spirit *and* have the ability to wreck a man with her kiss. But aye, 'tis all true, ye are and ye did. Thus, I was only irritated with myself for my uncommon lack of control, knowing I should nae have begun something I would want fully and heartily to finish but that I can nae—for my life, my future, and my fate lie in another century."

She didn't move, might still be holding her breath. The only perceived reaction was a brightening of her eyes. After a moment, Graeme gritted his teeth, realizing this was caused by her eyes welling with tears. *Bluidy hell*, but just what he'd wanted to avoid, hurting her. He opened his mouth, but knew no words to offer as a salve and a sigh was all that emerged.

Megan lowered her head, pinning on one of those false smiles of hers. She fussed with the cloth in her lap.

"Thank you," she said, her voice particularly small, "for explaining that so... carefully to me. I appreciate that you did not simply blow off my question."

Frankly, he wasn't quite sure which part of his answer had upset her, or if, in truth, she actually was distressed. He thought he'd painted her with a very benevolent brush throughout.

"But ye...ye are about to cry..."

"Yep," she chirped, bobbing her head, still looking down. "I know. Ridiculous, isn't it?"

Graeme had no idea what his response should be to that. He waited.

An entire thirty seconds passed before Megan lifted her watery blue eyes to him. "Sorry," She said and took a deep breath. "So...and just so I understand," she said, her countenance yet inscrutable, though no tears had actually spilled from her blue eyes, "you are upset and behaving coolly toward me because you...enjoyed the kiss too much. And you are angry as well because you're pretty sure you want to kiss me again?"

That was the essence of it. "Aye," he said slowly, a wee suspicious, wondering if this, now, would finally cause a larger outburst.

Instead, Megan favored him with one of her sunny smiles. This one was beyond anything of beauty, slow to start, paused for a moment as if she tried to tamp it down, before it expanded, her lips widening, her white teeth revealed, the smile reaching her eyes, which fixed steadily and happily upon him.

"Well, those are about the nicest words anyone has ever spoken to me," she said, her voice still slow and ponderous, as if she teemed with a wee bit of wonder. "Providing you were honest just then, feel free to play grumpy all day long and don't mind me, basking in the glow of the possibility of another kiss."

Graeme stared with an open mouth at her. Her eyes were crinkled with delight, her smile intact even as she returned her attention to the food on her plate. Sunlight streamed in through the window, highlighting red and golden strands in her hair, bathing half her face in breathtaking light.

By the saints, he was never going to be able to leave her.

Having cleared his own plate, and admittedly unnerved by the strange sensations evoked by the very idea, Graeme stood suddenly and returned to the banquet. The memory of Megan's teary-eyed stare and subsequent smile went with him. He clamped his jaw, focusing on the lavish offering of the banquet table, reminding himself as he had throughout the long night, sleeping in the blue-painted outbuilding in the company of one very annoying owl and naught but his arm for a pillow, that he had no business—no right, dammit—to think of anything outside of his objective, returning home.

Briefly distracted by a freshly delivered pan of the sausage and bacon, wondering why no cheese was presented at all, he filled his plate again, adding more eggs and some of the odd but tasty cakes curiously stamped with squares before returning to the table he shared with Megan.

He understood how Holly might have done it, survived in his time, when first she'd been sent there. Everything would have been so strange to her, much of it unreal. But maybe, as Graeme had learned, merging and mingling with the present day people and customs required constant awareness and an ability to simply replicate what was being done around you. Having Megan to learn from had been and was, quite frankly, a godsend. He'd lost count of the number of times he might have drawn his sword, so startled by so many things. Only her calm assurance that it wasn't necessary had stayed his hand. And she'd been right: he'd yet to see one other person bearing arms. He had much to learn and likely the intuitiveness that served him well seven hundred years in the past would be of little help to him now.

He wouldn't say that he was eager to get used to certain things—the scanty clothing worn by so many, the whirring monsters that were cars, standing in line and serving himself, among other things—but he could not deny a robust curiosity to see more of Scotland in this century.

He sat down, finding Megan with her head bent over a small black device, whose front was filled with images and words, he assumed, rolling past at the command of her lean forefinger. She held her fork in her other hand, poised over her plate, unmoving.

She glanced first at his plate, her eyes widening at its fullness.

"So I was trying to plan our day," she said when he sat. "I already cancelled my excursion out to Skye and was able to get a refund. I'm searching social media locally and so far, haven't seen anything, not one news story or clip about Holly. It would have gone viral, I'm sure, if any bit of news were out there. If she *is* back, it hasn't been made public."

Another part of blending in demanded that he pretend he understood every word she uttered, which he most certainly did not. But she was, or had proven thus far, clever, and clearly had more knowledge and insight in this time than he did.

She stroked her finger a few more times and shook her head.

"Nothing," she said before touching the device in a different manner that made the face of it turn black.

"Anyway," she said, giving Graeme her full attention, "before we do anything I need to do some shopping. My luggage got lost in transit—long story," she said at his blank look, to which she must be accustomed to by now. "So I need new clothes and Graeme, don't take this the wrong way, but I think you do as well. I mean, I think we need to dress you more appropriately, no offense. Or, do you have any other clothes?"

"Nae, the witch dinna give me time to pack," he pointed out but then acknowledged, "I ken I stand out, rather like a bluid red tabard in a sea of fine Scots' tartans," he said, looking down at his tunic and plaid. He reached down and uncinched a small and well-worn leather pouch from his belt, emptying the contents in his hands.

"Holy—! What are those?" Megan asked, leaning over, and without asking permission, running her fingers over all the coin he had in his possession. She picked up one of the dull silver coins. "What...oh, my God. Are these authentic?"

"Aye, but will it be enough to outfit me properly for this time?"

Megan laughed, holding up the coin to inspect better. "No, Graeme," she said lightly. "I'm pretty sure these won't be considered legal tender. But they are very cool."

Graeme returned the coins to the pouch and the pouch to his belt before addressing his plate again.

Megan returned her attention to the black rectangle on the table, bringing it to life again.

"What have ye there?" He asked, his mouth full.

"What? This?" She tapped the device. "It's my phone. I can make calls, Google things—well, you can do just about anything on here: text people, pay bills, watch movies, take pictures...anything. Geez, everything is so far away," she bemoaned, consulting the image available to her. "All right, looks like the closest place is just over an hour away. We can Uber there, shop for clothes, and then head out to where you think Newburn might be. Maybe I should find us a good, hard-copy paper map, rather than using my phone, in case we lose cell service."

He understood less than half of what she'd just said but didn't agonize over it, assuming more would be revealed to him the longer he remained here in this time, assuming also that clever Megan knew what she was about.

"Megan, ye ken the objective," he said when she looked up to him as if seeking his opinion on the matter. "And ye ken my limitations because of my circumstance. I leave the details in your capable hands." He hated the feeling, leaving his fate in the hands of another. His lack of understanding vexed him mightily in this regard, but little choice he had but to trust her.

"All right. Then I'm requesting an Uber now—well, in twenty minutes—and we'll get the shopping done first. Oh, crap. No cars available. They might not have Uber this far north. Oh, wait. There's something called Ubicabs." She poked at her phone several times and then lifted her face, smiling again. "All set. I've booked car for us."

Fifteen minutes later, in which Megan announced regularly the status of the car—*he's ten minutes away; he's seven minutes away; he's two minutes away, we should head outside*—they left the hall and stepped outside into the morning's vivid sunshine.

Walking behind her, he allowed his gaze to rake over her figure, nothing left to the imagination since her wee tunic was as clingy as her trews. He was fascinated by her trim waist and rounded hips and the way her bottom moved in those odd breeches. If he believed her wicked, he might have guessed she'd done it apurpose, garbing herself in those dearly familiar black trews, with a mind to bedevil him.

"That's him" she said, pointing to a car rolling up to them.

Aye, she'd said *car*, had said she was hiring one, but he hadn't followed the idea with any further thought. But now it seemed she might be expecting that he would climb inside the monster on wheels.

"I'm nae getting into a death box," he said, as she pulled open a door and oddly requested her name from the young man already inside the vehicle.

"What?" she gasped, staring at Graeme. "Oh, c'mon. Graeme it's...honest to God, it is not out to kill you." When he remained stalwart, hardly coaxed by her weak persuasion, Megan stood directly in front of him. "Graeme? Do you trust me?"

His answer came slowly, a tight nod, treating her to another of his fierce scowls, well aware of what manipulation would come next.

"Of course you do. So ask yourself: would I want to get in there if it were, indeed, a death box?" She clambered inside the small gray box and leaned down and looked up, patting the open space beside her as an invitation. "Please?" She cajoled, showing him one of her winning smiles.

Imagining he had little choice, if horses were not available to him, and because it gave Megan no pause at all, Graeme bent and climbed in beside her, his head scraping the ceiling, his knees butted up against the man's chair in front of him. *Bluidy hell.*

"Pull the door closed," Megan said, and then simply reached across him, her breasts flattened on his thighs and did what she'd requested of him, closing them into the car. "We're all set, sir," she informed the third person in the car, straightening and leaning back against the wide seat. She offered another radiant smile to Graeme.

"And dinna ken ye might motivate me all round the Highlands with only that smile," he said tersely. "Brilliant it may be, but 'twill nae win ye every battle."

Chapter Eight

They reached Fort William shortly after ten in the morning.

The car ride might have been uneventful but for Graeme's death grip on the head rest of the driver's seat, which sometimes included the poor guy's hair. He did settle after the first ten miles or so though his hands remained fisted in his lap for the duration. Megan's attempts to distract him by pointing out the passing scenery did not pacify him at all. For most of the drive, there were simply too few things of interest to point out. When they did pass a house or barn or pastures dotted with sheep, he showed little interest, his pallor nearly concerning, so much so that after a while Megan took hold of his hand and held it in her lap. He was specifically boyish then, giving her a stiff smile that might have been meant to prove he suffered no fear at all.

Possibly, Megan's pastiness for a while matched Graeme's, the cost of the trip raising her eyebrows. While she had the ability to pay the fare, never in her life had she spent over one hundred dollars on a taxi. The entire day would be expensive, she'd already surmised: having to buy herself *and* Graeme a wardrobe, enough items for at least a few days each. And they would need to eat again at some point and then hire a car to find Newburn, and still get a taxi back to Dornie.

Having lived through a childhood where she had nothing, Megan was very careful with her money, but still she had scrimped and saved for an entire year, had cleared one entire credit card completely of its balance, and had pre-paid as much as possible, all in preparation for this trip. One of her college professors had once casually mentioned that cheap people, people unwilling to splurge even a little bit, should not bother going on vacation. She'd kept that opinion tucked away for a while, deciding she would be much less thrifty on her trip, wanting to enjoy herself and not be constantly frantic over her funds.

Be that as it may, she thought with an internal laugh at herself, *Graeme MacQuillan's kiss was pretty pricey*. Her next thought, not the first time she'd asked herself this: Geez, how hard up am I that this is what I'm willing to do or sacrifice or give toward a man? More specific to this occasion: a man who might be zapped back seven hundred years into the past at any moment?

Megan was a little dismayed to see, no sooner had she stepped out of the car, an old, weather-battered missing persons poster for Kayla Forbes, several images of her beautiful smiling face faded with time. It had long ago been affixed to one of the street lamps of the Middle Street Car Park, where the driver dropped them off. She paused, gaping a bit, wondering if Fate and not merely the driver had dropped them right here at this corner near this sign.

Graeme, having only minutes to take in all that was supposedly new to him as they entered Fort William, now stood on the sidewalk, swiveling his head around, his jaw dropped as was Megan's, but for a very different reason. Likely, he was simply astounded by the numerous cars parked so close, along with a few smaller camper vans. There was another expansive loch and more mountains beyond that in one direction, the parking lot being close to the water. Opposite that, what held Graeme's gawking attention was the road, busy with cars and foot traffic, and street lights and what looked like the back of a shopping plaza, where several large delivery trucks sat near the loading ramps there.

He pivoted sharply and looked at Megan, his expression clearly asking: *are you seeing this, too?*

"This is Fort William," she said, waving her hand to indicate everything within sight, all of the town. "I'm not sure what it was called in your time, and I have no idea how this ranks in size and population as a town nowadays in Scotland, but I know its not as big as Edinburgh or Glasgow. And I think I read somewhere that Aberdeen is maybe the third or fourth largest city. Anyway, we're going to cross the street here and walk around to the front of this little shopping plaza."

They did so, walking on the sidewalk along a construction fence, which was covered with a blue tarp attached tautly to the steel.

Megan pointed out a woman waiting at a corner further ahead, presumably for the light to change. "By the way," she cautioned him, "traffic is *supposed* to yield to pedestrians—that is, cars are expected to stop for people walking—but you should assume that they might not. That woman is waiting for the red light to stop the flow of traffic, which is all the cars moving—so that she can cross the road."

They walked around a bend and turned down a lane between two one-story buildings, which brough them to an open space with a modern cobblestone road and a center pavilion of green grass ringed by neatly trimmed shrubbery with maroon leaves. A sidewalk split the grass and led to a statue of some guy leaning on a sword, the blade much thinner than Graeme's, and a church beyond. On the west side, which was the front of the plaza whose back side they'd seen from the car park, was a row of shops under a covered walkway.

Megan perused those shops but opted to try out first a larger store, which sat to the north by her guess, a standalone building, whose sign proclaimed it was Nevisport Mountain Centre and that it sold books and maps. She also knew from her Googling earlier that it had a wide selection of clothing, mostly geared toward hikers and outdoorsmen, but which she thought might suit Graeme just fine.

They had only a limited selection of jeans, none of which Megan recognized by brand name. But they also had a selection of *walking trousers*, as noted on the tags of lightweight pants, some of which were convertible, having zippers just above the knee to transform the pants to shorts. Megan found some Columbia brand *walking trousers* and began sifting through the rack.

"I have no idea about your size," she said, pulling out a pair of khaki ones, holding the pants and hanger up to his waist, "but I'm guessing a thirty-six inch length."

Graeme looked...well, so far from thrilled as he stared down at the pants.

Megan stepped closer and tipped her face up to him. "I might suggest you just suspend everything you know about clothing. Everything here, I imagine, will seem and feel weird, but I kind of feel like we—you—have no choice."

"Everything, lass, encompasses more than merely the garb presented so bountifully here or whatever I might be compelled to don. I ken I need to adapt, but..." he let that trail off, glancing around the store.

Megan did as well, taking in the aesthetics of the retail shop, the endless racks and table of clothes, the mannequins sporting the newest arrivals, a dozen shoppers browsing in different sections, the bright fluorescent lighting, the background music wafting from unseen speakers, which was regularly interrupted by pre-recorded messages announcing different sales going on and a plug to sign up as a rewards member.

Megan reached for Graeme's hand, finding it was again or still fisted tightly. All of him, in fact, seemed coiled stiffly. Two different veins stood out on his neck and a muscle ticked in his cheek.

Absently, meaning to bring his attention back to her, Megan laid her hand against his chest, which was as she'd already guessed, as hard as rock.

It did the trick, swinging his gaze down to her.

"Let's get this done and we can get back outside."

"Aye, let us do that."

"All right, but you have to try on the clothes first because I'm only guessing at your size." She'd worked several years during college at a retail clothing store in Des Plaines and so had some idea, but it was only a guess. He was huge and muscular but then trim-waisted and so tall. Briefly she explained the dressing rooms to him while she rifled through more pants, finding at least one pair of jeans that might work—not imagining that he would be comfortable in any modern skinny jeans. She added a few t-shirts in large and extra-large, almost giddy at the idea of seeing his arms and chest hugged by the thin cotton.

And then she broached the subject she'd thought on, wondered about, but wasn't sure how to ask.

"Um, Graeme," she said, feeling a flush creep up her neck into her cheeks. "What do you wear...um, under you pants?" she asked, twirling her finger around to indicate his pelvic area. To her chagrin, he didn't understand immediately. "Um, like, we have—or we wear—underwear, panties and well, boxers or briefs for men." Surely, her face was beet red now. She tapped her finger on the linen of his pants, just below the belt that hung low on his hips. "*Are* you wearing anything beneath this?"

And maybe he'd only been playing dumb, forcing her to struggle through that. His brow, just one, lifted suggestively at her while one corner of his mouth twitched with the beginnings of a grin.

"'Tis verra personal, lass," he said, his grin growing, "but I would be happy to show ye."

"Good Lord," she said, rolling her eyes, though her stomach flipped at the very idea. Never in a million years might she have suspected the fierce medieval warrior of being the sort to engage in mischievous flirting—which was not at all wasted on her though she replied, "No thanks, Casanova." Honestly, it was pretty hard to control her grin. "And just for that, you don't get a say. Boxers it will be." But she would have to wait until she knew his size before those were selected. With almost ten items of clothing hanging over her arm, she steered him toward the fitting rooms. "See, just step inside one of those doors," she said, pointing to the blue painted doors of each stall, "take off your shirt and pants and try on each one of these. Again, it will feel weird, but you'll get used to it. You'll have to. But come out here when you have the pants on, so I can check the size or tweak it if needed based on how these fit."

She flopped the entire selection of clothing into his arms and gave him a little shove through the door. And she wondered how difficult it must be for him, a sword-wielding, self-proclaimed warrior, to exhibit such wariness over almost every strange thing he encountered. He did not stride ahead with purpose and ease, but paused and walked slowly, his head still and always moving, taking in everything all around him. He must feel so closed in, so out of his element.

In the next second, she thought, geez, look at me, thinking about him as if he were truly from another time. However, she did not investigate this much further, unwilling to cast a pall over it—him, them, whatever was happening here.

Instead, she browsed the women's clothing, staying within sight of the fitting rooms, finding little of interest save for a gray fleece hoodie with hot pink piping along the hem and neck and drawcord. The hefty price tag advised it wasn't as cute as she originally thought. She would keep her fingers crossed for better luck at the other clothing store in the plaza, to find panties and another bra, and hopefully shorts or a pair of capris and a few more t-shirts. If she found a cute dress for dinners she might grab it, but she wouldn't worry about it if—

That thought dropped from her brain—was violently shoved aside, actually—by the sight of Graeme emerging from the fitting room. He padded out across the linoleum floor in his bare feet, wearing a pair of sage green trousers and possibly not anything else. His chest—Sweet Jesus, his chest—was naked.

One of her first thoughts in reaction was, *He's way too hot for me*. She'd always considered herself passably pretty, but not much more. She sometimes wished she had a curvier figure, including bigger breasts and hips that had a little more shape to them. Vanilla is what she'd regularly termed her body—nice, but plain; rather ordinary, without any distinctive feature.

Graeme MacQuillan was not vanilla. He was not ordinary. He was spectacular.

She'd seen more than her share of naked male chests in the ER, of all different shapes and sizes and colors. The sight of a man's bare chest was not unusual at all. But the sight of Graeme's chest most certainly was, being flawless in her quick estimation, her breath catching in her throat as he neared her. His shoulders were not only broad but thick, his pecs sculpted to steel-like perfection, his arms corded with muscle, his chest dappled with a light coating of dark hair.

He was not entirely perfect, though, his chest and arms covered in a multitude of scars, thin white lines and thick ropey patterns, a jagged one that was raised and cut across his left shoulder.

"Graeme...what are all these scars from?"

"War," he answered simply enough.

War, she mused, having never imagined...Good Lord, could it be true?

Megan blinked, her fingers tingling, nearly frantic to touch him. Her gaze slid lower to where the pants hung wonderfully but nearly indecently low on his hips, beneath the flat, well-defined plane of his abdomen.

Good God, but what was wrong with her? Not one thought in her head was decent at the moment. But c'mon! It wasn't as if she hadn't seen a magnificent body of a man before. Fine, those ones, any one worth a second glance, had either been patients in the ER, where she tried her utmost to always be professional, or they were seen on a twenty foot tall movie screen or in miniature, upon her phone, not so close and alive with vitality, staring her in the face.

Realizing she hadn't heard a word he'd just said, she swallowed and composed herself.

"I'm sorry...what?"

"Wool-gathering, are ye? Is it expected that they fit like this, so close between my legs I imagine a higher-pitched voice in a short amount of time?"

Oh, my God. "Um, well, yes, the boxers will, er, should help with that." Boldly, as if they were friends of long acquaintance or something even greater, she tugged at the waistband of the trousers, the backs of her four fingers meeting happily with his warm and solid skin. This simple action revealed by sight and touch that he was definitely not wearing anything underneath the pants. Another flush colored her cheeks, she was well aware, but was unable to do anything about it. "Oh, these are perfect. I mean, you'll need a belt probably, but they're not too tight and the length is good. How do they feel in the thigh?" She asked and then lifted her leg, knee bent, and requested, "Do this. Plenty of room, right?" She clarified when he did.

"Aye. Having noticed that the men of this time are all garbed similarly with these close-fitting, longer breeches, I ken this will have to do."

"Breeches," Megan said, lightly smacking her head. "That was the word I was thinking of, for those pants you were wearing. Okay, we just need to get you boxers. Hang on." She checked the tag on the trousers he was wearing for his size and sought out the boxers to fit him, returning quickly enough, wanting him and his magnificent chest back in the dressing room.

Graeme frowned as she returned to him, with several boxer shorts in her hand.

"I know it's not what you're used to," she said, "but you're go-ing to have to—"

"I canna wear that," he said tersely, pointing to the first pair, the fabric printed with a fairly subtle plaid.

"Can you at least—"

"Nae!" He snarled at her. "'Tis the MacDouall tartan. I'll nae sully my name nae my flesh by donning the tartan of a traitor." His frown deepened. "I dinna want ye touching it, Megan, nae anything related to the MacDouall."

"Seriously?" Yes, he was, said the hard line of his jaw. "Fine," she said, hiding that hanger and shorts behind her back, offering the next three pairs for his inspection, no plaid in sight.

A salesperson approached then, a lanky teen with pale blonde hair and buggy blue eyes, the tag hanging from the lanyard around his neck identifying him as Will.

"Can...I help you with anything?" He asked, eyeing Graeme with a wee hint of suspicion.

"No, but thank you. We were just trying to figure out his size."

"He does nae know his size?" He asked with a dubious frown. "Or to nae wander aboot bare of foot and chest?"

Megan narrowed her eyes at him and adjusted her initial opinion of him as a benign, unassuming kid.

"Um, no. He ah, suffered a TBI a while back—traumatic brain injury," Megan concocted hastily. "Yeah, so he's um, often confused. Anyway, I was hoping I could give you the tags of what we buy but have him actually wear it out of the shop. Would that be all right?" While the kid hesitated, Megan yanked the tag from the pants and unclipped one pair of the boxers from the hangar they were on, removing that tag as well. She handed the boxers to Graeme and the tag and hanger to the kid and said,

"Thanks," before he could tell her otherwise. "We'll need help in the shoe department as well in a few minutes."

"Grand," said the kid, staring at Graeme's very long, very white feet, his bland expression saying it was anything but grand before he walked away, shoulders hunched inward.

"How did the other things fit?" She asked Graeme, being mostly successful in her endeavor to drool no more over his mouthwatering body.

"Other things?" Graeme frowned at her, crossing one arm over his chest to scratch at the opposite shoulder. "Lass, it took me quite some time to recover from the encounter with myself in the wall. God's truth, Nearly had to pick myself up off the ground."

"Well, geez," she laughed, "just turn your back to the mirror."

"I tried, but then I could nae see if he remained and was staring still."

"You're joking, right?" She honestly couldn't tell. "*He* is you. You get that, don't you?"

"I'm nae daft, Megan. I understand what I'm looking at, same as what we viewed inside your chamber at the inn, within the bathroom—dinna make it any less unnerving, I say."

"Gotcha. All right, well assuming you know or can tell if a T-shirt fits you or not, find a couple that work well, and we'll take those. Oh, here," she said, stopping him before he turned away completely. She handed him the boxers. You'll want to put these on...underneath, that is."

Both dark brows shot up at this, eyeing the small item, which could have been scrunched and lost inside his huge fist.

"Yep," Megan said over her shoulder as she left him. "That's what they wear nowadays."

Ten minutes later, they were sitting in a pair of metal-armed, orange cushioned chairs, Graeme wearing a pair of socks—taken from a pack of five, whose tag Megan had also handed to the disenchanted Will.

She wasn't sure it mattered if he wore a hiking boot or hiking shoe, but assuming they sometimes might be traipsing around the Highlands on foot, she thought it might be better than only a running shoe, considering some of the more rugged terrain. Thus, she left the decision up to him, shoe or boot, and to Will's chagrin, Megan asked him to bring out several to try in Graeme's size ten and a half UK size, which converted to an eleven and a half in the States—or would, if he ever did find himself there.

After several different shoes and boots were sampled for fit, he decided on the boot.

"Feels closer to my boot," Graeme said, "being taller."

Will was way ahead of Megan this time, handing Graeme the other shoe to put on, tossing all the previously gathered tags into the empty box.

"Will I meet you at the counter then?" Will asked with entirely too much hope.

Megan decided they'd tortured him enough and nodded, gathering up the extra pair of pants and more boxers and the three T-shirts Graeme wasn't wearing. He was—thankfully or not, depending on perspective—wearing a heather gray tee that stretched deliciously across his broad back and fit just snug enough to tease Megan a bit more but not enough that he appeared to be posturing, showing off his fine form.

On the way to the counter a display of belts caught her eye, reminding her that Graeme would likely need one. She found his size and added that to the growing pile. At the check-out counter, Megan flopped all the items onto the worn butcher's block and hoped the total wouldn't require any cheek-slapping to revive her.

Will began scanning each tag, giving a few side eye glances to Graeme, who was absorbed with all the smaller products placed near the counter, the display full of things to appeal to the impulse buyer. Megan was normally immune to their allure, and knew today her grand total wouldn't allow her to look twice.

Graeme, on the other hand, was either intrigued or entranced, handling several different goods, including protein bars and a frog key chain, a small bottle of hand sanitizer and a pair of boot laces, the latter of which he lifted to his nose to smell.

Megan rolled her lips inward, hiding her grin but then saw Will skinnying his eyes at Graeme, which raised her defensive hackles. "This is his first time out since the incident," she said, wearing a face of angelic forbearance. She sighed. "It was only last week he recalled his name. He still doesn't remember me completely," she said, letting her voice break a bit.

"What say ye, lass?" Graeme asked sharply from ten feet away, suddenly realizing or now hearing what she was saying. "I've only just met ye, only came to this century yesterday."

Megan gave Will a look intended to imply, *See what I mean?* She tapped the side of her head and winced, another indicator of the brain injury she'd lied about earlier.

"Och, shite, poor bugger," said Will, his sympathies roused. He backed up a bit from the counter, looking underneath it, where presumably there were shelves. "I hae a coupon here, miss," he said. "It's only fifteen percent but I ken ye might need it."

"Aw, that's so sweet. Thank you, Will."

He leaned forward and whispered to Megan, "I wondered 'boot the draft coming oot his mouth."

The draft...? Oh, geez, he meant the way Graeme was slack-jawed over so many different things.

Somehow Megan managed not to burst out laughing. Instead, she shrugged her shoulders and glanced over at Graeme, who was nearly open-mouthed again, though now he wore an intense frown as well, staring at a teenage couple who just entered the store, both the boy and girl sporting blue hair, the boy's standing straight up about six inches from his crown.

She sighed again, handing her credit card to Will. "Yes, he still struggles with that motor skill. Thankfully though, he's improving every day." She leaned forward and whispered, "He does still sometimes think he's a medieval, sword-wielding knight."

Chapter Nine

Megan led them next across the cobblestones and into another expansive merchant market. Graeme walked beside her, carrying two bags by their narrowed roped handles. One bag contained more new garments she'd purchased for him and the other held the garb and boots and his plaid, which he'd been wearing when he arrived. The clothes were well-made, the seams near expert, he'd decided, but they felt strange on his body, the tunic hugging him too tightly, apparently the preference of twenty-first century people. He still wasn't sure of what to make of the braies, what Megan called boxers, but could find no fault with the light-weight breeches that moved well with him.

"I need to get some things for myself now," she said. "You can either follow me around or...I don't know, maybe browse a bit."

He was not yet comfortable with everything that staggered him, but he was getting used to *being* stunned by confusion and awe. Already he imagined that he might lie awake on this night, before sleep claimed him, and revisit in his mind all that was previously unimaginable and unknown but that was real in this time.

Graeme browsed with Megan always within short sight of him. He trusted her—mostly he did—but he trusted nothing and no one else in this century. His scowl returned, but then eased into raised brows, coming upon the form of a woman, having no face, wearing tiny scraps of materials over her breast and privates. The fabric looked to be silk with decorative lace curving around both pieces, and was colored a fiery red. Very provocative, but incredibly indecent, whatever the purpose of this unseemly display was.

"Stop drooling over the mannequin, Graeme," came Megan's laughing voice from a dozen feet away.

Shamed to have been caught gawking at the indecent exhibit, Graeme skirted around the lifeless body to where Megan was pushing through items on a shiny circular pole.

She pulled one out and held it up, using her free hand to turn over the wee parchment attached to it. Though this item was white, it was shaped similarly to what covered the fake woman's breasts.

"What is this?" He asked. "Why does the figure wear those wee bits of cloth?"

Without looking at him, she answered with near impatience, "It's a bra, Graeme. No one wants their boobs swinging all over the place. It's considered impolite, maybe ill-mannered—or loose, I guess you might say—to not wear one. Aside from sleeping at night, I feel naked without a bra on."

Having just ogled the replica female form and its *bra* in befuddlement, and now being unintentionally prompted by Megan's words, Graeme moved his gaze up and down her fine form, boorishly contemplating her being naked. In his mind, he made sure her hair was pulled back over her shoulders so that nothing stood between his hungry gaze and the sweet curves of her body, imagining her breasts high and round and her hips softly flared, where he might set his hands. He felt the twinge of his own body's reaction to the hazy, devised image and harassed himself for behaving as a green lad.

Her arms once more filled with items of clothing, Megan walked by him, stopping briefly, lifting her hand and laying two fingers between his eyes at the top of his nose. She pushed his skin upward gently.

"You frown too much, Graeme."

And she walked on, leaving her scent behind, one that had very nearly but not quite distracted him in the small confines of the unpleasant car, the scent warm and light but otherwise unrecognizable. He pivoted after a moment, just in time to see her disappear behind a length of fabric hanging in a doorway. A marker hung above the doorway but he could not decipher the script. Wanting to keep her in sight, he followed quietly, swiftly growing accustomed to his new footwear. 'Twas not so supple as his own boot, was a wee snug around his ankle, but he rather liked the sturdiness of the sole.

Through the first screen of blue fabric, he came upon five more doorways draped in a likewise manner, and realized an immediate thump in his chest, fearing he had lost her. He pushed through the first one, surprised to find only a small box chamber, each side wall outfitted with those looking glasses but having no outlet. His frown returned as he swept back the curtain on the second and then the third—where had she gone?

"Megan!" He called out loudly, throwing aside the curtain at the fourth door.

"Christ! Graeme! What the hell!"

He found her. Found her in splendid dishevelment, swinging round at him, crossing her arms over her naked breasts, wearing only her trews and one very irked expression.

She lunged forward and kept one hand over her breasts, tightly enough to push the rounded globes upward, and used the other hand to shove at his chest.

"Get out! Holy shit! You've crossed the line, Graeme!"

He stumbled backward, the magnificent view rendering him briefly witless, able to be moved by her small hand.

The curtain flapped closed in front of him.

"I dinna ken where ye—"

"It's a fitting room, Graeme!" She cried from behind the curtain now. "You were just in one. Don't tell me you didn't know what it is, or where I was."

He realized now, yes, but having lost her a moment ago had addled him briefly. And the doors in the wee chamber he'd used at the other merchant's shop had been made of wood, with curious slats fitted into the top half of the door, which did not go all the way to the ground.

"Lass, I-—"

"Just leave, Graeme," she said now, no longer yelling though her tone yet brimmed with irritation. "Wait outside."

Knowing where she was and that there was no threat to her, Graeme returned to the main chamber of the shop. Though he did feel like an arse for having erred so grievously, he was able to sharpen the parts of the image he'd entertained earlier imagining Megan unclothed. Little had he seen now, in truth—he would advise her of this when she calmed down—she having spun and concealed herself with the speed of lightning.

Megan emerged from the fitting room, seeking and finding Graeme, who hadn't gone far, scalding him with a singular glare. Just as he opened his mouth to apologize to her, she held up her hand in front of his face, her pale palm less than a foot away.

"That was inexcusable," she said tersely. "Even for you. Next time, try calling my name before you start poking your head behind curtains or doors."

"I am forever apologizing to ye, lass, but dinna believe any of it to be trite. I dinna mean to intrude. I kent ye disappeared."

"What? Like, zapped away by a witch?"

"I didn't get that far in my thinking," he said, not having thought of that possibility specifically. "I was only concerned." He did not remind her that she had invited him to follow her around.

Her mien softened. "Well, as lovely as that is, having someone worried about me, it is unnecessary, Graeme." She continued past where he'd waited close to that curtained doorway, saying over her shoulder, "I just need a few more things and we can go."

Another fifteen minutes later Megan now also carried several bags made of paper, and they stepped outside into the market square. The sun had reached its zenith but was fading, being overcome by hazy white and gray clouds.

"Let's sit here," Megan said, pointing to a bench made of metal. "I think it will be close enough to use the store's wi-fi. I can order an Uber or that other taxi service from here—oh, look, there's a museum nearby. We should—oh, wait. You probably...well, are you in any hurry? I mean the fourteenth century isn't going anywhere, is it?"

"Perhaps nae. I dinna ken how time is managed or how it works, lass," he said, "but I do recall Michael—he's the MacClellan— declaring that when Kayla and Eloise first met, they figured out there was some difference, some shift that took place between the centuries. When Kayla arrived apparently, Eloise had only been gone from this time for a few weeks and they met soon after. At that time, Eloise had already been with Nicol in our—my—time for more than a year."

"But that doesn't make any sense," Megan argued the implausibility of it. "How could—"

She cut herself off, reading Graeme's raised brow, which asked her to consider what she was saying.

"Right," she said. "How are we to make sense or expect rational parts and pieces with the impossible?" She returned her attention to her phone. "All right, we'll figure out the important stuff first and maybe save the museum for another day...if you might still be here."

Graeme stood in front of her as she sat on the bench, hands on his hips while he waited for her to do whatever she was with her phone device. He gave no reply to her last statement but chewed it over in his mind. *If you're still here* roused several thoughts, not least of which required him to think about not being here, not knowing Megan.

Mayhap the words gave her pause as well. She lifted her blue eyes from the scrolling images to look at him. His new garb had already wrought several curious stares from her, some of them more guarded than others—a great departure from how she'd stared at him when he'd come bare-chested from the fitting room.

He raised no ruckus at the time, and she could deny it all she wanted, but he was not so obtuse to fail to recognize admiration in a female gaze. He grinned inwardly now as she returned her regard to the phone. Aye, she'd clearly presented an obvious appreciation for what she'd seen then. Having caught her unawares and essentially bare-chested minutes later, he might have teased her—put her at ease?—by telling her that the high regard was mutual, if not greater.

"Graeme," she said lifting her face to him again, "can you look at this? Are you able to read this map?"

He sat down next to her, their thighs touching.

Megan showed him an unmoving image on her phone, a sea of blue with thin lines of darker blue snaking all over it. "So this is the map of Ross-Shire."

"I see nae map, lass, he said. "I see only blue."

She tapped her finger a few times and the image evolved and he understood from a thousand views from mountaintops in the Highlands and elsewhere that this was the eagle's view.

"Aye, I see it now."

"Okay, the inn where I'm staying is here. Its near these three lochs, where they all seem to join, Loch Long, Loch Duich, and Loch Alsh. Now here," she said, shifting the eagle's view with her finger, as if she'd sent him into flight, brown and green and nearly black lochs being pushed out of view, "is the broch where I found you. I cannot find any information of this Newburn or your friend, that laird guy, Lucas Thain. I haven't dug very deep, but I don't know if that will help. We could, and we might be forced to at some point, stop by like a clerk's office or an old church, certainly a library, where some records might be kept but for now—today—do you recognize anything, or at lease which direction it might be in. Do you know a loch by name that it might be near?"

Graeme considered her question, leaning closer to her to study the image. Nothing jumped out at him as something he might recognize. He would prefer to see it from the ground. "I could," he said, "I ken I might, at least, be able to navigate from Thallane, which sits near a loch called Cluanie."

"Clu-ah-nee," she repeated slowly. "I'm just going to spell it phonetically—um, okay, here it is. Oh, Graeme," she said with some excitement, tapping his thigh, leaving her hand there briefly. "Look, it's between here, Fort William, and Dornie. Perfect."

"And what now, lass? A bike?"

"I'll hire another car," she said, her gaze still affixed to her phone.

"And ye are sure, lass," he said, pivoting, looking at all the different boxed stalls inside the market town, "that there are nae horses to procure." He'd much prefer riding to suffering through another car ride.

"I'm sure. Maybe out somewhere more rural they might—or we'd at least come upon a horse or two to steal—"

"'Tis a hanging offense," he countered sharply, whirling on her, aghast at the very idea.

"I was kidding," she said. "Anyway, the car is ordered and will be here in...great, seven minutes. We have to go back where we were dropped off."

They collected their bags from the bench and headed out of the market square, finding the pathway Megan called the sidewalk and walking alongside the main thoroughfare, entirely too close to so many moving cars for Graeme's liking.

Curious about the tall tree trunks driven into the ground, with black cords suspended at their tops, Graeme noted each one's presence as they approached, deciding they were all spaced evenly, mayhap as much as four score footfalls apart. Each one was peppered with different notices, none of which he could read, some of them repeated on each subsequent thirty foot tall timber.

As they neared the fourth one, Graeme stopped suddenly, stricken with shock by the image staring back at him from one of these notices, to which he'd previously given only scant attention.

"What deceit is this?" He asked as he stepped closer, recognizing Kayla MacClellan's smiling face on one of the parchments.

"Graeme?" Megan stood at his side, looking at him and not the image. "Do you know her?"

"Aye, 'tis the MacClellan's wife, Kayla. I said to ye I met her. She was at Newburn—she and her husband, and the Cameron and his bride, Gabby, had met their to discuss their circumstance. Holly cried when she saw them. I dinna ken she'd ever met them, but as I'd said to ye at dinner, she identified the odd affectation Cora wore over her eyes—she named them *glasses*—and all those lasses gasped when she did, as if only a person from this time might ken what they were. I've seen them about in this century, the glass spheres," he said, making a motion with his hand to indicate where the strange affectation had sat.

"Cora Bennett wore glasses," Megan breathed at his side.

"Aye, she did, that's what Holly saw. Holly's tears were of relief, I now ken, that she'd found someone—three of them—who could understand what she'd endured. She was crushed in spirit, I dare say, when none of the lasses could advise about getting home. But aye, I just recalled, that's what drew the witches out. So said one of them—Samara, she was. She said she felt their energy and was called to it or some drivel to that effect."

"Tell me something about Kayla that would help me to really believe what you say is true," Megan implored, a hitch in her voice.

Graeme shook his head. "I met the MacClellan's wife but twice. I can tell ye plenty about Holly, as she is wed to Duncan, and I spent a guid spell of time with her."

"What can you tell me?"

"She is soft-hearted, as ye are," he said, the first thing that came to mind, but mayhap it only occurred to him because Megan reminded him of Holly in that regard. "She was nae well-received—as ye can imagine, being kin to the MacHeths—and yet she tried her damnedest to adjust to life at Thallane. She aspired to be a guid wife to Duncan, I ken that. As he was of her, she was a wee awed by him, tender regard, I ken it was. When first she came, most of her study of Duncan was done furtively, both intrigued and then a wee anxious mayhap, of this man—stranger at the time—who was now her husband. But she's nae timid—och, I almost forgot, was weeks ago now. Holly was trapped in the cellars at Thallane, a grisly place as ye might suspect. *Jesu*, but Duncan was wild to find her. Locked in one of the storage chambers, naught but darkness and the mice for company, for more than half a day. Next day, ye'd nae ever ken she suffered such trauma."

"Is that a prerequisite? To be a laird's wife, to live in a medieval castle? Fearlessness? Only the brave need apply?"

Of course it was not and many a weepy, timid maid he'd known. Though he'd seen—indeed caused—a few tears, Megan was neither of these things. "Ye would thrive there lass, of that I have nae doubt."

"Are...are you a laird?"

He wasn't sure he should take the liberty of reading too much into her query about the necessity of a laird's wife being brave, being followed so closely by her asking if he, himself, was a laird.

"I am nae the laird. That is Duncan. I captain his—the Mac-Quillan—army. I recruit, direct, train, and lead them into battle at Dunc' side."

"I see. Have you fought in many fights?"

"Too many to count. Is this our car?" He asked then of a vehicle slowing down, the driver leaning forward toward the window, squinting and eyeing Graeme and Megan.

"Yep, that's him," Megan said, heading toward it.

They folded themselves into this car, which was, thankfully, a bit more spacious. Resolved to become accustomed to both the speed at which cars sometimes moved and his lack of control over it, Graeme tightened his jaw and settled into the ride.

Unlike their first hired driver, this one was eager it seemed to make conversation with them, asking Megan if she were from the States, this lad with his obvious Scots' accent, seeming to know of such a place.

"I'm from Chicago," she happily supplied, "or just north of there."

"And ye, sir?"

"I am a MacClellan, hailing from Thallane in Wester Ross."

"Thallane?" Repeated the driver, his eyes visible in the looking glass hanging from the ceiling of the car, frowning and trained on Graeme and not the path in front of him. "Never heard of it. Ye booked a trip to Loch Cluanie," he said, his gaze shifting in the mirror glass, presumably toward Megan. "No Thallane near there, mate."

"Actually, we're seeking an...well, ancient, I guess, place called Newburn," said Megan, "and Graeme thought he might be able to remember it's direction from that loch."

The brows in the glass dipped lower but at least his attention had returned to the road.

"How do ye recall an ancient place that is nae there?"

"It was there, at one time," Graeme said. "I live there in—"

"He lives under a rock half the time," Megan blithely cut him off, giving him a gentle shove with her elbow.

"I live *on* a rock," Graeme corrected her. "Thallane sits on sturdy bedrock."

"Yes, dear," she said, her tone conciliatory at the same time it sounded a wee insulting.

He remained quiet then, allowing Megan to engage the driver in conversation, trivial enough that he supposed she was only passing the time.

Not for the first time, Graeme took note of how fewer trees and forests there were in this time, hoping that did not hinder his ability to navigate his way from where he knew Thallane had once sat toward what he knew as Newburn's direction.

They rode for less than an hour by Graeme's estimation, the road curving alongside three other lochs, which the driver announced as Loch Lochy first, which did not resemble the one that Graeme was familiar with, and then Loch Garry, and then briefly beside Loch Lyone, where the driver asked, "Sure ye doon want any of these lochs? Has to be Cluanie?"

"Aye, Cluanie," Graeme assured him.

Ten minutes later as they neared the requested lake, Graeme's brows lifted, hope dawning.

"I'll drop ye at the viewpoint," said the driver. "Was it last year, mate, or the one afore, when the air ambulance came just here, rescuing that numpty, fell and bumped his head on the rocks?"

"Aye," Graeme said distractedly, studying the landscape and the ribbon of shallow water running through hills and taller beinns. He exited the car as soon as the driver made it stop moving, having pulled off the main road onto a short fringe of smooth but lighter colored tar. Because the two bags of clothing, old and new, had sat in his lap on the drive, he brought those out of the car with him.

Aye, this spot he knew well, this south eastern summit overlooking the Cluanie water.

Absently, with one hand on the open door, Graeme reached his other hand inside to help Megan alight.

"Does it look familiar?" She asked, standing close, peering up at him.

"Aye, lass. This I ken." He moved her forward and closed the car door, tapping his hand on the top of the vehicle. "My thanks for delivering us safely, lad," he said. "We have nae further need."

"Um, Graeme," Megan said, watching the car roll about in a circle as it departed. "No further need? We're out in the middle of nowhere."

"Aye, but I ken where we are," he said, facing fully east, believing he recognized the ridgeline of hills closest to them. "Unless the mountains and glens were moved over the centuries, I ken exactly where we need to go."

"And we're going to walk there? I hired the car to drive us around in the direction you decided from here."

"He canna roll that vehicle verra far off this smooth roadway, lass. We need to walk it."

"You're serious? Geez, Graeme, you should have told me. I would have brought water and my backpack with...I don't know, other things."

"And I my sword, lass," he said. "But it only made sense to me once I stood here. Aye, I'd rather nae embark on any journey without my sword, but 'tis nae so far, naught but ten and five miles, and ye have insisted often that I have nae need of my sword."

"Graeme, I'm not worried about your sword," Megan stated, "but about thirst and hunger and blisters and"—she broke off, swatting her hand around in front of her face— "and bugs, apparently."

Graeme waved his hand in front of his own face, with less disgust than Megan had shown, less affected by the biting midges than she apparently was.

"We'll be fine, lass," he told her, "and we'll be able to satisfy any need along the way."

"This is what I get for hoping for adventure on my vacation," she grumbled, walking alongside him as he backtracked on the black road before stepping off and away from it, headed straight in a northeasterly direction.

They hadn't gone very far when a low rumbling of thunder was heard in the distance. The sky had slowly darkened over the last hour but 'twas still only light gray and not black with fury. He rather expected a light shower or a lasting misting rain but not much more, though he did sense that the wind had increased dramatically from when they'd been near the market.

Graeme glanced sideways at Megan, judging her reaction to the inevitable rain.

She was just now glancing overhead, her mouth wrinkled with a bit of exasperation that their trek might be mired in a swift summer storm.

Five minutes later, when they were sprinting across the jagged earth as rain pounded at them sideways, aiming for the shelter of the trees at the base of the hill they would need to climb, Megan called out, "This is *not* fine, Graeme! This is very *not* fine!" Her own bags bounced, and her strapped pouch bobbed against her hips and thighs as she ran, making her gait uneven.

He chuckled at this, pausing to take her hand to steady her, his face angled away from the stinging rain.

"Ye said ye wanted adventure, lass," he reminded her.

"Ugh! I should know better, should know to be careful what I wish—ahh!"

She screamed, her foot striking out in a long slide, the wet ground nearly causing her to fall. Only Graeme's strong hold on her kept her from going down.

They entered a stand of trees, not nearly as dense as he would have liked to offer them perfect refuge from the violence of this sudden storm. He pulled Megan forward, under the canopy of a fir with a reasonably thick trunk, its lowest branches just at about the height of Graeme's shoulders so that he was forced to duck to follow her.

Megan sighed and put her back to the trunk, the bags hanging limply from each hand.

The rain was largely unavoidable, coming so hard that even the trees could not offer complete protection. Graeme pushed

Megan around to the windless side of the tree, so that it buffeted them to some degree. He stood in front of Megan, facing her, allowing his back to bear the brunt of any wind and water that did come at them from another direction, which was not insignificant. He set his bags down and lifted his arms to either side of Megan's head to shield her face, his hands finding purchase against the stocky trunk of the tree.

Her chest heaved swiftly, a result of their mad dash. Her cheeks were marred with spots of red. Rain drops glistened on her lashes, joining several of them together creating a spiked effect, which somehow made her eyes appear larger, more luminous. She licked rain from her top lip, her gaze on Graeme, moving about his face, taking note of his sodden appearance.

Her magnificent chestnut hair was simply dark brown now, deprived of all the different shades, drenched and hanging limply all around her face and neck and shoulders. Graeme lifted his hand and swept back the locks drooping over her forehead, his gaze following, probing the soft skin revealed. When he lowered his gaze, he found that Megan stared at him still but had gone still at his touch.

Her lips parted and though it might have been done unconsciously, he took it as an invitation and lowered his head to feast on her, joining his wet mouth with hers. 'Twas not a modest kiss, but Graeme felt in control of himself now, more so than he had last night, when every nerve inside him screamed at him to kiss her and he'd had no will to resist. This, now, was a choice, one over which he debated not at all. She was in so many ways irresistible.

He parted her lips and plunged his tongue inside her mouth, teasing her to respond. She did, wonderfully so, her reception of a kiss as it had been last night—as needful as him.

He leaned his body into her delicious softness and moved his hand with tender insistence along her jawline, lifting her face to his. His hand kept moving then, wandering down over her shoulders and her arms bent between them, tugging at his tunic. Firmly, he moved one of her hands out of his way, then able to mold his own palm and fingers over the sumptuous roundness of her breast. Her entire body quivered in reaction to this touch, her kiss momentarily paused while she sighed into his mouth.

Graeme deepened the kiss, tugging on her bottom lip, driving and swirling his tongue in lush strokes. Thin though her tunic was, that and the previously explained garment that was a *bra* hindered his violent desire to touch her skin and hold her breast in his hand. He dipped his hand lower, sliding it beneath her tunic and then upward again, his movements aggressive, matching his desire for her. He pushed up under the bra as well, groaning into her mouth when his fingers encountered the bare and beautiful flesh of her small breast and taut nipple. He ground himself against her, his own desire surging to greater life inside his new boxers at the same moment.

He cupped and squeezed her breast, and stroked and teased her nipple until she wrapped her arms around his waist, pulling him closer. Wanting the sensitive peak in his mouth, Graeme growled against her lips as his hands began to lift her delicate tunic upward, "I need to taste ye, lass."

"Oh, Jesus, Graeme," she sighed. "Oh, I want that so badly." This, said even as she clamped her hands over his much larger ones, trying to force them back down.

He broke the kiss, their heated breaths mingling, the forgotten rain misting around them.

For a moment they both stared down at the four hands joined between them, unmoving now.

"I can't," she said, sounding as passionately saddened as Graeme felt at her words. "One of us is leaving, either me when my vacation ends or you when...whatever happens. I can't carry that with me." She sluiced water from her cheeks and blinked several times. "I can't be abandoned again, Graeme. I..." she paused, staring at his shoulder, her bottom lip trembling a wee bit. Her right hand disappeared from the top of his, rising to lay flat against his upper chest. She smoothed her palm over the saturated fabric of his tunic. "I feel as if all the hurts over the years, all the rejections and desertions and certainly the simpler goodbyes, would pale in comparison to yours. If I...if we continue to...it's only going to make it all the more unbearable when you leave or when I leave. I just know it."

Taking himself backward only enough that his erection no longer pressed against her, laying his hand over the one near his shoulder, he said, "I dinna want to cause ye pain, lass."

She nodded. "I didn't think you did, or would." She tried to smile, the effort falling short. "Fate's kind of stupid, isn't it? Or disorganized. Or maybe just drunk."

"Why is that?"

"This is only me thinking and talking and I'm only speaking for myself, but I...I don't know, but I almost feel like you and I are meant to be." She kept her gaze averted as she delivered this remarkable revelation. She looked beyond his left arm, her gaze mayhap upon the grass darkened and shimmering with moisture. "Silly, I know," she continued, "but that's how I'm beginning to feel, like maybe Fate had too many dark ales and he or she messed up our birth years."

A few snippets returned to him, things she'd said.

One of the families that raised me....

I have no brothers or sisters, no family at all as a matter of fact.

He supposed he would be safe in guessing that she guarded herself well, that loving relationships, such as a lass with a soft heart needed, hadn't come often or easily her way. She couldn't look at him now, even after meeting him so enthusiastically in their kiss, as she revealed small measures of her feelings—*I almost feel like you and I are meant to be.*

She said this, expressed her idealistic theory, in a small voice, as if she had little practice speaking so openly. Graeme surmised that one did not either suppose or wish such a thing as *meant to be* if there was no feeling at all attached to either the *you* or the *I*.

He sighed, wondering how in the hell she'd managed in twenty-four hours what no one had done in more than a decade: made him feel.

And yet, he would leave her.

He lifted both hands and laid them on her narrow shoulders, sliding them down over her arms, rubbing up and down a bit. When she lifted her eyes to him, he grinned faintly. "I'll have words for him or her, that blootered Fate, if ever we should meet."

Chapter Ten

The rain had finally cleared. Birds chirped overhead, darting from tree to tree. Megan thought they might be common wrens, or at least they looked like them. The sky was not blue, but teemed yet with swiftly moving thick gray clouds, suggesting they might yet see more rain. She was not completely soaked to the skin, her sherpa having absorbed most of the rain, but it was weighted with water now, hanging heavily on her. Her leggings were indeed soaked through, clinging annoyingly to her. A stiff breeze still whipped around them and though it was helpful in drying Megan's drenched hair—God only knew what that looked like—it caused chills to run down to her bone. Thankfully, she did always carry hair ties with her and had paused a while back to wrestle the sopping and tangled bulk of it into a ponytail, though strands were continually blowing around her face still.

Possibly they looked like two idiots, carrying their paper shopping bags on this nearly rigorous trek. But then no one was around to see them, so it really didn't matter.

They'd climbed and had descended on smaller hill—munro?—and now walked along a river tumbling choppily along over rocks and at one point over the carcass of an old tree, the trunk at least a foot in diameter. Where that had come from Megan had no idea; there were few trees within a hundred yards on either side of the river in this valley.

It was still breathtaking, the scenery, the moss-carpeted forests and majestic dark pines, the raw open glens, where Megan thought for sure she could see the bones of the earth, scarcely ob-

scured by a thin coating of heather and bracken. Even the isola-
tion of the landscape was fascinating and picturesque.

The terrain wasn't overly challenging, but it wasn't even
ground, and they had been walking for many miles now. Or
at least, it felt that way. But she'd yet to break down and ask
Graeme, *Are we there yet?*

For an hour after the rain stopped, after they'd left the shelter
of the tree, Megan suffered a terrific bout of melancholy, sad to
have left that tree and that kiss behind. Half the time she wondered why she'd bothered to stop him. Sure, what she'd said to
him was true; since he'd first kissed her, she'd been tormented
by some troubling sense that getting over him wouldn't be easy,
and then would only be made more difficult the more deeply involved she was—and kissing and any glorious thing that would
naturally follow would certainly qualify as more deeply involved.
The rest of the time she wrestled with the inevitable—whether
he was merely from Scotland or actually from another time, she
was from the States; their time together was limited.

"Ye've been quiet now, lass," Graeme commented as they
trudged along. "Almost a mile, nae a word."

"Frankly, I'm pretty miserable—with everything. I'm cold
and tired and hungry and we're out literally in the middle of
nowhere—which is gorgeous, don't get me wrong, but I'm not
sure how we're getting back to Dornie." She sighed, stepping
around a rough patch of earth, more jagged rock than grass.
"And honestly, I'm thinking I shouldn't have asked you to stop,"
she said, putting into words more than she normally might, but
kind of looking to see how he felt about it. When he didn't
respond immediately, she wondered if she'd been too vague.
"Stopped the kissing, I mean."

"Aye," he said, walking only a few steps ahead of her, his broad shoulders having provided a fine view when she wasn't appreciating the compelling landscape.

An entire half a minute passed before he added to that very non-committal initial response. When his voice next reached her, the rough timbre and the words themselves eased some of her melancholy.

"We'll have time yet, lass. Dinna believe I won't make sure of that."

The instant relief she felt told her that her earlier instinct that she shouldn't have halted their kiss was an honest emotion. On top of that, the thrill caused by his assertion warmed her from the inside out.

"Does this look familiar?" She asked then. "Or does it look similar to how it did in your time?"

"Aye and nae, lass," he answered. "I recognize the rolling hills and this river here and its winding shape, though it's narrower by far. 'Tis nae more settled now than then," he went on, "but in my time so much of this land is occupied by great herds of sheep and cattle, grazing and birthing, or being driven down to the market towns. Still, the landscape remains as wild and remote, nae inaccessible though the southerners see it that way."

"Are you worried, Graeme?" She asked. "That maybe you'll find Newburn, or what remains of it, but won't be able to get back home?"

"I dinna contemplate worry, lass. I'll get home, I've nae doubt," he said, his voice laced with fortitude, "whether today or in a fortnight or a year. I'll nae ever give up."

Never mind the fact that she regularly, after only twenty-four hours, spoke as if she did believe him, she had now to address the tightness in her chest over his declaration and his ardor about the matter. It was too soon to be hurt—to feel any emotion at all—over his fervent wish to go, to leave her.

Meaning to put those thoughts from her mind, Megan asked, "But how will they know you're there? The witches?"

"The one called Samara said that she was summoned to the Newburn by the energy of the lasses. Can I nae simply dwell upon the matter and call to the witch, Sidheag?"

Megan grinned, for how woo-woo that sounded, Graeme manifesting a witch.

"I guess you can try."

"'Tis nae far now," he observed, pointing to an unusual rock formation. "I ken that marker, *a ' chrùn*, the Crown we call it."

Megan considered the rocks, three of them, brown and gray and jagged, shaped like standing thin triangles, set close. They looked as if they'd used their pointy tips to force their way up from below the skin of the earth and now stood erect and majestic, being almost twenty feet in height, and indeed resembling an angular, spiky crown.

They left the river valley and marched over treeless rolling hills, and through spongy bogs, bumpy knolls, and across trickling streams. Emerging from a crisp and cool wooded vale, Graeme paused and stared straight ahead at the sea of green, the expansive flat grassland broken only by a rise straight ahead about a hundred yards or so. The rise was not insignificant but then it was a bit unusual compared to all other hills in the area, this one looking to be about the size of a football field but having a noticeably flat-topped profile.

Megan came abreast of Graeme, but only briefly, taking note of his expression, which she would have called staggered. He then broke into a run, sprinting across the grassland, hindered not at all by the tall, windswept grass that sometimes reached as high as his knees or those silly shopping bags that swayed wildly with each of his long strides.

She followed at a more leisurely pace, unable after so many hours of walking to even consider increasing her speed. By the time she reached the base of the mesa, Graeme had been standing up there for more than a minute. He was silhouetted against the sky from her point of view, hands on his hips while he stared at some fixed point, possibly unseeing, digesting what surely must be disturbing, to find no evidence that Newburn had ever existed, if this is where he expected it to be.

Megan paused and dropped her bags and purse, the former having made red lines in her palms and across the back of her hand. The sun had fought for the last quarter hour to make its presence known, successfully enough just now that Megan lifted her hand to her brow and stared up at Graeme. He was striking in form, looked every inch the proud and mighty warrior knight atop the hillock just now, bathed in the hazy and golden late afternoon sunshine.

Because he was so still, she did not call out but climbed the semi-steep incline and came to his side.

Without having to ask, Graeme offered, "I dinna ken what I expected, but to see it...I dinna expect this—nae sign, nae mark at all to say Newburn stood here, when I was here only a day ago in my mind. It does nae sit right in my heart, certainly nae my head."

He sounded nearly forlorn, as despondent as his deep voice could, she supposed. Instinctively, she laid her hand on him, her palm at his lower back. "I'm sorry, Graeme."

He nodded, his mouth crimped tightly, and stepped away, leaving her hand extended but no longer touching him.

He wanted privacy, she thought, or quiet at the very least, to process what he'd discovered, which was nothing at all, Newburn not being where he'd left it, essentially.

The grass was wet but then so were her leggings still, so Megan sat down, rather exhausted after their long trek. She said nothing, but watched Graeme, her heart breaking for him. If—somehow, some way—time-travel was real and he was indeed from another century, and as he said, had been here just yesterday, it must be awful and seem surreal to visit the same place and find it gone.

Having replanted his feet, his left knee bent to suggest some degree of either ease or resignation, and yet with his hands on his hips, he remained unmoving for quite a while. Long enough that the sun won its tussle with the clouds, chasing them away. Megan pulled the pony tail from her hair and ran her fingers through it, hoping it would dry quickly.

And then she simply sat. And waited.

There was no cell service out here, hadn't been any time she'd tried to call up a map on her phone over the last several hours, but the battery hadn't gone dead yet, which said it was now after six p.m. local time. At this rate, they'd be walking back to the inn in the dark. Still, she put no pressure on Graeme, didn't urge him to hurry up with his reflections or whatever he was doing.

Finally, after she'd changed positions several times and then had risen to her feet, hoping her leggings would dry as well, Graeme turned and strode toward her, closing the gap of twenty feet.

"Ye are verra kind, lass," he said, surprising her by lowering his head and giving her a quick kiss, "to allow me that time and space."

Megan nodded and then winced. "Did it...help? Whatever you were doing?"

"I canna say yet. But now I ask a larger favor."

"Bigger than hiking for more than four hours?" She asked, secretly praying it was not.

He made a face suggesting she might think it so.

"I wish to remain here, at least for what remains of the day and into the night."

Megan turned and surveyed the sweeping vista, meadows and mountains in every direction, as far as the eye could see. "Um...okay, but why?" Strangely, she knew no fear, was not clawed by any belief that this is where the serial killer came to life, that this had been his prolonged, carefully-laid evil plan all along. True, it might later madden her, seen through her *should have* lens if she were wrong, but she felt deep in her gut that she was not.

"I dinna ken how long it would take a witch to sense a presence, one in need or want," he answered. "The lasses, Holly and the others, were gathered for two days before any witch showed herself."

"Graeme, we can't stay out here for two days," she argued mildly but practically. "We don't have any water or food or...or anything."

"Nae that long," he responded. "If nothing happens overnight, we can make our way back to Dornie, ere the sun rises. But then I would want to return."

She digested this but did not dissect it immediately, asking instead, "Are you going to want to find Thallane as well?"

"Aye, but only if needed. I dinna ken I want to suffer another jolt as this, nae finding any evidence of *my* own home."

Megan nodded. "Do we...are we just going to sit up here?"

"Aye. If ye dinna mind. But we'll move off the plateau when darkness falls."

And so they did, sat where they'd stood, where Newburn once had stood. Megan asked Graeme to tell her about Newburn—what it would have looked like, sounded like, smelled like?

"Aye, I've ken the difference," he said. "Or rather, I imagine I never paid much mind to the noises I am accustomed to, but I ken straight away at your inn and then Fort William 'twas different here. Here at Newburn in my time, as at Thallane, you might hear horses whinnying and harnesses jangling. Wagon wheels dinna turn quietly as does the wheel of your bike. The smithy's hammer rings steadily. Livestock is nae silent, of course—and their scent, as ye might guess, hovers all about. I noticed the distinct lack of that here. Newburn, specifically, was having a bit of stone work done, masons pounding and scraping without ceasing at times upon my first visit."

He pointed out where Newburn as he'd known had stood on this flat hilltop, the keep or laird's manse in that corner, the stables there, the bakehouse around the rear where you would find the kitchen entrance.

For every answer he gave, Megan was enlivened to know more and asked follow-up or new questions. They chatted like that, all about Newburn and Thallane for more than an hour.

Graeme even described some of the people at his home, Thallane.

"Red Moll supervises the kitchen staff, serves as Cook as well," he said. "Gruff and feisty she is, but nae more dangerous than any barn cat. Roland is Thallane's steward—with capabilities beyond the average man; fair but then eager to ken a fine jest." He shrugged and grinned. "Sadly, too few come his way. Duncan's stepmother and stepsister, Doirin and Moire, reside at Thallane but nae for long. Dunc arranged Moire's marriage and her mother will be expected to depart with her to her groom's home after the wedding and feast." He glanced sideways and imparted, "Nae one will miss either of them."

And on it went, Graeme seemingly pleased to speak of his home and his kin, as he regularly referred to them. Having not yet encountered this very chatty Graeme, she wondered if he already suffered the loss of Thallane, if he missed his kin and home, and maybe worried—despite his assertion that he did not—that he might never see it or them again.

True to his word, when the last little arc of the sun slid down behind the western mountains, Graeme led them down and away from the flat hillock.

"We'll nae go far, lass, only remove ourselves from being targets in the open space and upon the ledge," he said, "but remain close enough that any illuminated entity will be seen."

Megan expected the chances of that to be very slim but did not tell him that. They walked toward the closest cover of trees, which was only a grouping of pines and one other tree, which Megan was unable to name. It had a broad leaf and more a shrub shape and configuration than a tree, many shoots growing rather than one trunk, its limbs expanding more widely than with any attempt to reach great heights.

They sat against its base, tucked under the dense canopy should more rain come. Megan flattened one of her shopping bags and sat on that, not of a mind to sit upon hard, possibly still damp ground for any length of time. Graeme got comfortable next to her, the growth of the tree's main bodies extending for a width of several feet, so that they sat side by side.

She yawned, her exhaustion unrelieved, and leaned her head back, hoping to God there were no spiders in this tree.

"Come, Megan," Graeme invited. "Make use of my lap. Lay your head down here."

That sounded as amazing in a cozy sense as it did awkward. She was not a prude but knew great moments of awkwardness and imagined that might certainly put her in such a situation. She liked Graeme, adored his kiss and wanted more, but strangely felt that she didn't know him *that* well that she might make herself so comfortable *on* his person.

"I'm fine but thank you." Before he might have pushed the issue, she asked, "What did it feel like, traveling through time?"

"Little do I recall," he replied. "'Twas simply a lack of light—but nae specifically darkness. Sounds odd, I ken, but that is how I perceived it. I felt verra light or as if I were buoyant, as if I were under a vast sea of water. I canna say if it happened swiftly," he said, snapping his fingers to indicate a flash of time, "or if it took hours or more to move me. I dinna remember any inclination that I was about to lose consciousness but ayc, dinna I, waking there in the auld broch with nae recollection of the journey?"

"All very peculiar, Graeme. I would have been freaking out." She yawned again and then thought to apologize. "You are not boring me in the least. I could listen to your voice all night long, but pardon me if I do happen to doze off. I am that whipped."

From the shopping bag at his side, he withdrew his odd plaid blanket.

"I have to ask," she said then, "what's with the blanket?" She knew tartans were a Scottish things, knew that clans wore their very own patterns, but she'd only ever seen them as kilts or hats or cloaks.

Graeme turned a ferocious frown upon her.

"'Tis a braecan, lass," he said, "or *braecan-feal* when attached to my person properly, belted and pleated. This is the MacQuillan tartan, kent by all in the Highlands. I wear it virtuously, identifying myself as kin to the MacQuillan."

"Oh."

Graeme's tone softened as he flapped out the length of it, clearly more than four or five yards. "However, it does serve many purposes, lass, and certainly can be employed as a blanket. And though ye will nae take me up on the offer of a lap pillow. Will ye at least lay yer head against my shoulder? I dinna mean to keep ye out here wholly uncomfortable. I'll wrap the braecan round both of us."

"Actually that's sounds very nice," she said while he stretched out his thick arms, spreading the braecan out fully behind them. "Thank you. My head keeps doing that sleep-bob thing."

She scooched closer to him and laid her head on his arm, unable to reach his shoulder while seated directly beside him, not with any level of comfort. Instantly, her cheek was warmed, the upper half of her cheek and temple pressed against the cotton of his tee while her lower cheek met nicely with his bare flesh under the short sleeve. She pulled the braecan around her where Graeme had draped it over her shoulder.

She sighed and turned her body toward him, expecting that soon she would need more of his warmth. She bent her legs upward, leaning them against his thigh. Graeme lifted his right arm and laid it over her knees, his hand hugging her shins. The familiarity did not offend her in any way, but actually warmed her in a different manner.

"Lass, I dinna see so many braecans about in this century," Graeme commented. "Do people nae longer have pride for their name and kinship?"

She had no idea. "Don't forget, I'm not from Scotland, Graeme. I'm sure there are still clans and...leaders of them, but I think things are different than when you're from."

"Are there nae battles between clans?" He asked. "Over land and wealth? Or simply for power's sake?"

"I don't think so," she replied. "I think those old clan wars have simmered down. Maybe all the fights are political now. People don't make war inside Scotland, against each other."

"Progress, I ken," he remarked, "if the fighting from within is nae more."

Not long after that, with Megan settled happily against him, Graeme asked quietly, "Do ye believe me now lass?"

Roused a wee bit from nearly falling asleep, Megan blinked several times and chose her words carefully.

"I *want* to believe, Graeme." She rubbed her knuckles over her eyes but kept her cheek against the warm muscles of his arm. "Certainly, I no longer believe you are a predator of women—a suspicion that lasted a little bit, by the way. For a short while, and because I could tell the names of those missing girls meant something to you, I wondered if you had lured them same as you might be luring me, pretending all this time-travel stuff and coming off a little confused but seemingly sincere, until you had them so wrapped around your finger, seduced by your...your smoldering gaze, that you could...I don't know, kidnap them, hold them hostage, and worse. I don't...I don't believe that's the case. Or at least I hope it's not."

"But ye came with me, here today," he reminded her, "and ye stayed, though ye had the option to leave."

"Because I really *want* to believe you." Otherwise, aren't I the nutjob, infatuated with either a seriously ill man or the aforementioned killer of women? "But—and we've talked about this—it's pretty hard without any proof to wrap my brain around something so...impossible."

A long silence saturated the cool night air until Graeme's voice came to her in the darkness.

"Ye ken my gaze is smoldering?"

She had hoped he'd have overlooked that part. She was pretty sure she could *hear* his grin.

"You know it is," she charged sleepily. No shame in admitting what was so obviously true, which was actually only an admission that she'd noticed it. "Even without mirrors in your time," she went on, speaking around her next yawn, "you would have to know that, what a woman sees."

"Enough time we have, lass," he said after a moment. "Tell me what *ye* see?"

Chapter Eleven

She never did answer, but damn, what he'd have given to know.

She'd fallen asleep instead.

He passed a rough night, weary but reluctant to sleep, restless but then unwilling to disturb Megan, who after a while clung to his side, having threaded her hand inside the crook of his elbow while she'd slept. She snored a wee bit, the sound not quite delicate but then not wholly unattractive. She was still perfect.

She'd been amazing all through the day, hadn't voiced but that one complaint, had allowed him time when they'd arrived to digest what had been found at Newburn—not one damn thing. 'Twas disconcerting, to have stood there where Lucas and Cora Thain, and Holly and the others might well be standing, in the exact same place but in a different time. What had become of Newburn? Of the Thains?

He'd spent those quiet moments, dozens and dozens of them, essentially attempting to conjure witches in his mind, believing himself as ridiculous as Megan sometimes or more often thought he was. At the same time, he was just so damn sure that either or both Sidheag and Samara would know he beckoned them. He felt that truth down to his bones.

All for naught, but he would not give up.

With morning came Graeme wondering what Megan surely had, though she'd not expressed her concern, how they might return to Dornie and the inn at which she resided currently. If he had been alone, the walk would not concern him. Though he was accustomed to riding everywhere, he'd found great delight in his new shoes, the comfort unparalleled, giving him no grief over so many miles. Megan had lagged regularly throughout their trek yesterday, forcing him to shorten or slow his stride on several occasions. Having asked and received so much from her already, could he really expect that she might march another dozen miles today?

In the end, they walked not quite half the distance between where Newburn was—or once had been—and the inn at Dornie. From the peaks of one of the taller beinns they traversed, Megan spied a road twisting through the glen.

"I wanted to see the majestic landscapes of Scotland, Graeme," she'd said, "but not so up close and personal or by hiking them for hours on end. Let's hitch a ride."

Hitchhiking, she'd called it after a while, though had lamented the rarity of cars on that remote stretch of road. Though she'd been pleased to walk on the smooth even track of black tar, her delight in that waned over the next hour, the amount of time it took to see their first car.

"Hitchhiking is not recommended," she'd said. "I wouldn't do it alone, of course, but I have you and I suspect no one in their right mind would try any funny business with you and your scowl. But good thing you aren't carrying your sword, or we'd never get a ride."

The car had stopped, the middle-aged man asking them if they were lost, raising a brow at the bags they carried. Megan's answer of "kind of," seemed to appease him and they were allowed entry into the vehicle. The man was kind enough to go out of his way to deliver them to the inn, but then annoying for how many times he reminded them of that very thing.

They'd been delivered to the inn almost an hour ago. Upon arrival, Megan had invited him into the chamber she'd let and asked if he'd wanted to use the shower. He did, approaching the chamber and the bathing device not so much ill-at-ease as he was curious. Quickly enough curiosity evolved to pure delight. He stood for quite some time under the hard spray of hot water, letting it splash onto his face and all over his head and upon his back. He made use of the soap and what Megan had called *shampoo* for his hair, as directed by her, and when he was done, he dried himself with those previously employed plush towels and availed himself to the teeth cleaning system, *toothpaste* and *toothbrush*, which Megan had generously offered to him.

Forethought would have meant that he'd brought his new clothes inside the bathroom with him, but fatigue had prevented that capability. Not intending to offend, he wrapped the over-large bath sheet around his hips and exited the bathroom.

Megan sat with her back to him on the closest bed, her legs crossed beneath her. She turned at his coming, her eyes widening.

"Holy shit," she said, her blue eyes moving slowly over Graeme's body. "Oh gosh, I'm sorry," she said then to a device she held at her ear, which had a springy, twisted cord hanging from it. "That wasn't meant for you. I'm so sorry. Yes, but that will be all, the coffee, waffles, eggs, and both the meats. Thank you."

She placed the device onto a matching gray box on the cupboard that sat between the two beds and hopped to her feet, facing Graeme.

"Are you trying to...? You could have—Geez, Graeme," she faltered, her cheeks turning pink.

He frowned, a wee surprised by her light outrage. "I dinna bring my garb into the bathroom with me."

"Right. Okay. Oh boy."

She sailed by him, purposefully avoiding looking at him, he was sure, a grin coming for her modesty, which was as charming as it was needless.

"I'll take my shower now," she said over her shoulder. "You can get dressed out here."

Before she closed herself inside the bathroom, she paused near the door, showing only half of herself, informing Graeme, "I checked again on social media and all the news. No word about Holly having returned."

"Aye, and thank ye, lass."

Twenty minutes later, in which time Graeme had donned another pair of boxers and a new pair of breeches and a fresh tunic, Megan emerged from the bathroom. She wore a garment of the same material as the luxurious towels, but this one appeared as a coat, having arms and a belt. Her hair was damp but not dripping, combed out neatly and hanging over one shoulder. She looked absolutely adorable, a wee too small for the overlarge coat, her bare feet curious for having too thin marks upon the top of each, which appeared to be very pale compared to the rest of her golden flesh, and then for the fact that her toenails were painted a bright and sparkling pink.

"Do you mind if I wear the robe while we have breakfast?" She asked.

Sitting in one of the chairs near the window, Graeme shook his head, finding no fault at all. "Nae worries, lass." She could dine naked if it pleased her. "Is that acceptable garb for the dining hall?"

"Oh, no, we're not going downstairs for breakfast. I ordered room service," she said, sliding into the chair across the table from him. "They'll bring it here to the room." She inclined her head at the smooth, folded parchment in his hand. "Can you read that?"

"Nae," he admitted. "Though I did try. I was studying the paintings on here. The artist is remarkable, the scenes so lifelike."

"Those are pictures, not paintings," she informed him and then immediately bounded up and out of the chair.

She collected her phone, detaching it from a thin and smooth rope and returned to the table, her fingers moving nimbly over the device. Briefly she held the phone up in front of her face, her arms extended a bit, and then leaned across the table, making the front of the phone visible to him.

Graeme leaned forward as well, looking at his own image on the phone and down at his tunic, his brow knitting for his lack of comprehension.

"There's a camera in the phone," she explained. "Cameras take pictures or um, capture images in a moment in time. See, here's other pictures I've taken. There's me and Jasmine when we first arrived—that's a selfie, me holding the camera and taking my own photo."

She swiped her forefinger over the image, and it was replaced by another and another, several images of lochs and mountains. She kept rotating the images, until more people appeared. Megan's face stared back at him in many of them. In every one of them, she was smiling.

"What is that on your face there?" he asked, recognizing only her blue eyes.

"That was during Covid—or the beginning of it," she said, showing a few more with her dressed similarly, in a tunic that matched her eyes in color, sometimes with other people.

"What is Covid?"

"It's an infectious disease, kind of like a plague, that swept across the entire world a couple years ago. We had to protect ourselves, so the masks and those glasses prevented us from getting sick. Ah, that was such an awful time. Almost the whole world was in lockdown, quarantined. But then these people would get Covid and come into the hospital—you know what that is, right? Okay, so they'd come in and because of quarantine, their families could not be with them. It was...it was heartbreaking, people dying alone."

She tapped her finger on the image of her leaning over a pale and smiling woman with crisp white hair, who wore a mask over her nose and mouth. The woman's eyes were bright but red rimmed and underlined by dark circles.

"That was Alma Stone. She was so sweet. I would take pictures of or with my patients and send them to their families. Poor Alma, eighty-seven years old, six children, fourteen grandkids, and three great-grandchildren, and she died alone. Broke my heart." She swiped again. "That's Ed Otto. Same thing, huge and close family, and he died with no one at his side."

There were more, dozens and dozens of them, her and her patients, all those people she'd cared for. In each image and despite all the gear on her face, he could see that she was smiling, her eyes behind the clear glass covering her eyes crinkled with good humor. And yet it had been heartbreaking, she'd said. He decided a time period could be established by the changes in Megan in each image. The more images she showed him, the healthier she looked. Those first ones of her in the mask had revealed signs of fatigue, the blue of her eyes wearier, fewer lines crinkling at the corners of her eyes. In those first images, she carried her own set of dark circles under her eyes, and her cheeks and forehead appeared much less robust of color.

"It was exhausting," he presumed.

"It was more depressing than exhausting, just so sad." She made a face, her mien suddenly forlorn, possibly recalling that period and all the heartache. "Honestly, I love nursing, I really do. But I'm a little worried that I've only been working in the hospital for a few years and...it's draining. I'm not sure I can see myself doing this for the next thirty or forty years. It's hard to see, day after day, so much sorrow and worry and loss."

"My wee tender-hearted Megan," he remarked, in awe of her.

Another healthy blush crept up her cheeks.

A sharp rapping at the door startled him and saw Megan bounding out of her chair.

"Breakfast is here," she forecasted, swinging open the heavy door.

A young lad entered, supporting an oval tray upon one of his shoulders. He crossed the chamber, walking directly toward Graeme, and lowered the tray onto the table, unloading each covered trencher while Megan rifled around in her small satchel beyond him. The lad barely made eye contact with Graeme before turning and facing Megan, pausing, the overlarge tray tucked under his arm.

Megan handed him a folded note and saw him out the door.

"God, I'm starving," she said when she had closed the door and returned to the table, sitting in the chair with her legs tucked beneath her, adjusting the plush robe but not before Graeme caught a glimpse of her bended knee.

She plucked each cover off the trenchers, uncovering an abundance of food, those things he'd overheard her requesting earlier: savory eggs and plump sausages, more of those stamped cakes, and strips of bacon, crispy and still steaming. In addition to this small banquet, there were two cups and a shiny black pitcher, from which Megan dispersed coffee, only recently known to Graeme but well-favored.

"Do you want me to prepare your coffee?" She asked. "Same as I did the other night at dinner?"

"Aye, please."

"It's helpie-selfie, Graeme," she said then while he waited. "Divvy up that food onto the two empty plates. You might be from another century and maybe are used to being waited on hand and foot but you're not there now and your hands aren't broken. You can dish it out."

He grinned at this but quickly got to work, dividing the fare between them, filling two plates nearly equally and leaving plenty of extras should either of them desire it.

Good company they kept then while they ate, Megan telling him more about her work inside the hospital while he, upon her request, shared more insight into his life at Thallane and in the fourteenth century.

When they finished eating, Graeme rather appreciating the private meal attended only by the two of them, Megan yawned and advised that she would love a nap.

"Would you mind?" She asked, and then was quick to clarify, "I don't need a lengthy power nap, just an hour to lose the brain fog."

Though fatigued himself as well but wanting to push through the lethargy, he had neither cause nor desire to deny her wish to rest. "Ye sleep, lass," he said. "I'll busy myself belowstairs or mayhap out of doors." He rose from the chair.

"Thank you." And she stood as well, once more searching through the contents of her leather satchel, approaching him after a moment holding up a small flat rectangle.

Briefly she instructed him on the use of the flat key that produced a blinking green light on the lock and then opened the door. "Tuck that in your pocket," she told him and then did this for him, shoving the small card into the pocket on his rear. "I think they serve cocktails all day on the back patio, if you're interested. But wake me in an hour and we'll continue our hunt for the witch." She bit her lip and screwed up her face a bit. "I'm not kicking you out—you can nap as well if you'd like. You just don't strike me as the napping type and I'm pretty sure you don't want to sit here watching me sleep."

"Dinna fash, lass," he advised and strode toward the door.

He glanced briefly at his plaid, folded neatly on the bed that might have been used by Jasmine for at least one night and then opted to leave it, even though he felt as undressed without that garb as he did without his sword, which was yet tucked away in the big blue outbuilding of the inn.

Unaccustomed to being idle, but with little else to do, Graeme made his way downstairs and then outside. He gave the gravel pavement just outside the door to the inn a wide berth as two cars were moving there and then ducked into the blue building to assure himself his sword remained. Satisfied that it was as he'd left it, he walked the perimeter of the property as he'd done once before, its margins easily distinguished by the neatly trimmed grass, which was in some places flanked by untamed brush and taller grass, and in one place, a stand of closely set birch trees.

He wound up eventually at the rear side of the inn, where a stone floor had been laid outside and where a half dozen round tables fringed by slanted back chairs did seem inviting. The *patio*, he assumed, which he'd spied from the windows of the dining hall, and where sat one other couple, their chairs close and their heads pressed together.

He chose the table and set of chairs furthest away from them and slid into the comfortable seat, enjoying a view of the loch. Though the sun did not shine, the water still glistened and danced with glints of silver.

He was soon approached by the same lad who'd served their supper the other night, Adam by name.

"A little R and R, aye?" Inquired the lad, his grin slow but seemingly genuine.

Graeme nodded, believing it was expected but not quite sure what he'd agreed to.

"Will ye have a drink while ye sit?" He asked next. "A Macallan 18, neat, aye?"

"Nae whiskey," Graeme decided. "Ale will be fine."

"What kind of ale will I bring?"

Graeme had no idea what his answer should be.

Possibly, it was his blank expression that prompted the lad to explain, "Mate, we serve twenty-seven different ales. Which one?"

With a negligent shrug, Graeme told him to decide.

"Sure thing, mate."

Adam returned shortly and Graeme sat with the richly colored ale, poured in a tall clear glass. He enjoyed the smooth, crisp flavor and was content to sit for a while, long enough to need a second serving of the dark ale.

When he was sure an hour had passed, he found his way back inside and up the narrow stairs, having to insert the key card, as Megan had called it, several times until the green light appeared and he heard the click Megan had advised he should expect. Though the door did not squeak or groan, he pushed it open slowly, not wanting to startle her from her sleep.

I'm pretty sure you don't want to sit here watching me sleep, she'd said earlier.

But he found that he did.

She lay in the bed closest to the windows and thus the table and chairs where they'd broken their fast. She had not climbed beneath the quilted blue blanket but lay on top, on her side, her knees bent and her hands tucked beneath her cheek. Graeme sat in the same chair he had more than an hour ago, stretching out his legs until they met with the hem of the bed linen, content to watch her. She was a lass of great animation, her face regularly corresponding with her mood and reactions. He'd seen her wide-eyed with surprise, and more than once she'd lifted but one delicate brow to show her disbelief. He'd witnessed her charming laughter and at least one occasion of tears, had seen her fresh and weary and had watched her attack and luxuriate in that sweet, nearly black cake, the sight more than captivating.

But despite last night's side-by-side sleeping arrangement, he'd yet to observe her in slumber, and now with this opportunity to do so, he was loath to give it up too quickly—the witches would have to wait.

He absorbed each detail of her face and body. Her hair was mostly dry now, fuller and messily arranged upon the pillow beneath her, one tendril of auburn curled around her neck. Her dark chestnut lashes made small crescent shadows beneath her eyes. Her rosy lips were crooked from her position, delectably so, looking as if she puckered them. Lines that in her wakeful hours frequently apparent were wholly absent now, her slumber peaceful.

Graeme scratched at his jaw and continued to watch her, ignoring the sense that he intruded in some fashion.

He was not without emotion, but he had known a hollowness inside his chest for more than a decade, ever since he'd lost his wife and son. Mariam had been his first—his only—love. She was as different from Megan as was this century from his own, quiet and circumspect, hard to make laugh, though this had only presented a constant challenge to Graeme and was not an obstacle. She was placid but not timid, and childlike—this noted only in retrospect, he being too young himself at the time to have considered her such. He'd never known her to be anything but content. She'd been so easy to love.

The prospect of a child with her had filled him with great joy and they had each, alone and together, eagerly awaited the coming of their babe. He'd thought more than once how ironic that the thing that had wrought such bliss should be the very thing that had taken all joy from him for so long. Aye, he mourned still, but time—as had been maddeningly predicted by many and often when he'd lost Mariam—had indeed lessened the ache.

He hadn't loved since, not like that, had been unable to know even the slightest stirrings of emotion, not anything more than the wee bits that were required to assuage his personal needs, always so impersonally.

Once more, with his elbow on the arm of the chair and chin in hand, he let his gaze wander over Megan.

He could not disavow the truth, which he'd known not from the first moment he'd met her, but decisively from the first moment he'd kissed her, that unintentionally or not, she was pouring a bit of herself into that void in his chest, filling it worthily, effortlessly. Not for the first time, Graeme mulled over how much more difficult it became, hour by hour, to consider leaving her.

Despite this concern, he could no longer resist the temptation she presented and moved to kneel at the side of the bed. Gently, he drew that lock of hair from around her neck, smoothing it back away from her face.

Her lashes fluttered but were slow to open and quite frankly, the slow but immediate smile that wakened her face upon seeing him was not going to make his eventual exit any easier. The effect of it was not lost on him, but was part of the reason that he leaned forward until his chest met with the side of the bed and lightly brushed his lips across hers. Megan did not demur, but lazily lifted her arms and twined them loosely around his neck.

"Ye wanted to be wakened," he said against her mouth.

"I did," she said as he moved his lips back and forth. "Possibly, I imagined a gentle shaking of the shoulder, maybe even a tickling of my foot. This is so much better."

"I agree, lass."

He pursued more, wanting to taste her and feel her, deepening the kiss, stroking his tongue inside her mouth. The first time he'd kissed her there had admittedly been some desperation attached to the action, potent curiosity and the very beginnings of desire driving the impulse. This kiss was different, was all about want, about need, for more of her. Without breaking away from her lips, Graeme rose a bit and fitted himself onto the bed beside her, drawing her into his embrace.

Megan's arms tightened around him. That was all the acceptance he needed, and his initial tender touch became hungrier, unyielding. Megan responded eagerly, moving her lips and tongue in time with his, until a groan of satisfaction was pulled from deep within his chest. The air inside the chamber was cool but her kiss was not.

He moved his hand down her arm, over the plush fabric of her robe, and then around to the middle of her collarbone, where her soft skin was exposed. He slid his palm lower, forcing the robe to open for him.

He'd just moved his hand left, feeling the first curve of her breast when she drew her hand away from his neck and covered his, her grip rigid enough to compel him to stop.

Graeme lifted his face and searched her blue eyes.

"I think you are...fascinating, Graeme," she said as her prelude. "Beyond that, maybe. And so handsome and kudos to you for not freaking out so much as I would have if I were thrown willy-nilly into another century. And...and well, you must know that I'm attracted to you. Obviously I am. I want you to like me and I want you to kiss me and I want to do so much more than that but what is the point? Either you are leaving or I am." She paused, considering his reaction, which surely at this moment only suggested he was aroused and wanting more. "Why would I purposefully and knowingly set myself up for a great big heartache?" She asked.

He did not dismiss her query as insignificant, did not belittle her concern in that regard. He leaned up on his elbow and looked down at her. "Would ye nae pluck the rose because it will die before long once separated from the plant?" He inquired. "Do ye avoid sunshine knowing rain must eventually come? Do ye refuse the wine because your head will ache come the morn?"

"Not quite the same, Graeme," she said, wincing a little for having spurned his comparison. "Can you...pursue this and then just walk away—or be taken away? And you're okay with that?"

"I am nae," he answered honestly, having thought briefly as she did. "Nae one wee bit. But I'd bemoan far greater all I didn't have or experience with ye than lament what we did share."

She was still hesitant.

"I will nae force ye, lass, as well ye ken by now."

She nodded and searched his face, looking into his eyes, and then her hand left his, moving again up and around his neck. "I just wish...things were different. But I hadn't thought about it from that perspective, and you might be right," she said, threading her fingers into his hair as she pulled him down to her lips. "I might regret more everything I *didn't* do with you. Right now, I don't want to think. I want to feel."

Chapter Twelve

You've gone mad, Megan West, she scolded herself, but the admonishment contained no force.

She wanted this, wanted him.

At this point, she was all in apparently, and had been possibly shortly after meeting him.

She'd just spent an absurd amount of money on three more nights at this hotel. Yesterday's shopping and car hires had seriously clogged up more of her credit card. She was taking her former professor's words to heart, truly living it up on vacation. She hadn't done any or all of that simply out of the kindness of her heart—she really would worry about her debt once she returned home. She'd done it because she was infatuated with him—strange tales of time-travel, unsavory garb, and menacing sword aside, along with everything else about him that frantically waved red flags and so much uncertainty before her eyes on a regular basis.

But his kiss was...well, it was soul-stirring and knee-weakening, and she wanted more of it.

"Don't think poorly of me, Graeme," she said, "but I've already wondered how you would feel, naked and pressed against me."

"*Jesu*, lass," he seethed against her neck, where he'd gone to kiss and lick. "Ye stiffen my shaft with words such as those. But dinna believe I have nae yearned for the same."

And suddenly she was inside some really raunchy, steamy novel of rakes and debutantes or warriors and maidens and she didn't care. *Stiffened shaft,* indeed. She wanted it, wanted all of him.

He returned to her lips, his kiss now demanding and coercive, taking from her as much as he wanted her to give. There was a magnificence to his kiss and taste—he'd apparently taken up her suggestion, had a draft or two on the patio—that was impossible to either resist or ignore. The devotion of his kiss, the way his tongue swept so expertly over her lips and inside her mouth stirred her. It fed her. She leaned into him, sliding her hand between them, a bit surprised by herself, taking the initiative as she never had before. Need, it must be. An overwhelming desire.

The fabric of his pants, there at the zipper, was warm where his erection pressed against the fly. Megan moved her fingers up and down and heard herself groan in response to the size and shape and hardness of him. And then, as if the kiss had started a fire and her hand at his crotch was only adding kindling, they began shucking clothing, lips and tongues connected and then parting as needed to remove his shirt or for those few seconds when he cursed and had to take time to undo the laces of his boots and get rid of those. Megan slid her arms out of the robe, having yet to dress, glorying in Graeme's reaction, the way he paused at the side of the bed, in the midst of dropping his pants, his gaze filled with wonder, she might have guessed, for the way his green eyes glided over her body, slowly, with so much reverence.

Not immune at all to his impressive body, she resisted the urge to lick her lips as he dug his thumbs between the waistband and his hips, pushing the pants and the boxers down and off. He stood naked before her, the size of his *stiffened shaft* wreaking havoc between her legs, where her body clenched with anticipation.

"Oh, Graeme," she breathed. She felt as if she were the one misplaced in time, tossed into some bower of the gods, little Megan West from Des Plaines, Illinois, unworthy of his magnificence—except that his continued ravenous regard said that she was not.

Instinctively she lifted her arms to him when he came to her, and a gasp was drawn from her at first contact, for how solid and warm he was against her aching nipples. The kiss was renewed, enlivened by their nakedness. He tangled his fingers into her hair and intensified the kiss, exploring deep inside her mouth while his hands began another equally titillating exploration.

Sex was not new to Megan. Sex with a good-looking guy was not new to her, either. But this was Graeme, who outshone any and every single guy she'd ever had interest in, far surpassing those few she'd gone to bed with. Vaguely, she wondered if she were dreaming, if her nap had become deliciously erotic.

No, she wasn't dreaming, she decided. She wouldn't be able to feel the exact and scorching heat of his kiss, or the spark of flames lit by his hands as they trailed down her neck and over her shoulders. In dreams, it would all be hazy, the feeling, the emotions. This was real and thank God, so that she could experience everything. Her senses were on fire. He was freshly showered, the scent of the hotel's sandalwood soap enveloping her as much as he did. His hair was soft, and his flesh was hard. Though her eyes were closed in hazy delight, she saw still the briefly flashed image of his brilliantly sculpted chest, so much more beautiful than her.

If she were dreaming, she was fairly certain she wouldn't know the absolute and breathtaking beauty of Graeme touching her nipples, grazing the pads of his thumb roughly over the hardened pebbles. Her body clenched delectably, at the surface and all the way to her core, burning for him, to have him inside her. When he lowered his face to her chest, she threaded her fingers through his hair. His clever teeth plucked at her nipple, while his hand squeezed and lifted her entire breast. He used his tongue on the peak while his teeth held it in place. Megan whimpered his name—a dream in itself, to sigh his name while he did these things to her—and withdrew her hands from his hair to grasp at his hips, pulling his erection against her.

"Megan," he growled, an ache detected, lifting his face from her breast. "I canna wed ye, nae in this time." Pain, remorse, and hunger were etched in every cord and vein of his face and neck. "If ye mean to save yourself for your eventual husband, stop me now. Otherwise, command me to finish this, lass," he seethed raggedly. He rose upward and kissed her senseless once more and then begged, "Dinna ask me to stop now, Megan."

"There is nothing to save and no one to save it for," she said, her brain fogged with the luscious cloud of sexual delight. "I'm not a virgin, Graeme, and if you're okay with that, then I happily give myself to you. For now, in this moment, and for however long we have together."

Those words struck her as uncharacteristically romantic but then so powerful, saying them aloud, making that commitment, which was everything she wanted right now, and for as long as Graeme or Fate or Delta Airlines would allow it.

Graeme sealed her affirmation with another weakening kiss and then slid down her body, his hands skimming over and pausing at her breasts even as he continued to move down on the bed. When he drifted his mouth across her belly and then lower,

Megan let her head fall back as all clear and rational thought escaped her. *Yes, please*, her body whispered with urgency. She inhaled swiftly at the first touch between her legs, his lips and breath dancing over the Brazilian triangle that cost her seventy-five bucks a month to upkeep. He pushed her knees up, spreading them apart gently.

She shuddered and sighed at what he did to her, his tongue teasing and tormenting, his lips and breath fanning the flames that he created. A flush suffused her, tingling along every inch of her body, along her limbs and over her breasts under his hands, prickling with sensation everywhere. Megan could not have opened her eyes if she wanted to, at once languorous and then taut with a keen and powerful expectation. She arched her back and gripped the bed's comforter, murmuring whatever came to mind, willing to be enthralled by Graeme and his touch, so very far removed from being disappointed. Pleasure drifted over her, teasing her, always within reach but eluding her attempts to seize it. This was part of Graeme's enslavement then, adjusting the pace or the depth of his stroke, his touch breathtakingly intimate, astonishing for its flawlessness.

And then her pulse quickened with greater excitement and noises she foggily thought she should tamp down erupted from her. She lifted her bottom against his lips and cried out softly, her body tightening and expanding simultaneously. A violent joy soared throughout her, skipping across her body like a stone over the water, sending waves of pleasure everywhere, at her core where he labored so dreamily, across her belly clenched with the intense release, up to her aching breasts, and downward, curling her toes.

Megan embraced it, reveled in it, had no thought to resist the fullness of it. Until this moment right now, never had she wished more fervently that a moment should remain, that pleasure would not ever fade. But it did, of course. Her body quieted, her giddy pulse returning to normal.

She opened her eyes finally to find Graeme watching her but could give him little more than a wobbly smile, one of profound admiration. She thought she should try to sit up, thought she should return the glorious favor.

"Ye come apart so beautifully, love," he said, his voice husky.

A bit mindless, she said, "I'm so happy to come undone."

"There's more, ye ken," he said, moving his knees up until he perched between her thighs, delighting her with a wild kiss.

Instinct moved her hand, reaching for him before he would have entered her, wanting to touch him, know him. Her fingers encircled him, and she suffered only a brief regret that the even strokes of her hand along his rigid velvet skin did not at all compare to what he'd done to her, what he'd given her.

"I need to be inside ye, Megan," he said, forcing her hand away with a forward shove of his hips.

She whimpered at the first touch of his probing length and smiled and let out an unexpected shaky laugh, so delighted by his first smooth and satisfying thrust, which filled her wholly.

He paused, for which Megan was thankful, wanting to relish this, the beauty of it.

They expressed the sensation in murmured words, spoken at the same time.

"God's bones, lass, but ye are heaven."

"That's...it's just perfect."

Sweet heat engulfed her, and she trembled as he plunged again and then again, the seductive motions of his hips thrusting forward coupled with the way he filled her igniting a fever of longing renewed, a thousand times greater than any she'd ever known. "Oh, God, yes," she moaned as he kept up the rhythmic tempo, one hand hard and strong under her ass, the other soft and tantalizing on her breast. "This is heaven," she whispered brokenly, yearning and throbbing once more.

"Ah, Megan," he ground out against her, before searing her with his kiss.

He drove deep and hard, increasing the rhythm, driving her mad with the temptation of a second release. She reached for it, wanting him to know the joyful anguish as well, clenching her core around him, eliciting a deep, vibrating groan. Megan climaxed only seconds before Graeme thrust a final time, going perfectly still while he shuddered as he came inside her. She let the fiery bliss wash over her, soaking it up, lazily skimming her hands down Graeme's tensed arms, over the steel of his muscles. She felt as if she blossomed from the inside, flowering and flourishing in Graeme's capable hands.

Graeme shifted again, in and out, with excruciating slowness, wringing a small sigh and idyllic shiver from her, her entire body sensitive, tingling now, prolonging her orgasm until she was completely and contentedly drained.

The heat of her body slowly returned to normal once more, but she knew she was not the same, would never be the same again. It simply wasn't possible. This was something she'd never done, had never before let someone inside. Not physically, the sex itself, but otherwise, granting Graeme entry to places inside her mind and heart that she normally held so close and tight, walled off from the world. Oddly enough, it did not cause her to panic but strangely saturated her with that other thing she'd purposefully kept at bay for so many years: hope.

At length, Graeme slid off her and slumped to her side, in the middle of the bed. Barely a second passed before he gathered her into his arms, anchoring his leg over hers, his chin resting on the top of her head. Megan snuggled against him, burrowing into him as much as she was able.

"I'll want more, lass," he said, his tone lethargic.

"Yes, more," she agreed, drifting a bit, further sleep inescapable. "Much more, preferably soon, hopefully more often than not."

"Aye to that, love—more and often."

***

He'd only meant to kiss her, hadn't much been able to resist. He truly hadn't intended that it would have gone any further, certainly could not have imagined that it would progress as it had, to that soul-wrenching conclusion.

Jesu, but this lass!

Aye, he should have known though, having only been made hungrier by the few kisses they'd shared. Once she'd lifted her arms to him, he'd been lost. As soon as she'd uttered those beguiling words, *I don't want to think. I want to feel*, he'd known there was no turning back.

But how now? How could he watch her leave? How could he ever leave her?

Light streamed in through the windows, through the transparent curtains, bathing her lithe, naked body in pale and shimmering light, her skin aglow yet with the dew of their lovemaking. Graeme kissed the top of her head and tightened his arms around her.

He would never consider that the afternoon had been wasted, but they did not leave the bed for several more hours. They'd dozed, or at least he had, waking and knowing an instant recollection that something tremendous had occurred and in the next second realizing Megan's presence in his arms.

He wasn't ready to move, or certainly not to relinquish this moment. He wanted more with her, was wide awake now, filled with thoughts of her and more desire. He should have known, might have guessed it, that having her was only going to whet his appetite for more, not quench it entirely, not for long.

Graeme began to move his hands, testing her wakefulness. She was sleepy but not sleeping, murmuring, "Mmm," as she moved her hand over his chest. And that was all it took, all he needed. He lifted up and over her, pushing her onto her back again. plundering her mouth with a blazing kiss.

His cock sprang to life and Megan groaned, feeling it rise against her.

"We'll never get to Newburn," she said between kisses, her small fingers closing around his shaft, stroking as she had before, goading him to greater passion, to forget all else.

"Newburn and the entire fourteenth century can wait, lass."

Graeme sat up, his back against the head board, knowing exactly what he wanted with her. He reached for her. She took his hand, her grin intrigued and prodded by a tug of his hand, moved one leg and then the other until she was straddling him. Immediately she wrapped her arms around his neck and plied him with a kiss, so brilliantly soft in his arms.

His hands found her breasts, their high, rounded shape already known and loved. He pushed them up and together while they simulated with their mouths and tongues what they'd done so superbly before, what they were about to do again. Graeme lowered his hands to her slim hips and broke the kiss. Her gaze was heated, still, waiting. She was breathless again.

He'd been lost before, hadn't thought to create an image to keep with him, had closed his eyes when first he'd sunk into her tight sheath. Not this time.

"Keep your bonny blue eyes on me, lass," he said hoarsely as he tightened his grip on her hips and brought her down on his shaft.

A noisy, titillated breath escaped her. She held his gaze, her beautiful lips parted, her hands reaching for the top of the bed behind him.

He did not slam into her, but glided inside with careful precision, filling her but not completely. A tortured smile lifted her lips. She knew what he wanted now, a wee whimper escaping for his desire for controlled strokes, his hands at her hips dictating their pace.

She wanted no part of that, but squirmed and writhed to have her way—all of him. She closed her eyes, her head lolling back, the arch of her neck so graceful, perfect. Graeme wondered if she had any idea how bloody arousing, how very desirable she was.

Aye, he wanted to take her by the hips and crash her down on him as well, but this first. She shifted, giving a sweet and sensual undulation of her hips as she rode him, applying her lips to his temple and cheek and down over his jaw and neck. Heaven, indeed, the way her sheath closed and throbbed around him. Another moan came, and she fought against his pace, what limits he put on them so far, wanting him deeper.

His own grin was pained. It was a glorious torture.

Finally he gave her—them—what they wanted, slamming her hips down hard until she was seated fully around him. She cried out a gorgeous noise and found release with the second hard thrust. Her walls compressed around him, heightening his own arousal. Megan went liquid in his arms, on his pulsating erection. Graeme wrapped an arm around her and stood, keeping her in place. He took her to the only bare wall of the chamber and continued to thrust into her. She didn't need to hang on to anything but him, but she leveraged herself, one hand on the arm of a light to his right, her other on the tall bureau to his left. It was an open, provocative pose, splayed out against the wall, her small breasts bouncing up and down to the rhythm of his thrusts, her legs wrapped around his hips. His release came hard and fast, his jaw clenched, driving into her one last time, closing his eyes, reveling in this.

"Damn, Megan, you feel so bluidy guid."

When he'd been still for several seconds, he dropped his head to her shoulder while her arms abandoned their anchors and moved around him, over his shoulders and down his back. Eventually, Graeme straightened but did not withdraw from her, simply gathered her closer and kissed her, lazily, slowly, with as much appreciation as he could muster just now for how amazing she was. He couldn't think about the next time just now, he was that depleted, happily so, but he hoped like hell that he would be able to do this at least another thousand times with her.

Megan West had made him her willing captive, body and soul.

And his heart clenched with something akin to pain, something that resembled or was sorrow itself, knowing there would not—could not—be a thousand more occasions of this.

***

She couldn't decide if she should file what they'd done under her ignoring red flags and searching wildly for love, for any sort of affection, or if this was only a case of the ever-practical Megan, meaning to be the perfect child and teen and adult, simply falling off the wagon, the temptation of Graeme MacQuillan impossible to resist. There might be something said, also, for the fact that of all the guys in whom she had ever shown any interest, whose notice or regard she might have wanted, none of them had ever treated her as Graeme had. She felt his desire, in his words, in the way he looked at her, in how gloriously he'd just made love to her. If she were parted from him now at this moment, she would go to her grave believing that there was some affection attached to their sex. She could be wrong, she was a terrible judge of people, but she didn't think she was this time.

Gathered in his arms with her head in the crook of his shoulder, their heartbeats finally slowing to normal, Megan stilled the fingers she'd been scratching across the broad expanse of his chest.

"Graeme, would you say you are getting used to the twenty-first century?" She barely recognized her own voice, imbued with a dreamy, delightfully satiated quality.

"I like *ye* in the twenty-first century," was his pleasing though less informative reply.

Fearful of the answer, Megan couldn't bring herself to ask, *Enough to stay?* He'd made it abundantly clear—almost from the start, one of the first things he'd said to her—he needed to get back to his time.

"I canna recall the word ye used, lass," he said after another moment while his hand stroked lazily over the side of her arm, "when ye said ye were only visiting Scotland. But why? Whom or what do ye visit?"

"Vacation," she reminded him. "I wasn't specifically visiting anyone. I don't know anyone here. I was just visiting Scotland itself. I wanted to see it. I have a list of places I want to see. Ireland. Prague. Australia. All over the world." She recalled how she'd determined which place to travel to first. "When I decided I was serious about traveling—which is just for leisure and because my little world in Illinois is rather small—I said to myself: all right, the next place I hear mentioned or see something about, one from my list, that's where I'm going. And the next day at work, one of my patients was from Scotland," she said, recalling John Anderson, a seventy-six year-old from Fraserburgh in Aberdeenshire, who sadly passed away after only a few days in the hospital, only one of those in the ER under Megan's care. "I decided that was my sign. I booked my trip the next day, originally just as a solo traveler, but then Jasmine made this big fuss, why hadn't I invited her? Why was I going alone?" She needn't rehash what had happened with that arrangement as Graeme had witnessed it.

"But if ye journey to any of these other places, ye will nae travel with Jasmine again," he presumed.

"Um, no. I don't think so. I'd rather go alone."

"Ye have no one else...?"

"No."

"Because ye have nae kin," he supposed. "And how is that? Ye were nae raised by wolves, so what became of your kin?"

"I have no idea," she told him, shrugging against his chest and arm. "I was orphaned very young. I never knew who my father was—my mom left that blank on the birth certificate. And then my mother died when I was four, so I don't remember her at all. My grandmother raised me until I was seven but I'm guessing that wasn't so great since I retain very few memories of her or that time. Most of my childhood memories begin and include the different foster families that raised me."

"Nae verra solid footing, a beginning such as that," he remarked, kissing the top of her head.

"No, I guess not." But it was all she knew.

He didn't ask or add, but she wondered if he thought, as she did, that yes, it was lonely.

She didn't let it bring her down.

Megan was fairly certain she could not be brought down from today's high.

She couldn't remember a time, or if ever, she'd lounged so cozily after such great sex—two magnificent occasions of that, by the way—her partner still wanting conversation with her, wanting to know about her.

When she rose to shower before dinner, she was still wearing the smile that had been hers all afternoon.

Chapter Thirteen

The next week of days went by entirely too fast for Megan's liking. Even as she lived it, was still immersed in it, she feared she wouldn't be able to recall properly or with such detail all that was wonderful and momentous, or even the smaller details that made her Graeme's happy and willing accomplice in bed and outside of it. When her phone wasn't acting up, turning on and off whenever it wanted to, she took picture after picture of him and them, supposing she would cry over these when her vacation was done, or Graeme was gone.

Earth shattering sex aside—she would never believe she wouldn't remember and revisit every succulent detail of Graeme's lovemaking—he was simply perfect as a companion, amenable to each of her requests and suggestions, teeming with information about his life and the Highlands in the fourteenth century. Plus, he provided true joy simply watching him eat what he called *the marvels of this century's kitchens*.

They had agreed that they would devote each afternoon to the hunt for the witch at Newburn, or where Newburn had once stood, it's location pinned on her phone. She'd gotten friendly with a hired driver and asked if he wouldn't mind picking them up every day at the lodge at the same time, driving them out to search or wait for a witch or some other magic that would take Graeme away from her. The mornings were reserved for other things; they ordered room service the very morning after he'd first made love to her with such feral passion and had barely left the bed until noon; that afternoon they'd biked around the loch, Megan singing her heart out, her joy boundless and screaming inside her—not that the grand Highlands needed the addition of a rousing Lady Gaga song sung off-key—and then they'd enjoyed lunch on the patio before David, the driver they'd hired, arrived to take them to Newburn's site. The next day began with a bus trip down to Fort William—much less expensive than hiring a car; she'd wished she'd inquired or known about that sooner. They had breakfast at a small café that was also a bookstore, where Megan bought four books in her favorite genre, cozy mystery. The day after that, Graeme had suggested they rent one of the long canoes available and leased by the inn. He'd paddled them from one end of the loch to another and back again, seemingly tireless, while Megan had read aloud from *Invitation to Mayhem*, which was the second book in the series. Megan had read *Invitation to Murder* more than a year ago.

She'd finally gone on the tour out to Skye. They'd caught the ferry from Glenelg, Graeme giving her no grief at the sight of the noisy metal barge or the trip across the water. They'd visited the Highlands' famous Fairy Pools, where it was said that fairies had once and perhaps still lived. The deceptive tropical blue of that water suggested a tepid temperature, which was not the case at all. The water was icy when Megan had dipped her fingers in it.

She'd booked them an excursion in and around Loch Ness, explaining the legend of the sea creature to him. He'd slanted a dubious brow at her, which had wrung a smile from her.

"You were moved through time by a witch," she'd challenged, "and yet question the possible existence of a much-revered sea creature?"

Their excursion included tours of local villages, beginning in Fort Augustus and progressing to Drumnadrochit village, where they visited the Loch Ness exhibition center, which Graeme proclaimed presented more speculation and imagination than evidence of any mysterious creature.

Their wee adventures were not without their own little missteps, Graeme proving peculiar and unexpected in different ways.

At the fairy pool Graeme had given her a good scolding for tempting Fate by daring to touch the water. He'd brusquely pulled her away from the inviting pool, to the consternation of several others at the same spot. Megan had soothed his upset with a laughing kiss, telling him that he was stuck with her for now.

"Dinna...just dinna do that, lass," he'd said in a stilted voice, giving the water a hard glare as he'd ushered her away.

At the café/bookstore, the barista taking and making their order had been chatty, asking as had a few others since her vacation had begun where in the States she was from and how she was liking *our wee Scotland*. Though admittedly very nice looking, he was simply making conversation, just being friendly. Graeme had thought otherwise, sidling up to Megan, his scowl returned as he curled his lip at the guy, his displeasure having grown when the guy handed over their coffees and sandwiches, saying harmlessly, "Here ye are, fair Megan."

Graeme had taken exception to this. "Have ye sought leave to address her so familiarly?" He surprised both Megan and the barista by asking. "If it's a courting ye're about, I suggest ye find another lass on whom to practice your uninspired efforts. She is mine."

"Mate, chill," instructed the kid, suddenly bereft of all good humor.

Megan had been forced to clap her hand over her mouth to keep from laughing outright and out loud. She'd swiftly voiced abundant apologies to the startled guy, giving the swiftly concocted and very lame excuse, "He's kidding. He's working on his role as warrior prince for the play at the theatre next week," before she'd ushered Graeme away from the counter, having no idea if Fort William either had a theatre or put on plays.

"What the hell was that about?" She'd hissed at Graeme, though she was still smiling as they'd claimed a small bistro table near the back of the shop. *She is mine* was both endearing and arousing. There was no threat to her affection for Graeme, she might have told him but did not. By this time, her heart was well and truly invested.

"What said he? *Mate, chill?*"

"He was asking you to relax," Megan had replied, "basically telling you he is no threat."

"He is nae threat," Graeme had assured her arrogantly.

Still semi-amused, Megan quipped, "Yes, dear."

When they'd rented the canoe, the string bean kid working that booth at the dock had asked if they required a rower.

"A rower?" Graeme had repeated, his frown instantaneous as he'd looked over the boy's skinny frame, not bothering to hide his skepticism of the boy's capabilities. "More sword practice, lad," he suggested to the kid, who at that moment looked as if he were stoned for the way he stared at Graeme, as if he didn't quite understand what he was saying. "Ye need bulk in those arms," Graeme recommended. "I dinna ken how you might guide a birlinn and nae see those wee limbs snap off for the exertion."

Megan had shoved him forward toward the canoe, showing her key card to the kid so that her room would be charged for the rental. "Sorry about that," she said, hoping her grin showed none of her embarrassment-by-association. "His ship just recently landed from Mars."

To Graeme, she'd suggested gently, "Maybe a few less of the personal attacks on these people only trying to do their jobs."

"Ye expect that lad," Graeme had argued, "who is nae wide enough to bless himself, might operate the bìrlinn better than I?"

Megan had rolled her eyes. "Not the point, Graeme."

This morning, they'd decided they would revisit the broch where she'd first discovered Graeme, having some hope—his not hers—that the witch or *a* witch might appear and zap Graeme back to his time. Once more they borrowed bicycles from the ones supplied by the inn. While in Fort William the other day, Megan had bought two umbrellas and two rather pricey rain coats, since she didn't want those cheap plastic ones that might serve to keep them dry but would do nothing to prevent the chill she felt each time it did rain. They would come in handy today; though it wasn't raining steadily or heavily, there was and had been all morning a persistent mist falling. She'd also purchased a good canvas backpack for Graeme, after he'd lamented that he didn't like leaving his plaid—braecan, he regularly reminded her—behind at the inn every time they went out.

"You are bringing your sword?" She asked Graeme as they left the hotel room. He hadn't brought it with them on any of their excursions to the Newburn site.

"Only because I can," he said, making adjustments to his belt so that the sword was strapped vertically on his back. He put his arms through the backpack straps and affixed that over his sword. "Ye said I could nae have it in a hired car, but on the bike I can."

Megan chewed the inside of her cheek, watching him ready himself for the ride. A thought occurred to her, one that maybe had been tucked away in her subconscious: he had everything with him that belonged to him. If he left now, she'd have nothing by which to remember him, nothing but those pictures on her phone. What would happen as memories began to fade over time? How would she remember him and every splendid moment they'd shared?

He'd shaved yesterday, using her razor, needing a quick bit of instruction. She missed the rugged and sexy stubble and the feel of that scraping across her skin but she equally adored the sensual lines and chiseled angles of his clean-shaven face and jaw.

"Ready?" He asked, straddling the bike, the same one he'd used to ride around the lake, a bit larger than hers, the middle bar a bit higher.

Megan nodded, showing him a wistful smile, the best she could do while dread clawed at her heart.

Nothing good ever stays.

Darren Robinson, a kid she'd once fostered with, had said that to her when the family they'd been with for almost a year, which might have been Megan's favorite home, had been forced by the husband's job to relocate out of state.

It was rather like the old adage, *this too shall pass*, but considered from a different perspective, a sad reminder of the truth that even the good things were only ever transient.

The melancholy stayed with her throughout their ride, which was not so easy as the first time simply because the ground was more drenched than it had been on that occasion. She endured so many misgivings about the entire affair. Might she simply board a plane back to the States in two days and never know what became of Graeme, or if any of his wild tales had actually been true? She debated whether this, most of all, might be what tormented her all the rest of her life—second only to the probability that she might never see him again.

They saw no other person on any part of their ride, not on the main roads or on the bike paths or along the sparse trail that took them over rolling green hills. Along those rising and falling knolls, Megan's bike slipped several times in the mud, which was by now splashed all over her sneakers. Miraculously, she righted the thing each time, managing to keep herself from landing in the muck and mud.

It was early afternoon when they arrived. Graeme opened the gate, and they walked their bikes on through and up the incline. It looked almost exactly as it had on that first accidental visit here, when she'd found Graeme inside the ruins of the round house. Once more, the small hill was dotted with lazy sheep and the sky overhead was a restless gray.

Leaving the bikes around the back side, behind the nearly complete still-standing wall, they stepped down into the depressed circle where Graeme had lain, more than a week ago at this time.

Megan smiled. "You were terribly rude, by the way," she said. "Threatening me with a sword and launching yourself at me while I was trying to escape."

Graeme sent her a tender smile. "I must have ken, right from the start, I dinna want ye to get away from me."

"I'm sure that's what it was."

"'Twas the first guid look I had at your eyes, lass," he said, "when I pinned ye on the ground, the blue so vivid, so brilliant. I could nae let you leave me."

Warmed by this admission, even as she was sure it had nothing to do with his demand at the time that she help him, Megan kicked at some of the wet brown leaves coating the ground inside the loch. "You brought all your stuff with you today, but you did not any time we went to Newburn. Are you expecting that today is the day? That the witch will come?"

"Peculiar, is it nae?" He asked. "I had nae sense that this would prove any different than any of the time wasted at Newburn, and yet I packed the saddlebag, rather intuitively I imagine, in that way."

Perhaps the somber face she could not hide brought him to her. He covered the slight distance between them in a few strides and took her cheeks in his warm palms, planting a soft and slow kiss on her forehead before he gathered her into his arms. They stood in that embrace for a long moment before Megan once more spoke of the inevitable.

"I'm not going to like it at all if you're somehow magically taken away," she said and then made light of it, "and not only because I'll have to escort two bikes back to the inn."

"Nae more than I, lass, when I contemplate ye getting on that car that soars through the sky as would a bird—which I still canna comprehend."

"Three more days, Graeme," she reminded him sadly, seized by a now familiar twisting of her heart.

"Stay," he said, his voice ragged, possibly as close to begging as he'd ever come. "Stay with me, Megan."

"So that you can leave me when the time comes? If it does?" She pulled away from his arms.

He sighed, his expression tortured. "Then come with me."

She gaped. "To the fourteenth century? Graeme, I have an entire life back home in Des Plaines."

"Ye dinna," he argued, his scowl seen for the first time in days. "Ye have nae family. Your closest friend abandoned ye without a backward glance, with nae any contact through your device there as ye expected. Ye say the healing is wearing on ye—your words, lass. To what do ye return?"

Megan shrugged. "Normalcy?"

"Is that what ye want?"

"Graeme, my childhood was chaos," she tried to explain, "tossed around from one foster home to another. I've spent my life searching for something—the family I never found, of course, but also peace. My life may be dull—and it is—but there is peace. There is so much to be said for my very boring routine, the consistency of my hectic job, my own apartment and my bike and the few friends I do have—they are familiar. I built this life myself," she said, tapping her chest.

"Ye can have more," he gritted with some desperation. "Build a life with me, lass."

"Stay here with me," she offered as an alternative. Her throat clogged, tears imminent. "Come to Des Plaines with me."

"Lass, I...I have people—kin—to return to, who wait for me. I dinna say as much to hurt ye, Megan. Ye ken I would nae—"

She nodded abruptly, understanding his point, dropping her gaze for a moment to compose herself. "Truth is truth, no harm done." Lifting her watery gaze to him, she whispered, "I'm sorry, Graeme. I'm not brave enough to risk even my pitiful little life for...."

"For me?" He asked, his jaw hardening.

Megan tilted her head, wearing an anguished expression. "To return to chaos. You're asking me to choose something I don't understand, something I'm not even sure is real."

"Why do ye devote yourself to me, to my quest, if ye dinna believe?" He challenged.

She was pathetic, she'd already established that, and so there was no sense lying to him. He would know, anyhow. He had to know by now.

"I wanted to be with you," she said in a small voice.

He sighed and ran his hands over his eyes and the stubble of his jaw and then planted his fists on his hips and contemplated her silently. "Ye are brave," he said after a moment, harshly, as if all of it, the entire discussion and situation, frustrated him. "Of course ye are, to have made the life ye have, to wear smiles and give of yourself so generously when nae one has returned the favor."

Hoping to dismiss even this wee praise, with which she was not comfortable, she made light of it. "Well, yes, I have my own brand of bravery. I mean, I'm not Steve Irwin brave, tickling the balls of dangerous animals—God rest his soul—but I'm not afraid of raw cookie dough, there's that. And while I do look both ways when crossing, sometimes I don't wait for the hand to turn green. A rebel, I know." Of course, he didn't understand her references, so she grinned cheekily at him. "And this one time, this guy I met said he was from the fourteenth century, and I was like, great, let's get you back there."

That he understood, one corner of his sumptuous mouth quirking. "Aye, as I said. Brave, ye are."

They stayed all afternoon at the ruins, this endeavor as fruitless as all the rest. At one point, Graeme had pushed away from the low wall he'd been leaning against, looking around with some tense expectation, as if he heard or felt something. But nothing happened and he returned his perch to against the stone while Megan, seated atop a level section of the two foot wide crumbling wall, returned to her book.

They returned to the inn shortly after six, the bike ride back taking away another hour of their time. Their moods had adjusted, fitted now to their dissatisfaction, not specifically with each other but with so untenable a circumstance. Splendidly they might be enjoying each other now but the truth was, they had only just met a week ago. Though disappointing, it was not exactly unexpected that neither was willing to give up real life as they knew it to remain or go with the other.

That night, Graeme's lovemaking was the most tender it had ever been, his kisses soft and lingering, their joining devoid of the previous urgency and hunger. He loved her leisurely, intentionally, bringing her to the brink of the purest delight many times before he finally sent her magnificently over the edge. Her release was the most beautiful thing she had ever known but it did not come without a tinge of sorrow, wondering if this would be the last time they would know this, wondering if he considered that as well.

**

They had only days left, if that. Either she would leave Scotland, or he would finally be taken backward in time. It would be at the broch, he now knew. He'd felt it yesterday, a change in the air around them as they'd lingered at the ruins. 'Twas the same as it had been at Newburn that day, when the witches had come, a shimmering weightiness to the air, almost similar to the sense one got when a grand storm was brewing, but...different as well, charged with a wee otherworldly character, that awareness.

He hadn't told Megan but knew he must. He planned to return there today. He had all morning then to convince her to go with him, not only to the site of the broch, but home with him.

He sat in the chair by the window in her chamber, watching and waiting while she was on the phone with someone named Delta. She'd explained to him that while she wasn't willing to journey back in time with him, she was prepared to delay her own departure but needed Delta's permission to do so.

As ever, he was pleased to sit and watch her. She was dressed today in a thin and clingy tunic and a ridiculously small garment that she called *shorts*, which had wrought a severe reaction from him when he realized she intended to wear them not only in this private bedchamber. The idea of other people, males specifically, gawking at the creamy smooth flesh of her lissome legs drove him nearly to distraction.

He would have expressly forbidden her to step outside this chamber wearing only those shorts, putting her legs on display in that fashion, but that he understood now it was common to reveal so much skin in this time. Inappropriate, he still believed, but not exceptional by twenty-first century standards.

Otherwise, she was as bewitching as ever. Though he preferred her hair loose and draped over her shoulders—or better, spread about the pillow while he was loving her—there was a charm to her ponytail, which hid none of her bonny face from him.

"I'm just asking what is the cost to change this flight I'm booked on for another, say at the end of the week," she was saying now to the phone, a device Graeme still could not comprehend. "How much would that be?" She asked next. "Christ, are you kidding me? Sorry, sorry. It's just that I'm asking to change a reservation already made. I didn't expect to have to give an arm and a leg and a few internal organs as well."

Graeme frowned at this.

He might have liked to remain, for a wee bit anyway, to learn more of this century. Megan had advised that he was experiencing so little of it, in reality. She'd called Fort Willian, which had staggered him as much as it had intrigued him, a small town compared to so many other places. She'd claimed there were structures in other locations, buildings that reached into the clouds the way the mountains here did—improbable, he'd thought, secretly accusing her of a wee bit of exaggerating. She'd spoken at length of those flying *planes*—hard to imagine—and had showed him what she'd called a *movie*, which they'd viewed on her phone—more than an hour that he could not retrieve, wasted on the god of thunder, an implausible tale. A god that made use of a hammer to fight his enemies? He'd been more confused than entertained, compelled to pose many queries, enough that Megan had turned her phone black, mumbling, "Maybe a sitcom next time."

She wanted him to see Des Plaines, the place that she called home, had said she would have liked to show him the park around which she rode her bike and her favorite museum—where artifacts were contained—and the hospital where she healed people.

She spoke of places and not people.

When he thought of Megan in his time—and he did, regularly—he imagined introducing her to Duncan and Holly, if she were still there. He would proudly present her to Roland, Thallane's steward, and show her off to Kennera, Thallane's healer. He imagined her meeting all those other lasses lost in time. He would take her to the graves of his wife and son and tell her these were his loved ones once upon a time and would always hold a place in his heart.

And now she did.

Megan tossed her phone on the bed when she was done, blowing out a frustrated sigh.

"They cannot accommodate me," she said and then pursed her lips. "Or rather, they cannot accommodate what remains of my measly budget. I have to fly out on Tuesday or apparently, according to my checking account and credit cards, never leave Scotland."

"'Tis coin ye need?" He surmised.

"Yes, money."

She moved toward the chair opposite him, but Graeme leaned forward and took hold of her hand, bringing her to him, where she fell gracelessly into his lap. She leaned into him, laying her head on his shoulder.

"Ye would have nae need of coin in my time, lass," he said, by way of temptation.

"I imagine even in the fourteenth century, people need money, Graeme."

"I would take care of ye, lass. I've said as much. Ye would nae live richly, but ye would live well."

"Please, Graeme," she implored. "I'm bummed enough. Please don't ask me again to come with you. I'm already pretty torn up inside about having to leave myself. Don't ask me to make that decision."

Though disappointed in her aversion to even consider or have a full discussion about the possibility, he understood her reserve. He might find that he had no choice but to stay here in this century, but he would not do so willingly. He wanted and needed to go home.

He sensed that she was as torn as he, though. Few words had been spoken, but he knew that like him, she dreaded their inevitable farewell, the very idea of never seeing each other again.

She clung now tightly to him, wriggling her arms around his waist while he sat in the chair and held her, an anguish gleaned in her embrace.

Graeme inhaled the fresh, clean scent of her, her hair infused with the aroma of her shampoo. He made slow and steady circles on her back with one hand while the other held her silky soft legs close to him.

"Maybe we should say goodbye now, Graeme," she suggested, a noticeable catch in her throat. "I think it would be easier than—"

"Nae, lass. I'm nae ready to do so," he said stiffly. "Dinna ask that of me."

Chapter Fourteen

They went again that afternoon to the ruins of the ancient broch. Once more nothing happened, for which Megan was secretly relieved. Selfishly, she rather hoped that he was forced to say goodbye to her, with her leaving, as opposed to the other way around. And then she felt bad for having known that relief since Graeme was noticeably quiet that night when they dined at the inn. So pensive was he that he didn't even comment on the Chocolate delice, which had appeared on the menu again. He ate it all, and pretty fast, but he said nothing about it, possibly hadn't even realized how great the indulgence was.

Megan struggled with the weight of her own worry. She wasn't ready to leave, not Scotland and certainly not Graeme. But what choice did she have? She could neither afford the hefty price tag of re-booking her flight home, thereby extending her stay, nor the possibility that she might lose her job, if she were to request a leave of absence or simply be a no-call, no-show. And yet she racked her brain for ways to compensate the lack of the first—money—and spun her brain round and round more, trying to imagine any scenario that would placate the powers that be at the hospital and afford her time off from her job.

It was wholly and recklessly irresponsible to consider simply abandoning real life in Des Plaines, all for a guy from another century. That would most certainly be a case of looking for love in all the wrong places, she determined, even as she sometimes tried to justify it in her head. And frankly, part of her questioned why she should be expected to give up everything when Graeme had said adamantly that he would not.

"What will you do when I'm gone?" She asked him as he pushed his dessert plate away. "Where will you stay? Or sleep or eat?"

He lifted a grim face to her, as melancholy as she, she might believe.

"Ye dinna concern yourself with that, lass. Ye've enough to contend with." He was quiet then, though his regard was steady.

"This sucks," she lamented.

"Which means?" He asked, lifting one brow.

"It's awful and stupid and... I don't know, unfair. Among other things."

"Do ye regret then everything we've done?"

"No, Graeme," she answered honestly, holding his pensive green-eyed gaze. "I don't. It's going to break my heart, I'm sure. But I wouldn't take back anything."

"Nor I."

Later that evening, returned to Megan's hotel room, she received a call from Jasmine. Her friend managed to pretend that nothing was amiss, that she hadn't abandoned her on vacation in a foreign country. Too troubled by genuine problems, Megan let it go.

"Are you having a good time with Kyle?"

"Oh, gosh," Jasmine exclaimed. "We're having the time of our lives."

She went on to name all the sights she'd seen and tours she'd taken, that schedule much busier than the itinerary she'd planned with Megan. Not one snippet of whining to be heard.

"What have you been doing? Is that creepy guy, Graeme, still around?"

Megan actually laughed at this. Jasmine thought him creepy but had no problem leaving Megan in his company. Never one to quickly write off another person—everyone made mistakes—Megan was in this instance slammed by a want to distance herself from Jasmine, both now and when they did get home and were back at work together.

"He's here," she said now. "He's really very—"

"Oh, shit," interrupted Jasmine. "I gotta go. Kyle is waving frantically at me. I'll see you at the airport in two days, right?"

No mention was made of what Megan had once proposed, that they would at least spend their last few days together in Glasgow.

"Yep," Megan answered tersely.

"Great. See you then."

Megan's goodbye was made to a dead line, Jasmine having already hung up.

While Graeme took a shower, Megan sat at the table and pulled out her small journal and a pen from her purse.

The journal was empty, bought specifically for this trip, where she'd meant to record her own diary of everything she'd seen and done. She experienced a brief pang of disappointment because she hadn't written down anything and hoped she did not have any larger regrets later.

Presently, she made two columns on the first page, separated by a straight line made with the side of her phone. She titled the left column, *Reasons to Go Back Home*, and the right column, *Reasons to Go Back in Time with Graeme*, and then tapped the pen against her pursed lips while she considered in what order she might put the things that screamed loudest initially.

In the left column she wrote first: *Safe and normal.*

Beneath that, she added, in rapid succession:

Time-travel is not real.

Good job.

Quiet life.

Ordinary, but stable and predictable. No surprises.

In the right column, she immediately jotted down two words: *Graeme MacQuillan.*

She heard the shower turn off and re-read what little she'd jotted down.

She added, under Graeme's name:

No one would miss me.

Possibly, I would miss no one.

Just before the bathroom door opened, spilling steam out into the hotel room, Megan wrote in all capital letters, pressing firmly on the pen: *Just do it. Be brave. Take a chance. Go to the ruins of the broch with him and go back to the fourteenth century.*

She laid her hands over the words she'd written, staring at them, wondering if she did have the courage to do so, and then closed the small journal when she sensed Graeme watching her. She pivoted, lifting her face, the journal forgotten as she found him lounging against the corner of the wall, where the small foyer and bathroom door were separated from the main part of the room. He wore only the big bath sheet, the terry cloth hung low on his hips. His hair was wet and pushed back from his forehead, his naked chest still a sight she hadn't quite gotten used to.

"Get in there, lass," he said, "and make use of the shower or dispense with your garb and climb into bed. I want you naked in my arms."

Megan smiled at him. Later, she might add: *sex, lots of toe-curling, mind-blowing sex,* under that right column.

"Aye, aye, captain," she said, hopping out of the chair and meeting him in the middle of the room.

She stood on her toes to kiss him. "I will shower, thank you very much." Another sweet meeting of lips. "And I promise to return naked but only if *you* promise that I will find you naked as well."

"Ye dinna need to fret on that, lass," he said, playfully whipping the towel away from his gorgeous body. "I promise," he teased and kissed her again and then swatted her butt, sending her on her way. "Go now before I decide I canna wait."

***

They left the inn on bikes again the next day, earlier than they normally ventured out looking for the witch, directly after they'd broken their fast, which they'd done this morning on the patio since the sun was once more bright and the air was warm. The roads and trails were favorable, the rain of days ago long since soaked into the earth, the ground dry today. As he had on the two previous excursions to the broch, Graeme had packed up all his belongings, carrying his sword on his back and making good use of the saddlebags Megan had purchased for him.

He glanced behind him now, checking on Megan's progress. She kept up well as she regularly did when they were not on foot. She wore an expression that was not entirely unfathomable, but he could not say from that quick glance if she were irked or sad. They'd spoken little since they'd taken off, this mood vastly different from the companionable breakfast they'd shared together, where Megan had regaled him with tales of what she called modern medicine. She'd spoken of the things present day barber surgeons were capable of. She'd not been sulky but animated, had drawn images on the outdoor paper napkins of a terrible break she'd once seen in a patient's leg, sketching how the bone had poked through the skin, not anything that Graeme was unfamiliar with. The lad's leg had healed, she'd said, marveling that after many long months, and with nary a scar, the lad had suffered no lingering effects, neither a limp nor any residual pain.

"Graeme, you'd be surprised what they do nowadays in medicine," she'd said. "Well, some of the surgeries are not particularly medicine, not for the sake of healing. People change their looks with surgeries," she'd said. "They can have their noses altered and their jawlines reshaped, their skin tightened to remove wrinkles." She'd leaned forward, her eyes alight with mischief. "Some women get boob jobs. Breast augmentation, technically." She cupped her soft hands six inches in front of her, her palms facing her breasts. "They make their boobs bigger."

"Why?" Was the only response he could conceive.

"Ding, ding, ding," she'd said merrily. "We have a winner, posing the proper million dollar question."

He'd chuckled, more so at her charming enthusiasm and bright smile than her words, only guessing at their meaning, that *boob jobs* were frivolous.

She was not smiling now and hadn't since he'd asked her if she were ready to leave. Then, she'd only nodded glumly, compelling Graeme to suggest, "Ye dinna need to go with me, lass. Mayhap it would be better if ye did nae anymore."

For a fleeting second, he could see that she considered it. Only for a second before she shook herself and feigned a greater interest in riding to the broch with him.

"No, I want to go with you," she lied.

He wondered if she actually meant she did not want to be left behind. She'd once said exactly that, had expressed a mournfulness over a family that had briefly raised her and then had moved away, leaving her displaced until another family had been found to care for her. *Which they...did not*, she'd said then, having lowered her eyes, biting her lip, mayhap having revived a sore memory.

Graeme gripped the handlebars and lifted his arse off the saddle, riding faster and harder, not to reach the broch but to expend a frustrated energy. Heedless of the uneven path that was sometimes grass and sometimes dirt, and was often rocky, he rode faster and faster, his chest burning not for his exertion but for the pain known inside.

He would end this today, he determined, could no longer bear her sadness or the nicks to his heart, every day wondering if this would be the last time he would see her. Tonight, he would take himself off and away from her, would steal away in the night, would say only a silent farewell rather than being torn from her, in front of her. Better still than watching her be taken away in one of the mammoth machines she'd called a *bus*, which she said would bring her to the place where she would *catch a plane*. And leave him.

Today was not the day anyhow, he presumed, slowing his grueling pace at Megan's shout, distant now. The air was not heavy, had no substance to it, was not laden with the mischief of witches. The sun shone brightly, the sky unspoiled blue as far as the eye could see. There was no place for unearthly magic to hide.

He stopped completely, setting his booted feet on the ground on either side of the bike, in sight of the broch a few hundred yards ahead.

"What was that about?" Megan asked, breathless when she caught up to him and came abreast of him. "Did you sense something? Or see something?"

"Nae, lass," he answered with a shake of his head. "Purging demons, that is all."

She returned his grimaced smile, possibly understanding what demons he spoke of.

They rode a bit further, dismounting and deserting the bikes just inside the gate before they climbed through the dry, wind-blown grass up to the ruins. Graeme hopped down and turned, grasping Megan's hips while she clung to his shoulders as he lowered her into the sunken interior with him.

"Another day, another chapter," she said, sitting on the carpet of rustling leaves, presumably since the ground was dry today, pulling her book from her bag. "Do you want me to read it out loud again?" She asked.

"Nae today. I fear I canna give it my attention in this hour," he said. "And frankly, lass, I dinna ken how a pair of felines—nae better than barn cats, as it sounds—can assist that lass in ferreting out a murderer."

Ah, her first true smile in the last few hours, her blue eyes crinkled at the corners, sparkling in the sunshine.

"Sometimes reading requires the suspension of disbelief," she defended pertly. "You know? Kind of like believing that time-travel could be real."

"Your point is made. Another time, mayhap," he offered, even as he already knew there would not be.

Over the next half hour, Graeme prowled the interior and sometimes the exterior of the ruins while Megan never moved, happily lost in her implausible narrative. It seemed as if aside from Graeme nothing and no one moved; there was no wind, not even the occasional breeze to stir the summer air or move any hanging leaf; no clouds appeared, none at all, gliding lazily about the sky; not even a single car sped along the black-topped road.

He returned to the depressed interior at one point to find Megan sitting with the book and her eyes closed, her face tilted up to the sun.

"Ye finished?" He asked of her reading.

"No," she said, lowering her face, opening her eyes. "But I re-read the same page over and over without comprehending or retaining any of it so that it seems pointless."

"Distracted?"

"Are you not?" She returned.

"Nae so much as ye, I gather. I dinna ken today is the day. I canna sense any disruption in the air."

Megan stood, brushing off her bottom and winked at Graeme as she returned her book to her bag. "Looks like you're stuck with me one more night."

She took one step and then another toward him and then stopped, her brow creasing with a frown, lifting her hand to point beyond him. Graeme whirled around just as Megan said, "There was...there was lightning. But the sky is blue...every-where."

He saw nothing but a second later heard and felt a low rum-ble of thunder. He pivoted again, looking south over Megan's head.

"*Jesu*," he breathed.

The sky was no longer blue in that direction, but roiling with thick black clouds, throwing everything below into dark shad-ows. Impossible, he thought. 'Twas only a second ago, the entirety of the vast sky was clear. Another pivot, another incredible sight, clouds rolling in from every direction, swiftly, the circle of remaining blue sky growing smaller and smaller by the second until all those churning clouds met and the sky was nearly black.

In the next second, a hard rain pounded down. Graeme squinted his eyes and lifted his hand, still gaping at the scene he'd just witnessed, how quickly and terribly the storm had risen.

"She's here," he said to Megan, having to shout to be heard over the pelting rain. "I can feel her."

"Are you sure that's not the brewing storm?" Megan shouted next to him.

"The witch may well be the storm, love."

A flash of lightning avoided all the trees and mountains that were closer to the sky, smacking with a small burst of flame upon the ground twenty yards away from them, near the gate. The wee fire was quickly extinguished by the torrential rain.

"Graeme...?"

He turned to her, instinctively taking hold of her hand, stricken by the look on her face, her expression fraught with panic for what she—and he—assumed was his imminent departure. He was furious that he'd been given no warning and had not the time to give Megan a proper farewell, had not the time to send her away so that she did not bear witness to his leaving, and whatever that might entail.

She would be left behind. By him.

If he did nothing to prevent that.

"Megan, I canna leave ye," he hollered over the storm, yanking her into his arms, kissing her desperately, his hand clenched firmly around hers. "I canna leave ye, love." His voice was ragged.

"You're staying then?" Joy bubbled in her voice, against his lips while rain splashed all over their faces, sometimes bouncing from his cheek to hers.

"Nae, lass," he said fiercely. "I canna stay either." He pulled back and cupped her face in his hands.

Her expression faltered, either dawning with understanding, a hint of shock opening her mouth and widening her eyes or arrested as it was in confusion, not realizing what his words meant.

There was, he thought—and would think for quite some time—a second, mayhap two that she might have twisted out of his arms, away from his tight hold. If she'd wanted to. If she in fact knew what plan he had just conceived and now was determined to play out.

"Graeme?" She questioned, curious about more than only the tempestuous storm, but possibly about his rigid, tormented gaze. "Graeme!"

"I canna let ye go, love!" was the last thing he recalled saying while they stood inside the broch and the wind and rain whipped all around them. He wrapped his strong arms around her, pressing his lips to her temple.

***

The sky was neither black nor blue but returned to that agitated gray that had overseen more than half of her time in Scotland.

That was Megan's first thought.

Her next thought was an understanding that she was laying on the ground, outside, on her back, and both she and the ground were wet. She first moved her hand, lifting it up from what felt like a puddle of mud. Mud indeed, said the hand she inspected, warm gooey mud, caked all over her fingers and under her nails. She lifted her other hand but found that though wet, it had escaped the mud bath.

Megan sighed and only then did it occur to her to wonder what had happened, why she was laying on the soaked ground, and...

And then it came back to her. She and Graeme at the ruins. The furious storm. Graeme taking hold of her so aggressively, kissing her madly, telling her he couldn't let her go.

Lightning had flashed. Had lightning struck them?

She tried to sit up. What should have been a very simple act turned into a feat of wonder once accomplished, for how weak and uncoordinated she felt. And then it seemed it took her brain another moment to catch up, so that she only stared all around her, recognizing nothing save for Graeme's lifeless form laying about ten feet away in the middle of a quiet and treeless field.

Where was the broch? And the hill upon which it sat? And the bikes and the gate?

Why was—

Graeme!

She swung her head back toward him—my God, why had that initial sight of him, laying motionless on his stomach, not scared the shit out of her? She'd totally skimmed her gaze right over him, having realized that he was unmoving, but not initially panicking! What was wrong with her?

She tried to stand, struggling with that much more so than when she'd tried to sit. Nothing worked, her legs and arms slow to respond to her commands. *Is this a dream?* One of the really fantastic but annoying dreams where all limbs felt as if they were made of molasses, rubbery and not subject to the brain's will?

Unable to stand, she crawled over to Graeme, clawing her way through mud and short grass, flopping on top of him when she still couldn't fully control her extremities.

"Graeme," she cried, pushing her chin off his back, nudging him roughly with her hands.

He didn't move.

Megan flexed her arms and hands, stiffening all those muscles, hoping to imbue them with either strength or at least the ability to obey. Somehow she was able to turn Graeme over onto his back. She knew when he woke by the way he went rigid and when his arms began to flail wildly.

"Graeme, it's me," she soothed, pushing one of his strong arms away from her, settling her mud-free hand on his cheek.

His arms fell down, landing at his side, one hand flopping onto his flat stomach.

"Bluidy hell," he groaned but did nothing else.

Unable to support an upright position any longer, Megan drooped onto him, her head landing on his chest. But her legs were crunched awkwardly and in order to straighten them she had to twist a bit, collapsing onto her back beside Graeme.

She felt as if she'd just finished a triathlon and every muscle and bone and all her flesh screamed in aching protest. She wasn't sure how much time passed before she turned her face toward Graeme.

He was looking at her, his expression baffling.

"Are you—why are you smiling?"

"We did it," he said, his voice raspy. "We did it, lass."

"Graeme, please tell me we're not...oh, no. We didn't. Tell me we didn't." Panic seized her. Was it possible? "Why did you hang on so tightly to me?"

"I could nae leave ye behind." He was still smiling.

Megan stared at him, stunned speechless.

No. Just no. They hadn't. It wasn't possible, she reminded herself. Something had happened, obviously, but no, they hadn't traveled through time. "Graeme MacQuillan, if you're right and I'm in the fourteenth century—or any century that is not the twenty-first—you and I are going to have a problem." How could he!

Possibly sensing her distress, realizing she was not as thrilled as he was, he cautioned gently, "We dinna ken that we were moved, lass, will nae ken until...until we find something to say what year we are in."

Finally, Graeme rose to his feet. Maybe having lain there for a few minutes had allowed him to have full control over his body so that he seemed to rise effortlessly.

He towered above her and reached down a hand to her..

"Do not touch me," she gritted through her teeth, fright clawing its talons deeply into her. "Don't you ever touch me again."

There was no hill and no broch, no gate and no bikes. Graeme and Megan began to march across the field. Slowly her body returned to normal, her initial trudging becoming regular walking, though hers was more an angry stomping.

Graeme's attempts to speak with her, telling her he thought he recognized where they were was met by a crisp and cool, "Don't talk to me now. Don't say another friggin word to me until I know I'm still in the twenty-first century."

"Lass, if ye would give me—"

"Stop!" She cried, covering her ears with her hands.

And on they marched, for more than an hour, Megan's rage simmering until she felt as if she might burst with it, which was not relieved at all when they finally came upon something other than mucky trails in open glens and forests of dripping trees.

She stared in awe at the massive fortress, which sat atop the same elevated hillock, which appeared to have the same backdrop as that of the site they'd visited in their search for Newburn, a space of rolling hills and beyond, larger mountains covered in a forest of pine trees. The extraordinary but startling castle grew larger and larger as they neared it.

"'Tis Newburn, lass," Graeme said, his voice both proud and pleased.

No. Newburn was gone. They'd visited the site, this very spot. It was gone.

But this...Megan gaped and felt tears well, though not for the austere beauty of the huge castle, whose front corners were flanked by square towers and an imposing gatehouse over the three story gate, but for what actually might be her present reality.

A short wall extended down and away from the larger, more formidable curtain wall which surrounded the immediate castle and yard. The shorter wall, not any taller than herself, she judged, came down in two arms from the two front corners of the castle's curtain wall and meandered almost crookedly down the hillock, the arms stretching wide there to contain a number of small thatched-roof huts that lined both sides of the rutted lane.

People moved up and down that lane and others walked along the top of the wall, soldiers she presumed, as hinted by their clothes, similar to what Graeme had once worn, though with the addition of dull silver helmets. The massive but relative-

ly narrow gates were open, a slice of the interior of the yard showing more milling and moving people within as she and Graeme
approached.

Megan's steps slowed, disbelief and fury warring within her.

Graeme stopped walking, turning to face her, interrupting
the staggering view.

"Ye believe me now?"

She couldn't speak. She shook her head, blinking rapidly,
tears falling just as the rain returned. Her lips trembled. Trapped
in that fog of incredulity, she allowed Graeme to once more take
her hand, to lead her on. His pace increased the closer they got,
until they were jogging through the rain and through the gate
as someone overhead shouted Graeme's name. She had a fleeting
impression of watchful people, bales of hay and wood, the whin-
ny of a horse, of fires lit inside smaller, open-front structures in
the courtyard.

And then Graeme burst through the huge, arched door of
the castle. Inside, they were nearly accosted by two men, lunging
to their feet, whipping swords out from their belts. A woman,
standing with a striking man on the wide staircase to the right,
gasped and covered her mouth. Several others inside the expansive, timber-ceilinged room gasped and stared.

One of the sword-wielding men, larger and brawnier than
Graeme, returned his weapon to its sheath and rushed forward,
pulling Graeme into a big bear hug.

"God's bones, lad," the man hollered.

The couple on the stairs came racing down, the man holding
the woman's hand. They forced their way past several others, this
man with eyes the same color as Graeme's throwing himself at
Graeme.

"You bastard," he rasped at Graeme as they embraced. "Scared the shite out of me."

When he was done, the woman launched herself at Graeme.

Megan's mind didn't work properly now, was slow to process the abundance of detail, so only vaguely did she consider that the woman looked very similar to a picture of Holly Wright she'd seen possibly a thousand times. It might have been her, her dark blonde hair and animated brown eyes looking about the same, but that this woman, like the few other women present, was dressed in some weird long gown, wearing a rope belt around her skinny waist.

"Oh, thank God," cried the woman in Graeme's arm. "Oh, gosh, I was so worried."

"All is well, lass. I'm pleased to find ye here," Graeme said. "I thought for sure ye might have been flung somewhere else."

"No, Graeme," said the Holly Wright lookalike. "Only you were moved."

"'Tis guid," Graeme acknowledged, sounding a wee breathless.

The green-eyed man who had come down the stairs with the brown-eyed woman narrowed his eyes at Megan, his gaze moving up and down, staring at length at her leggings and tennis shoes. His brow lifted slightly when his eyes landed on her hand, which she only now realized was held firmly by Graeme.

Megan blinked and watched more people greet Graeme, men and women all dressed in period clothing, long gowns of different colors, and breeches and shirts that reminded her again of Graeme's clothes, which were tucked into the canvas rucksack still on his back. The young women who'd welcomed him back, with such joy as if they might have feared they'd never seen him again, held much of Megan's stupefied attention.

It was impossible, implausible, but she recognized each of them.

Kayla Forbes.

Cora Bennett.

Gabrielle Noble.

When those greetings were done and while Megan's gaze jerked from one missing girl to the next, all of whom were smiling, Graeme asked the other green-eyed man, "What are you still doing here?"

"Still doing here?" the man repeated, puzzled. "I only arrived a day or so after you...left."

Graeme frowned, his confusion evident as well. "I've been gone nearly a fortnight."

"Graeme," said Holly Wright's doppelganger, her tone laced with sadness. "It's been but a few days."

"Nae," argued Graeme, dumbfounded. "A full ten days at least."

Bits and pieces, details and a startling reality smacked Megan in the face.

He hadn't lied.

It was true.

Those missing girls were here...apparently in this, the fourteenth century.

Megan tugged at her hand with force, reminding Graeme of her presence, which he seemed to have quite happily forgotten.

"You son of a bitch!" She raged at him when he faced her. "You just...without even...how could you?"

She pulled back her free hand and let it fly, her small fist connecting sharply with Graeme's hard jaw.

Graeme absorbed the blow, giving a good shake to his head to clear it. He rubbed his jaw lightly, still holding her hand.

Then he smiled at the couple she now presumed were Duncan and Holly.

"This is Megan," he said proudly, evidently impervious to her weak assault.

Chapter Fifteen

Despite the reckoning from Megan, which prickled yet on his jaw, Graeme could do nothing about his grin, still processing the truth, that he'd made it—he'd returned home.

Megan wasn't the only one glaring at him, however.

Sending a quick glance to Megan, a tight-lipped Holly stepped directly in front of him and hissed, "Please tell me that you didn't forcibly bring this poor woman to another century?"

This question eclipsed Duncan's lower, more hesitant, "What the bluidy hell are ye wearing?" as he frowned, looking Graeme up and down, at his jeans and T-shirt and hiking boots.

Megan, who'd been silent and trembling for so long before she'd lashed out at him, found her voice again, answering Holly's query.

"Oh, he did," she charged, her voice shaken but strident. "He wouldn't let go of me, wrapped me up in his arms when he knew—he knew!—what was happening." She finally shook his hand off, using her free hand to claw at the clamp of his. "I will never forgive you, Graeme. Never."

These bitter admonishments were keenly felt and finally his grin dissolved.

"You are Holly," Megan guessed correctly, and then faced the other women hovering close. "And you're Cora. You're Kayla and you're Gabby. The entire world is searching for you—I thought he was lying when he said you were all safe and well. Holy shit. I didn't believe him. I thought he was a serial killer, who'd kidnapped all of you—he was calling your name when I stumbled upon him," she said to Holly.

Graeme clarified evenly, "I had just woken. I dinna ken if ye had been tossed forward with me."

Holly shook her head. "But then...how were you able to trust him?"

"What were you doing for ten days, Graeme?" Cora asked at the same time.

Megan's chin quivered again. "I don't know what made me believe he wasn't dangerous, but now I'm wishing I'd listened to every friggin' red flag that fluttered so forcefully right in front of my eyes. I wouldn't be stuck here—" she stopped herself, closing her eyes. "I wouldn't be somewhere I don't want to be."

"It'll be fine, Megan," Holly assured her—falsely, thought more than one. "We'll sort it out."

Cora Thain mouthed to Gabby, *How?*

And just then, when it seemed Megan was about to lose all control over herself and her emotions, Megan lifted her chin and lengthened her spine, and drew in a deep breath through her nose, looking from one lass to the next.

"If any of you knew *how* to return to the twenty-first century, I imagine you would not be here now. It is not fine. Unless you do know how to get home, please don't tell me all will be fine."

Gabby interjected in a small voice, filled with a wee hope. "But Graeme just went forward and now came back. Nothing, it seems, is impossible."

Megan pinned her with an uncompromising glower. "Why didn't you return then?"

"I...guess I didn't actually try," Gabby admitted, sending a glance over her shoulder to Aedan.

Megan ran her hands through her hair, still damp from the earlier wild storm and the subsequent misting rain.

"I'm sorry," she said, wearily. "I'm...not myself. This was—I didn't expect..." she lifted her shoulders and let them drop, unable or unwilling to finish.

Cora said, "Megan, we've all been there—right here where you are. It's not easy, we get that. We just want you to know—what we've just said to Holly a few days ago—we're here to help, however we can."

"Even if it's only a shoulder to cry on," Kayla added.

"Come," said Holly, taking Megan by the shoulders. "Sit down. You look exhausted."

The women moved away then, Holly leading Megan away, sitting her down at one of the trestle tables where they continued to fuss over her, offering food and wine, a bath, whatever she wanted. Megan waved it off and their talk became muted for the slight distance, and when the ladies all sat round that table with her.

Graeme's cousin and laird, Duncan, stared harshly at him, his mien stiff with a grave disappointment. "Did ye bring her purposefully?" He asked.

Graeme nodded. "It was in my mind, and aye, why I would nae let go of her when I sensed the witch was near."

Lucas Thain, the first to greet him, narrowed his eyes at Graeme. "The witch said if there was love, a pair could nae be separated," he said, having lowered his deep voice.

Graeme's grin returned, having discerned the question in Lucas' tone. "Exactly."

Lucas Thain snorted out a laugh. "All for naught, lad, if she dinna forgive ye."

"She will." Either his own love or her tender heart would prompt forgiveness. He moved his gaze to Megan again, who was now weeping softly into her hands while those lasses attempted to console her.

Forgiveness would come, but perhaps not today.

Michael MacClellan shook his head, chuckling at Graeme, clapping him on the shoulder. "God be with ye, lad. There's a tall beinn to climb."

Duncan, seemingly of a mind to let Megan be smothered and mothered by the other twenty-first century lasses, then asked, "But you've been there? To the...the future?" Hands planted on his hips, he shook his head with a wee self-loathing. "God's bluid, that dinna sound right, those words from my mouth," he grumbled.

"I have," answered Graeme, his regard still trained on Megan. "Unreal it is, as fantastic as it is illusory. And yet much of it looks little changed from this here now. Aye, but at a place called Fort William—"

"Kayla was once there," Michael interjected.

"Eloise and Gabby, as well," Aedan supplied.

"Aye, it teems with things we could nae imagine unless seen—cars and buses and wire cables hung all about. Lights that turn on with a switch, warmth that comes from vents in walls and *Jesu*, the shower—'tis akin to standing under a waterfall, heated to a perfect temperature. I may well bemoan the loss of that. Otherwise, I'll be pleased to nae ever see it again. 'Twas nae home."

"And if you had nae managed to return...?" Aedan prompted. "Would ye eventually..." he paused, shrugging, searching for the words, "have resigned yourself to stay there?"

"Given no choice, aye, but I'd nae stop trying."

"Would ye give up though, truly, with Megan at your side?" Michael asked, his frown bedeviled.

Graeme grimaced. "'Twas nae long enough to tell."

Michael sighed. "I asked Kayla to give up all attempts to return after only two weeks. I dinna truly consider what she sacrificed."

"Cora as well," Lucas chimed in. "All of them, I'd wager, might struggle often with what they'd lost."

Aedan chuckled without humor. "And we are the brave ones, are we nae?"

"Nae," said Michael, pivoting to fix his gaze on his wife amid the four other lasses, Megan included. "They are."

Sometime later, having hardly taken his gaze off Megan, surmising she might wish only a quiet place to lay her head and rest, Graeme approached her from across the room.

He addressed Cora first once he reached the gathering of lasses.

"Might we have a chamber? Megan will surely wish to retire for a wee bit?"

Cora nodded. "Of course. The chamber is ready—I'm sorry, Megan. We shouldn't have kept you so long."

"Oh, gosh," said Holly, "and here we've just been jabbering all this time and you probably wish to shut the world away. Which room, Cora? I'll take her up."

"I will take her up," Graeme inserted while a shuffling occurred in front of him, all the ladies standing rather at once.

Megan did not refuse his offer, but sent a meaningful look to Holly, seen only in profile from his vantage point, but remarkable for the pleading she sent Holly's way.

"It's fine, Graeme," Holly said, giving him a tight smile. "You know she's in good hands with us."

Gritting his teeth, reluctant to force his presence on Megan when she was clearly angry with him still, he watched them leave.

While he reminded himself that he hadn't wished to be without her, that he'd had some suspicion that she might feel the same, he did now realize how impetuous and selfish his actions had been. Mayhap if he'd been given more than only seconds to have come to the decision and acted on it, he might have made a different choice.

He was offered bread and cheese and ale and swiftly consumed that, having a ferocious hunger. He spent some time with the four lairds inside Newburn's hall at the chief's table. Though he'd been gone for what felt like a very long time, there was little changed of which he needed to be apprised.

After a while, he took himself outside, wanting to reacquaint himself with so many things, including the crisp air of this evening and this century, presently devoid of any sense of a witch's presence. Lucas Thain had advised that his steed had been kept well for him, and Graeme found him thus, the lean but massive destrier pawing the ground inside his stall even before Graeme had reached him. He saddled up the big black and indulged himself and his steed to a spirited ride in the gloaming, pleased to have this hearty and solid saddle and beast beneath him, quite sure he would not bemoan never having to ride a bike again. By his reckoning, he had never reached so swift a speed on the bike as the destrier was capable of, which meant the only advantage of a bike, had he known such a thing in this time, was that it could not easily be made the target of an enemy arrow or other missile, its killing or maiming meant to fell a man.

As he rode, he thought of Megan—and then fleetingly wondered when he did not.

Are you hungry? She'd asked him ten days ago. Among so many others, that image was burned into his recall. He'd known at that moment that she'd immediately questioned why she'd asked him that, had bitten her lip, beguiling in her uncertainty, in her willingness to push through it. Och, and then her smile when he'd answered in the affirmative, her eyes lighting and her chest expanding with relief or pleasure. He might have been lazily smitten with her in the first few hours before this, but this was the moment he'd acknowledged the existence of a satisfaction known, to have made or caused her smile.

Providing you were honest just then, feel free to play grumpy all day long and don't mind me, basking in the glow of the possibility of another kiss.

To his dying day, he would likely be able to recollect vividly the slow, burgeoning smile that had creased her face then, which had come at length after she'd questioned why he'd made so hasty and stiff a retreat after he'd kissed her that very first time. For some time after that while they'd broken their fast, she'd worn a wee grin, which sometimes was enlarged, and sometimes tamped down, as if she wanted to keep it and other private thoughts attached to it, hidden away.

He recreated other images in his head: Megan sitting on the handlebars that first day, facing him, holding his sword, which was not much shorter than she, the wind and their ride disheveling her hair, forcing it toward him, tendrils as fingers, regularly stroking along his cheek and chin; her expression when Jasmine had announced her beau would be journeying with them, how she'd stifled her own disappointment, had admirably shown Jasmine what she wanted to see; Megan in that plush, oversized white robe, one whose belt on numerous occasions he'd had the pleasure of untying, opening to reveal the treasure of her sensual body; she in those images at the hospital, all that time and care afforded to those patients, smiling through fatigue and sadness; Megan, just last night, naked and beneath him, her fingers tight around his neck, begging him, *No more teasing. I need you inside me.*

He scrunched his nose then as he rode, meaning to dispense with the sudden heat and tingling there, and then wheeled the destrier around, heading back to Newburn.

Twenty minutes later, he crept through the quiet hall and encountered Holly on the second floor.

She sighed when she saw him.

"Where is she?" He asked, his voice low in consideration of the hour.

"Graeme—" she began, haltingly.

"Where?"

Another sigh. "Upstairs," she said, pointing her finger toward the stone ceiling. "Third door on the right."

He went on, knowing Holly watched him, mayhap with a wee regret for having divulged this. He climbed the stairs and slipped soundlessly inside the chamber Holly had indicated.

A small and dying peat fire glowed softly, the chamber awash in a faint orange glow, revealing an unmoving figure on the bed, little seen beyond the thick counterpane but the wealth of Megan's glossy hair, draped about the pillows.

Graeme stood at the bedside for several minutes, having told himself he wanted only to see her. 'Twas never enough, though, he realized, and never would be. He doffed his boots and shirt and trousers but left his boxers on, climbing into bed with her.

She woke softly, not startled, but turning slowly toward him. Her face was briefly illuminated, a drying trail of tears highlighted. She met his gaze, a wee anguished but he believed not displeased by his presence. With great certainty and need, Graeme gathered her into his arms.

And she let him, rotating fully around into his embrace.

She'd been given a clean, dry shift, her arms bare, folding at her chest as she burrowed into him.

And she wept, more, again, but said nothing.

Graeme soothed her with a warm hand gently stroking over her linen clad back and kissed her tears, telling her over and over again that he was selfish, and how sorry he was.

***

Megan was wakened by laughter wafting up from below. It was short-lived, just someone's—a man's—bark of a laugh sounding briefly throughout the castle. *Keep*, she corrected, as it had regularly been referred to yesterday.

She rolled over onto her back, not entirely surprised to find that Graeme was gone, and then was in no hurry to give up the coziness of the soft bed. And there was much to consider, all that she'd discovered yesterday, little of which made sense.

Greatest shock of all—as if the fact that time-travel was actually real wasn't that, unless she was simply trapped in the longest dream known to man—she had just found all those missing girls.

Here in fourteenth century Scotland. Little was she appeased by one part of this truth, that at least she now knew for certain—dream scenarios notwithstanding—that Graeme had not lied to her. This scarcely offered any relief.

Groggily, she slid her hand along the empty side of the bed, where Graeme had lain last night. She was still furious with him for what he'd done to her, for forcibly bringing her here with him, but she was at least honest with herself in one regard: as pissed as she was, she considered that this present fury might be easier to deal with than the ache of having lost him, if only he'd been moved through time.

And as sweet and comforting as all four of those young women had been, their sympathies and simply the very consolation of their presence hadn't done much by way of compelling her to want to stay any more than she had yesterday.

But oh, how fantastic in an unreal sense, how... mindboggling it all was, how each of them had come through time. Kayla, as she'd recalled yesterday afternoon, had simply walked through a forest—searching for Eloise, who was also missing!—back in time, only to stumble upon Michael MacClellan, buried in the earth for two whole years. Astonishing.

Gabby Noble had been innocently strolling along a beach on the opposite side of the country when she'd been sucked through the ground—horrifying—only to waken and spend three weeks in distress, having no idea what had happened and unable to communicate with the family with whom she'd found shelter. She'd met Aedan Cameron while running from her life, first from a pack of wolves and next by a band of cutthroat reivers.

Cora Bennett had actually met the witch who'd so ruthlessly moved her through time.

"I'm still so embarrassed," she'd said, "for how gullible and just how...senseless I was. But I still maintain I thought it was some kind of hokey marketing thing."

She landed plop in the middle of the aftermath of a battle, meeting Lucas Thain within the hour, being given refuge with him and his moving army because she'd given him some warning of another army headed their way.

Holly, who was the most recent to go missing, had only been here a month, had been taken from the same broch in the twenty-first century, the same broch where Megan and Graeme had been caught up in that witch's storm and had been flung back here. Megan already knew her story, having been told by Graeme about her being passed off as a MacHeth, and betrothed and then wed to Duncan.

She'd shrugged during her telling yesterday. "I didn't set out to deceive him—I didn't even know him. But Sidheag said it was the only way to get home."

Megan recalled that name, Sidheag, mentioned by Graeme as being the name of the witch.

Aside from the very astonishing time-travel business, Megan couldn't quite grasp how at ease each of them were. They laughed often, most of that instigated unwittingly by Cora, who possibly didn't know how curiously funny she was. They all just seemed so...not resigned, not at all; these women were improbably happy, truly happy to be here, even as they spoke at length about their families back home, those that had any to miss them. Kayla lost herself briefly yesterday, torn up with tears for missing her mom and stepdad and sister. But otherwise, and as far as Megan could tell, they'd adapted well and blissfully.

She had no plans to do the same.

She just wasn't made that way. She was definitely guilty of problematic romances and had known her share of unhealthy and unsatisfying relationships—and she might well include Graeme MacQuillan in that mix—but aside from love and romance, Megan had lived her life striving to be perfect. It had started young, of course, as soon as she realized that every family was seeking the ideal child. She was responsible and practical, was neat and clean, was not a rebel. She considered her struggles in school to have been one of her greatest failures. Except that a counselor had pointed out that it was not, since she'd made a success of it, had finished high school and had navigated the very difficult nursing program while working full time and without the support of family as most students had.

Taking up with Graeme initially—against those caution flags waving—might have been the boldest thing she'd ever done. And frankly, she was certain so many things would have gone differently if Jasmine hadn't abandoned her.

Even in a few previous relationships that had begun with more question marks than any certainty, that had ended good, bad, and ugly, she simply wasn't a person who threw caution to the wind. Though she was practical and normally decisive and unafraid of hard work, she didn't take the bull by the horns without careful consideration. Jumping in the deep end was not her style. She was a toe-dipper.

She was, therefore, simply not the type of person who would dive in head-first—*sure, I'd love to live in the fourteenth century.* Examining it with greater rationale, which admittedly she'd used little of over the past week plus, Megan determined that while Graeme might have thrilled her profusely by saying he didn't want to be without her, even that passionate admission carried no great weight. That was today, or had been yesterday, but what of tomorrow?

Closing her eyes, she willed away the melancholy. She didn't want Holly or Cora or the others to worry about her, didn't intend that her—hopefully—short-lived excursion to this century should be recalled with any grimness or sorrow.

She sat up just as a knock sounded on the door, the rapping light enough that she didn't suppose it was Graeme.

After a quick glance downward to be sure she was covered appropriately—the light nightgown they'd loaned her was surprisingly soft and comfortable—she called out "Come in," which ushered in Cora and Holly.

They wore matching expressions, hesitant and quizzical, their brows raised.

"How are you?" Holly asked.

"I'm good," she said. "I am. I'm just going to take this one day at a time."

They came further into the room then, their faces evolving to more cheer, maybe a bit relieved that they didn't have to contend with tears again today. Holly appeared to hold the clothes Megan had worn yesterday, her leggings and the pink tie-dye tee, which Cora had promised last night would be laundered.

"Great," said Cora, a long rust colored garment hanging over her arm. "Graeme wants you to—well, all of us do—want you to come down and head out to the village. You can meet Sidheag."

"The witch is here?" Christ! Why didn't someone say this yesterday?

"She is," Holly quickly assured her, "but she's not super healthy. Or she is, but apparently, as we've learned, moving a person through time saps all their strength."

Serves her right, Megan thought uncharitably.

"Like, really weakens them," Cora added. "She was nearly co-matose the first few days."

Megan's brow furrowed. "Then...she wasn't the one who moved us, if she is still weak?"

Both women shrugged. "We're not sure," Holly admitted.

"Anyway, I brought this," Cora said, lifting the rust colored fabric in both hands. "I didn't know if you wanted to blend in or....?"

"If there's any chance of going back," Megan replied, "I think I'd rather wear my own clothes, but thanks."

Cora nodded and shoved her glasses up on her nose. "I miss leggings," she lamented.

"Among other things," Holly reminded her with a grin as she set the bundle of Megan's clothes on the bed.

"Do you want us to wait for you?" Cora asked.

"Yes, please," said Megan, rising from the bed. She'd changed out of the clothes in front of them last night, didn't need privacy now to swap them again. "And please," she said as she pulled the nightgown over her head, "please don't let me alone with Graeme. I can't...I don't want to be persuaded by him or his...by anything. I want to go home."

Chapter Sixteen

Having watched Cora and Holly ascend the stairs to fetch Megan earlier, having been advised that the léine Cora Thain carried was meant for Megan, Graeme decided it was not a good sign that when Megan appeared, she was wearing her own clothes, those damnably enticing trews and that clingy soft tunic.

He'd recovered what few possessions he'd brought with him to Newburn originally, when he'd been charged with escorting Holly away from Thallane, and was thus able to freshen his own garb, returning to the comfort of the familiar breeches and tunic, his plaid once more proudly worn over his shoulder and across his chest.

Megan barely met his gaze when she entered Newburn's great hall, though his steady regard of her showed that she did sneak glances at him now and then. She appeared refreshed herself, bearing no sign that she'd cried recently, mayhap not since she'd fallen asleep in his arms last night.

Lucas, Michael, Aedan, and Duncan had all strictly forbidden that their wives be allowed to see the witch, Sidheag, whom Graeme had since been informed remained nearby, too weak to make herself gone perhaps, per the conjecture that possibly it hadn't been she who'd returned him—and Megan, too—to this time.

However, upon their arrival in the hall, Cora Thain marched purposefully to her husband, standing on her toes to whisper something at him, which wrought an immense scowl and what looked to be a swift and earnest trading of arguments. Eventually, Lucas glowered anew, curling his lip with displeasure at his petite wife, who at the end laid her hand upon his massive chest and favored him—melted him, Graeme would later presume—with a beseeching look.

"Cora will walk down to the village with us," Lucas announced stiffly in the next minute, "strictly to accompany Megan." He glared further at his wife, commanding, "But she will nae go anywhere near the witch." With a sigh, he lifted his attention to the others gathered around. "Decide for yourselves who else may or may not walk with us."

"Bluidy hell," seethed Michael, sending a scowl to his wife.

"She needs us now, Michael," said Kayla, unmoved by the severity of his countenance. "I'm going."

"Me, too," said Gabby Cameron.

"Gabrielle, ye may nae—" Aedan began, only to be silenced by the tilted head and raised brow of his wife. "God's teeth, but ye will nae step foot inside the cottage."

Duncan and Holly exchanged a look, he conceding without argument. "Same rule applies, love. I will nae take any chances."

So it was, the party of ten exited the keep and walked down the hill and off to Newburn's village, beyond those closely planted crofter's huts in the immediate shadow of the fortress. It did not escape Graeme's attention that the women formed a protective circle around Megan, as if there was some intent that he should have no access to her.

Though there was some conversation amongst those lasses, it was softly given so that none of it reached his ears and on the whole, they progressed rather quietly.

And any concern of these husbands that their wives should not enter the small but tidy cottage was all for naught when they neared the place where the witch had been kept and found her not within but sitting just outside the door, perched on a squat drum barrel, upended to be used as a stool.

Graeme recognized Sidheag immediately, having kept that form of a wretched hag he and others had been witnessed to another façade she owned, that of a much younger, less hideous woman. He did not recognize the crone sitting on the other side of the open door, similarly upon a small cask employed as a seat.

"'Tis the other one, Samara?" Graeme asked Duncan of the second old woman as they approached.

Despite the gravity of this circumstance and the purpose of their visit, Duncan grinned. "'Tis Goldie, a mortal resident of the Thain's village."

Graeme grimaced, sorry to have mistaken the ancient, possibly innocent woman for a witch.

Michael commented under his breath, "She dinna appear to be as weak as she was."

There was some warning in his remark, each of them aware of the witch's indiscriminate power.

When they stood upon the lane directly in front of the croft, the lasses were advised by wary husbands and a few motioning hands that they should proceed no further.

Knowing Megan wanted an audience, Graeme took hold of her hand and led her forward, only a few feet in front of the others. He felt a quiver of fear in her hand, the effects of it tingling along his hand and forearm. In response, he squeezed her hand comfortingly.

But she didn't look at him, her gaze trained on Sidheag. He wondered how she knew which hag was the witch but soon realized that the steady and shrewd gaze Sidheag fixed upon her might have answered any question. Goldie sat with her head bowed, her attention centered on the stick she was whittling with a small and sharp knife.

Causing chills to race up the spine of more than a few, Sidheag smiled grotesquely and said, "And here ye are, Megan."

"*Jesu,*" cursed Michael MacClellan behind them. "And ye wonder, do ye nae, why ye find your kind persecuted?"

Megan ignored him, her gaze trained on Sidheag. "You brought me here?" She asked in a firm voice, anger simmering.

"I did nae," answered Sidheag, "but I ken ye would come." She finally removed her glassy blue eyes from Megan to look at Graeme. "And ye made it back, I see."

If she hadn't brought Megan, then she certainly hadn't brought him back. "Nae thanks to ye, if ye are to be believed."

"Was right here, all this time," said Sidheag. "Goldie kens that."

"Mm," said the other crone, without lifting her head from her pointless industry.

"But how do I get back?" Megan asked.

"Ye dinna. Ye canna, nae now."

"So you're not as powerful as you pretend to be," Megan challenged tersely. "You like to play with lives but it's just that, games. You aren't capable of anything more."

Sidheag chuckled, a raspy sound, at the blatant manipulation. "I dinna play, lass. I only move people to where they should be."

"But you just said you didn't move me."

"I dinna."

"And who are you—what right do you have—to be meddling in people's lives so catastrophically?"

Sidheag moved her gaze beyond Graeme and Megan, to where four other couples stood. "I see nae tragedy."

Megan bristled. Her hand clenched Graeme's. "That is not for you or...or any of your kind to decide!"

"Nae, it isna. Fate decides this as it does that, has its hand in everything, always."

"You or whoever did this to me had no right," Megan snapped. "I want to go home. Now. You had no right—"

Sidheag waved a surprisingly strong hand, dashing it through the air dismissively, rousing Graeme's ire.

"Bah, rights," she derided. "'Tis all ye mortals speak of. Rights have no power over destiny, child."

Megan was not cowed. "How about personal choice and freedom? Do they get any say?"

Sidheag looked at her, tilting her head with some sympathetic aversion. "Choice was made, lass. Inside, at any rate. We dinna hear words so much as feel the emotions."

"Bullshit," Megan contended. "You or whoever did this didn't hear or feel any such thing. I didn't want to come here."

"Did ye nae?"

"No, I—" she paused, lifting her face to the sky.

Graeme felt it, too, some change in the air, which suddenly felt thick and agitated, as if a storm brewed. He spun around, seeing that the others noticed it as well.

"Christ Almighty," Aedan cursed.

Five swords were drawn, almost simultaneously. Behind Graeme, Sidheag snickered.

Ten gazes searched all around. Graeme saw that Goldie was barely disturbed, lifting her face but briefly before she returned to her whittling. To his eternal puzzlement, he noted that those

few people who were out and about in the village today—a pair
of women speaking at one of their doorways; two lads racing
along the lane, the trailing one hollering for the frontrunner to
wait; a stocky farmer, pushing a wheelbarrow straight toward
Goldie's cottage—gave no sign that anything was amiss, did not
acknowledge in any way even the advent of the laird and mistress
and their eight guests. It was as if they, mayhap everyone that
stood in front of this hut, were unseen presently.

As quickly as the air had changed so too did it settle.

And nothing was different, all persons still accounted for,
Megan's hand still attached to his.

Or so it seemed.

"I ken ye could nae stay away," Sidheag drawled.

Mortal eyes continued to dart around, finally rewarded by
the sight of the witch, Samara, walking out from between
Goldie's cottage and the next. She was without the illuminated
aura that had blanketed her last time Graeme had seen her, but
she was unmistakably the witch, her feet not quite touching the
ground as she pretended to walk.

Graeme pulled Megan closer to him.

"Samara!" Cora cried with obvious exasperation. "You're like
a moth to the flame, with the way you keep showing up. What
now?"

Cora was ignored.

Sidheag cackled, squinting up at Samara. "Ye've more for
which to atone, it seems. Doubly so, by the looks of it," she
added, tossing her narrowed eyes at Megan and Graeme.

"It was intended only to right the wrong you'd done, Sidheag, and bring the MacQuillan man back to the here and now.

He," Samara said with some accusation in her tone, directing her frustrated gaze at Graeme, "would not let go of her hand."

"Aye, but she felt it, the enchantment, then and now," Sidheag either guessed or somehow knew, her shrewd gaze unnerving as it sat so boldly on Megan. "Trouble brewing, nae a storm, she surmised. And she did nae want to let go. She trusted him, did nae want to release his hand any more than he did hers."

"That is not true!" Megan asserted, lunging forward, angrily shaking off Graeme's hand when he at first resisted. "Are you the one, then?" She asked Samara. "Send me back. Or reverse it, whatever you have to do to—"

"Hush, child," Sidheag infuriated many by snipping at Megan.

A moment of wide-eyed, enraged shock passed between all the mortals.

All but one.

Goldie, who'd seemed to be utterly unaffected by all the otherworldly business happening in her midst, finally spoke. "So much meddling," she observed, her voice as craggy as the beinns, not bothering to lift her head as she spoke. "Have anything to do with the ancient doctrine, passed down through the ages, that any witch who joins two mortals in love can one day earn her own humanity?" Finally, she lifted her face, passing her wizened gaze around the lairds and lasses. "Witches cannot mate," she explained, "the daughters of shadow are strictly that—daughters, women. But if—"

"Bah, legend," scoffed Sidheag.

Samara narrowed her eyes and challenged Sidheag. "Then why, old daughter, do you persist in joining each pair that is designed but broken by time?"

"Guided by the hand of Fate, same as ye."

"Mother Moireach will not agree," Samara predicted. "Hence my presence, as yours is requested by the eternal daughter."

"Have ye done nae wrong?" Sidheag asked.

"I have made my peace with Moireach," Samara contended. "You have avoided yours for too long."

"This is charming, your little family squabble," Megan said, as curt as Graeme had ever known her to be. "But is someone going to send me back where I belong or what?"

A wicked wind blew across the village, waving loose hair and flapping the ends of plaids and léines, sending a swirl of dust up from the ground, swiftly along the lane.

"Christ," fumed Duncan, "and what now?"

With only a fleeting, mutually thin-lipped glance exchanged and without any bright light or evidence of any magic, both Samara and Sidheag disappeared, their fullness dissipating, like mist scattered by a person charging through it.

Megan tossed back her head and groaned. "C'mon! Really?"

Graeme realized and appreciated her frustration but recognized at the same time all the relief shown on the faces around him. They might be sorry for Megan's dilemma, but far greater was their exultation in this respite from the presence of witches.

***

They remained three more days at Newburn, half-expecting and half-dreading the return of the witches, or at least one of them. They discussed at length, ad nauseam in fact, the perfidy of witches, the odds of their return, the chances that Megan might be granted her only wish.

Everyone was on edge and on the third day, Michael and Aedan said they would stand no more. They were off, they declared, headed to their respective homes—with some intent, Graeme was sure, to remove themselves from the place where the witches had visited and shown themselves so freely. He did not envy Lucas Thain's position, being that it was his home which they'd frequented.

Graeme said as much privately to Lucas, who reminded him, "I canna remember which of them said as much, but dinna neglect to recall that they were summoned here in the first place by the energy of the lasses. Once they disperse, I have to hope the energy will fade."

Graeme ably read between the lines. He and Duncan were invited to depart as well. He didn't blame the Thain. Lucas wanted his home back, wanted any threat removed from his much adored wife. Shortly after that conversation, Graeme consulted with Duncan about removing themselves from Newburn.

"Aye, I ken we should," Duncan agreed. "I feel for your lass, Graeme, but I'm nae keen to have Holly in the peripheral of those sorceresses." He swiped a hand over his cheek.

Graeme nodded, certainly not riled by Duncan's protectiveness regarding Holly. Despite Megan's continued coolness toward him, Graeme himself was not of a mind to make her too available to the witches.

"*Jesu*, I forgot all about the other issue confronting the Mac-Quillans," Graeme said then. "What did ye do or are ye planning for the MacHeths?" He asked of the closest neighbor to Thallane, and their most exasperating enemy, the ones who had pre-

tended Holly was Ceri MacHeth, the sister Duncan had expected to wed to instigate the end of so many petty skirmishes and
slights. "No peace now since they'd foisted a fraud onto ye as
your bride."

"Aye, and I'd nearly forgotten, with everything else going
on," Duncan acknowledged. "Nae sooner had ye left with Holly
than the lads caught three MacHeths up near the Lady Fingers
Hills, making off with a dozen cattle."

"They dinna quit," Graeme growled, incensed at their daring.
"I ken they're ailing, starving mayhap, with few prospects because of Hugh MacHeth's obnoxious character—more enemies
than allies he's made—but they just dinna learn."

"I expect they might now," Duncan remarked. "I was done
with the constant catch and release of all the miscreants he sent
about his foul work. I ken I'd done my part, but peace will nae be
ours, Graeme. I took a hand from each thief, sent them back to
Hewgill House, their hands tied around their necks."

Sadly, Graeme agreed with Duncan's assessment. "That will
nae deter him."

"I fear nae. Another reason to return to Thallane. Too long
we've been when I ken a retaliation will come."

"And maybe that's what he's been looking for all these years,"
Graeme suspected, "Pushed enough to make you act and now
he'll claim he has fair cause to embark on a grander scheme, all-
out war."

"I dinna dismiss that as a possibility." Duncan turned toward
the door to the hall. "I'll ready the lads. I'd brought Baltair and
Connor and Roari."

"Five swords," Graeme calculated. "Plenty to see us home."

"Aye. God willing." He inclined his head toward the interior of the keep. "Gather the lasses. I dinna expect ye will allow Megan to remain here—dinna ken Lucas is too keen on that."

"Not an option," Graeme informed him. "Whether Lucas is or isn't amenable to it, Megan is coming with me."

They parted company then, Graeme pursuing the second floor and Cora Thain's solar, where she and Holly and Megan had convened earlier, after saying farewell to the Camerons and MacClellans.

He rapped curtly and stepped inside at the call for entrance, finding the three ladies all sitting on the floor, Cora with a ledger in her hand, recording words with what he assumed was a pen, but which did not appear as any he had ever beheld.

"We will take our leave of Newburn, Mistress," Graeme said to Cora, who had been most gracious and sometimes disturbingly unflustered by what had transpired here over the course of a week, "and give our appreciation for your hospitality and forbearance."

As one unit, Megan, Holly, and Cora came to their feet.

"I hope you're not leaving because of anything Lucas might have said," Cora replied. "He's such a worrywart."

Holly laughed aloud at this, grinning at Cora. "Many descriptors come to mind for your husband, Cora. I assure you, worrywart is not even in the top five hundred."

Carelessly, Cora waved this off. "Well, obviously, he's magnificent in every other regard," she said with a gratified smile, "but seriously, he worries like a grandmother."

"You're impossible," Holly said, "and wonderful." She and Cora embraced fondly. "I'm going to miss you."

"Oh, gosh, me too," cooed Cora. "But I'm so happy you found us—you have Graeme to thank for that —and now we can write to each other, all of us—me and Kayla and Gabby already do. Oh, and Eloise, too. I'm sure you'll meet her soon. If you think Lucas is crazy protective, wait till you meet Nicol. Anyway, we'll happily expand our time-travelers' pen pal club to include the six of us now. You, too, Megan."

"Oh, I won't—" she started, crunching her fist at her chest. "I mean, thank you, but I'm hoping to not be here that long to have the opportunity to join your secret club." She grinned at this, her expression seemingly heartfelt.

Cora hugged her next. "Consider the invitation open ended."

"Thank you, Cora, "Megan said, holding her tightly. "For everything."

"Ooh," Cora said when all of them began to move toward Graeme at the door, "we should celebrate Christmas together! Wouldn't that be awesome?"

"Actually, it would be," Holly said. "I would like that very much. I'll ask Duncan if we can host at Thallane." Holly stopped in front of Graeme. "Did I thank you, Graeme? For having some foresight or sense that you should bring me here to Cora and not return me to the MacHeths as...was planned?"

"Ye dinna need to, of course." He lowered his head and confided, "I ken it wasn't going to be permanent, either Dunc's ire or that wee separation."

Holly patted his cheek and grinned at him before she stepped out into the corridor.

Megan hesitated, but he didn't think it was only because she would have to walk by him to exit the chamber.

"Maybe I should..." she said, wringing her hands in front of her. She tore her anguished gaze from Graeme and laid it upon Cora. "Would your husband—he probably doesn't want me here—but would—?"

"Nae, Megan," Graeme inserted firmly.

"Now wait, Graeme," Cora cautioned. "Megan, you will always be welcome here—"

"She goes where I go," Graeme insisted curtly, stepping into the room.

Cora was swayed by Megan's anguish and not by Graeme's rising fury. "But don't you think—for now at least—that it might—?"

"Nae, she comes with me."

"Does *she* get a say?" Megan asked tartly.

Graeme turned a feral frown on her, the last few days without a softening from her having soured the grand high emotions of returning home to this century. "Ye dinna. I brought ye here. Ye stay with me."

Megan surged upward, straightening her spine as she glared at him. "Not that you ever had any rights, but you certainly forfeited whatever ones you might have known when you dragged me kicking and screaming into this century."

He sneered at her. "I dinna recall so much kicking and screaming," he gritted out, "as I do the weeping and clinging."

Megan gasped. "You bastard."

He ignored the slur, having been just now a wee despicable for goading her. "Ye will abide by me. I will make sure ye return to yer precious modern world," he ground out. "I did it myself, found a way back. I'm sure I can manage it for you."

He would, he vowed. It would likely tear his heart from his chest, but he would figure out a way to give her what she claimed to want.

Chapter Seventeen

Five horses sat by seven people rode away from Newburn a wee bit later, Lucas and Cora Thain seeing them off from the gate. Megan had put up little fuss over the arrangement, saddled with him upon his easy-going destrier, having watched Holly happily be settled in front of her husband on Duncan's steed. After a tensely murmured, "I suppose I have no choice," she'd allowed Graeme to lift her onto the horse, seating her sideways, and hadn't squawked at all by the strong arm he'd placed around her waist.

Baltair and Connor rode the lead, having a good sense of their direction and route, having made the trip back and forth between Thallane and Newburn several times now. Duncan and Holly followed, their conversation low, meant to be private, Graeme understood. He and Megan were next in the short line, and Roari trailed them, lagging about twenty or so yards, his shrewd gaze no doubt in constant motion, left, right, and backwards.

"Naught but half a day, lass," he'd advised as they'd set out. "I ken you're angry yet, but I will be pleased to show ye Thallane."

Without any remark about the present condition of her ire, she had asked, "Is Thallane as big as Newburn?"

"Nearly similar in size," he'd acknowledged, "but situated differently, being cast out onto an arm above the sea."

"Thallane is on the water?" She'd asked, turning her head further toward his chest. "The North Sea?"

"Aye."

"There might be some consolation in that," she's supposed, though little hope influenced her tone. "But then, isn't the broch closer to Newburn than Thallane?"

"It is. And I've considered such. I propose we return first to Thallane and then set out again in a day or so, supplied and prepared to spend a few days at the broch so that ye might be returned home."

"Do you promise? I mean, this isn't some ploy that only hopes I'll start to like Thallane and want to stay, is it?"

"Nae, lass," Graeme had replied, his voice resigned. "I might be right peeved to discover any partiality for Thallane had swayed ye when any fondness for me had nae."

That had been hours ago, that brief exchange. Since then they'd spoken little but for Graeme's curt caution that she hang onto his arm as they descended a steep slope and then Megan asking where and when she might relieve herself before they made a short stop for those needs.

When the small party was on the move once more and Thallane but an hour away, Megan tipped her face up to Graeme, the motion seen in his lower periphery.

"It isn't that I don't have a fondness for you," she said now, returning to his earlier remark. "It's just that my anger over your high-handedness and being in this...this situation—this century—won't just evaporate."

"I've said, have I nae, that I'd get ye home?"

"You have, but really, what are the chances of that actually happening?"

"Ye might—" He stopped abruptly, noticing Baltair's hand, raised at his side, his elbow bent and hand giving the halt signal.

Graeme narrowed his eyes as Connor ducked in his saddle, peering out or at what or whom Graeme could not say. He glanced around, looking for someplace to conceal Megan, if the need arose. In the next second, just as two riders burst out from the forest through which they would trek to reach the sea before they headed north, Baltair waved his hand forward twice in quick succession, giving the sign that all was well.

Graeme recognized Boyd and Paedir, two lads from the MacQuillan army, a wee alarm raised by their arrival.

They bypassed Baltair and Connor while Graeme urged his steed ahead, coming abreast of Duncan and Holly. The newcomers drew up sharply in front of Duncan.

"MacHeths are on the move, laird," said Boyd, a trusty lad of even temperament.

"Where are they?" Duncan asked.

Boyd shrugged his slim shoulders. "Last seen just sitting, laird, out near that strawberry hill."

Little to be ascertained by that information. The place of which he spoke, where strawberries were abundant in the early summer months, sat just east of Thallane and might just be the MacHeths skirting round Thallane land to get somewhere else. Ah, but they weren't to be trusted.

"How many?" Graeme inquired.

Paedir eyed him gravely. "All of them, captain, more than a hundred possibly."

Duncan's scowl advanced. "Who watches now?"

The lad's face colored a wee bit. "That's just it, laird. 'Twas only Fergus, chasing sheep, happened upon them. He come straight back to the keep, and this morn Hendrie took a unit out to search, but they've nae returned. Boyd and I, laird, kent we best find ye in the meantime." He transferred his gaze to Graeme. "We discussed it with Roland, captain, best laid plans and whatnot, since ye were nae there."

"Ye did well, lad," Graeme allowed.

Duncan shifted his regard to Graeme, speaking his thoughts aloud. "Might be naught but them hoping to escape any reprisal as I'd alleged in the message I'd sent, returned with those thieves and their hands."

"Might be them," Graeme countered, "meaning to seize the upper hand by way of an offensive."

Duncan chewed the inside of his cheek, nodded faintly. "Aye."

"A swift pace will see us through the gates in less than an hour," Graeme remarked.

"Aye, we'll send out more units then," Duncan decided. He then addressed Boyd and Paedir. "Fall in behind Baltair there, eyes wide, heads turning."

"Aye, laird."

"Are these the same MacHeths that...?" Megan asked.

Graeme kept his steed beside Duncan and Holly, the entire group increasing their speed.

"The verra same, lass," Duncan called over as they raced toward the trees.

"This can't be good, Duncan," Holly stated, having to raise her voice to be heard over the growing thundering of hooves.

"Dinna mean it's bad, love," Duncan declared loudly.

They were forced to slow down inside the forest, Duncan calling out for Boyd and Paedir to stay back from Baltair and Connor in the lead, closer to the remaining five. Graeme knew he wanted greater protection around the lasses, just in case. They cleared the trees after only a few minutes, closer to home already. And just when Graeme was imbued with some sense that they would meet with no trouble, he saw that Baltair and Connor had stopped at the crest of a small knoll.

Graeme exchanged a speaking glance with Duncan as they rode on, catching up with the forward pair.

There was no reason for scouts to stop unless....

Unless something stood in their way ahead of them.

"God's bones," seethed Duncan, having reach the summit seconds before Graeme.

Graeme reined in next to the others, a sparce line of targets standing in front of an army, not quite a hundred strong by his calculation, but formidable nonetheless, they being only nine and having but seven swords.

The MacHeths, either having taken umbrage at the open threat Duncan had sent off to Hewgill House or believing they had nothing to lose by mounting this offensive now. Graeme might suppose that one or more of the fifty soldiers Thallane and the MacQuillan army had acquired at the wedding of Duncan to Holly, whom the MacHeths had tried to pass off as one of their own, might have been sent as a spy or had become disillusioned with the strict order and constant instruction of the MacQuillan force. He or they might have alerted Hugh MacHeth that neither Duncan nor Graeme was in residence, and they had simply gathered to wait, presumably to slay the laird and captain, disconnected upon their return, before they turned their sights on Thallane itself.

The truly sorrowful part was that Thallane was nearly visible from this location. They would have kept on, west toward the sea and then skirted north a wee bit, through the glen where the river went to the sea. It was there, that wee speck in the distance, where the land jutted out to the sea itself. He could nearly make out the towers.

"We canna fight," Duncan decided just as Roari finally caught up and joined the line atop the hillock.

"A dozen or more circling round each direction," Roari informed them. "They'll be directly behind us in just a few minutes."

"Shite," Graeme seethed.

There was no time to escape, no time to even redistribute persons on the horses, sending Holly and Megan away, back to Newburn, away from this danger. The enemy was upon them, and Graeme knew as well as Duncan did, despite the overwhelming odds, that the lasses were safer where they were. No one would defend or safeguard them so well as he and Duncan. He would breathe his last—like as not, it seemed on this day—but before that he'd do everything in his power to assure her safety.

"Best chance," Duncan presumed, "is to thin them out. Ride out in four directions. We can bust through a dozen easier than four score."

"Aye. Roari," Graeme said, swinging the lad's attention away from the enemy and over to Megan before he met Graeme's gaze. "Do ye ken you could make it back to Newburn?"

Roari patted the neck of his swift courser. "We've nae taxed this boy overmuch, sir." He appeared wholly undisturbed, either by the threat ahead of them or what he might face behind them, in a return journey. "He'll get me there, under two hours my guess."

"Nae yet," Graeme advised. "When we move, it's all at once."

"Come round, lass," Duncan said to Holly, moving his hand away from her middle, putting the reins in his right hand.

"What?" Asked Holly, wide-eyed.

As was Megan, Graeme had to imagine. Against his chest he could feel the quickening of her breathing.

"Behind me," Duncan clarified, "to allow me to wield my blade."

Graeme dismounted, confronting Megan at the same time. "Likewise, lass," he said reaching up to bring her off the horse. Quivering indeed, the reverberations of her fright felt along his hands and arms. He hugged her tightly, but just for a moment, kissing her forehead. "I'll nae let any harm come to ye, lass," he said, knowing a fleeting mournfulness. Whether or not he could preserve such a vow, this would dissolve further any wee fondness she might have felt for him once upon a time.

Without another word, he mounted again, reaching down his hand to her.

Megan's face had drained of color. She stared blankly at his hand but did not lift hers.

"Megan," he prompted, there being no time to squabble now about nonsense, how she wouldn't be in this situation if not for him.

She startled at the sound of his voice and then jerkily re-arranged her small satchel so that it crossed over her breast diagonally, the bag hanging behind her now. Without looking directly at him, she slapped her hand in his.

"Astride, lass," he advised, lifting her up behind him. "Put your arms around me," he instructed, his voice hoarse with emotion. "Put your head against my back and come what may, dinna ye let go of me."

He felt her nod against his back.

"I'm afraid, Graeme," she said in a small voice.

"As am I," he admitted. "But I meant it, Megan, they'll nae get to ye but through me."

"Please don't die," she cried.

"I dinna plan on it." He regarded the army just in front of him and the hills and glens beyond them, Thallane just beyond to the north. So close.

"Roari's going back to Newburn," Duncan said. "Connor, Boyd, see him through the line convening behind us, best ye can. Holly and I and Baltair will head directly north. Graeme, you and Megan make for the old cairn near Lundy's wall," he said, pointing due south. "Paedir, you're with your captain. I dinna need to tell ye to give the MacHeth line a wide berth. They'll have the angle on us; we need to outrun them."

"I'll head straight at them—" Baltair offered.

"Dinna be daft," Duncan said tersely.

"But laird," argued Baltair, "ye ken a great number will convene on the one coming straight at them. Fewer then to give chase."

Duncan's nostrils flared and he pointed a finger at Baltair. "Ye commit to that, and I'll kill ye myself."

When Baltair offered a reluctant nod, Duncan shifted his attention to Graeme. They shared another grim stare, both understanding and silently acknowledging that the odds were absolutely not in their favor.

"God be with ye, Dunc," Graeme said.

"And ye, Graeme."

***

With her cheek pressed against Graeme's back, Megan shared a panicked look with Holly, mounted now behind her husband, her cheek likewise plastered to his back, her expression no less grim than Megan's. Holly tried to offer a comforting smile to Megan, but it came off as only a terrified contorting of her mouth.

"Let's move," Duncan commanded, turning his horse to the right.

"MacQuillans we are," Graeme barked out. "*Nolite tradere.*"

"*Nolite tradere!*" was echoed back to him, louder and more robustly by the soldiers.

As the laird had ordered, their party did move all at once, Holly soon gone from sight as Graeme turned their horse south. They went, all of them, from zero to sixty in mere seconds, as fast as their horses could reach top speed. It was awful. With nowhere to put her feet to leverage herself, she could only hang on while she bounced wildly behind Graeme. Sadly, she wasn't sure that if she did manage to stay on the horse, that this would assure that she managed to end the day still alive.

With her face angled to the right at Graeme's back, she then had a clear view of the MacHeths' response. There was actually a bit of scrambling, as if it hadn't been pre-determined who would chase which group so that many horses crisscrossed in front of others. But soon enough, she and Graeme and Paedir were being pursued by at least a dozen mounted, screaming men, some with weapons raised, swords and axes, and more than one brandishing a long spear with a pointed metal end. She didn't think it mattered that at least none of them wielded bows and arrows, as she'd noticed several Newburn soldiers either milling about or upon the curtain wall who carried bows and quiver as part of their uniform.

Barely able to breathe, and suddenly chilled by a cold sweat of fear, Megan watched as those in pursuit, chopping at the distance between them by coming at an angle as Duncan had warned, slowly but steadily gained on them.

This, then, was her introduction to the fourteenth century. Those few days at Newburn had not been, might be viewed in hindsight as nothing more than a gentle dipping of her toes into this strange era. Even with her anger, she'd been comforted by the presence of Holly, Cora, and Graeme, too. She'd been cozy in a warm bed, had dined on unusual but tasty food, had been intrigued by the fortress that was Newburn, had even heard herself laugh a time or two in response to something Cora had said.

In retrospect, all quite...ordinary—as far as being hurled chaotically into another century could be considered such.

This, now, was not ordinary. This was beyond terrifying, was closer to a nightmare than reality, Megan's first twenty-four years on earth never having presented anything even remotely close to this as a possible circumstance she might encounter. Another reason to be super pissed at Graeme, for bringing her here. This would not have happened in her real life in the twenty-first century.

But none of it mattered now, not how or why, or what might have been.

"Graeme!" She called out a warning as the closest riding man came within twenty yards of them. Even as she'd seen no bows, no arrows, she whimpered at the thought of being impaled by a flying missile, come from behind without warning and possibly skewering straight through her into Graeme.

"Hold on, lass!" Graeme called back.

A second later the horse's feet left the ground. Megan's eyes widened and she clutched tighter at Graeme's waist, seeing a flash of a narrow gully pass beneath them. The horse faltered, the landing not entirely smooth. He didn't stumble completely but was stalled for a second struggling to keep upright and moving as Graeme no doubt was urging him to do. Oh, but those few seconds cost them dearly, the enemy and their smooth landings being able to gain yet more on them.

"Paedir!" Graeme called to the lad somewhere ahead of them. "Come about! To the fight!"

Oh my God, no!

She would have kept running until she could no more. Graeme, she supposed, was not made that way. Or possibly, he didn't like that Megan's back was exposed, the first thing one of those crazed MacHeths would come upon at the rate they were going.

He wheeled the horse around with such force, with such sharpness that Megan listed precariously to the right, nearly losing her seat. For one split second they were almost unmoving, Megan able to right herself and cling even tighter, just in time as Graeme urged the horse forward, drawing his sword as he charged at the coming horde.

What happened next was both fantastically unreal and then wholly inevitable. Horror made her squeeze her eyes tightly closed at the first startling clang of swords meeting. She wasn't sure how she could know the sound of a steel blade meeting with flesh and more gruesomely, with bone, but she heard it and understood immediately what it was, and the ugly croaking grunt that followed, given not in Graeme's voice or from his body. More alarming clashes and clanks followed, sometimes in rapid succession, Megan supposing some of those must belong to Paedir.

Graeme grunted loudly with each thrust or swipe or parry, sometimes lifting himself in the saddle, bringing Megan's arms with him. The horse beneath them moved jerkily, presumably steered by Graeme though she could not be sure, but so erratically that she was jolted left and right, and forward over Graeme's back at one point when he leaned so far forward. She would swear she heard the whoosh of a sword cleaving through the air just above her head.

And then Graeme snorted and seethed and jerked in front of her in a way he had not in the last few agonizing seconds and Megan knew he'd been struck. The horse stalled at the same time and Graeme grunted again, and Megan opened her eyes, fear choking back any sound she might have made. With her head turned to one side, she saw that two men were angling to take a stab at her, and that Graeme was moving the horse in such a way to protect her and present himself as a target instead, taking another swipe or stab and then another, beginning to slump in the saddle.

"No!!" She cried out, jerking her hands against his sides. "No! Stop! Graeme! Stop!"

He did not.

At one point, he maneuvered the horse sharply and the strike meant for her skimmed along the back of his neck, slicing the skin but not deeply, the bloody blade only inches from Megan's face.

"Stop! Please!" She implored him. "Drop your sword."

"Nae while I breathe," he said, his voice raspy.

And he would have continued, taking every thrust, half of which should have pierced her flesh and bone but did not for the way he expertly managed his steed.

Megan could not bear it, tears spilling from her eyes.

Having no idea how she might make him concede, believing he never would, she moved her hands and then pushed off from his back, desperate to put distance between her and him. As she fell she tried to dive to one side but did not find much success. She landed hard on her shoulder and hip, and immediately covered her head, aware of hooves smacking the earth very close, afraid of being trampled.

"Megan!" Graeme roared.

But he was not so close as the enemy, who were instantly upon her. Someone leapt from his horse and dragged her to her feet by her hair. How she didn't cry out, she wasn't sure. She did not fight the assault, but lifted her hands to show she would not resist, her tormented gaze looking for Graeme.

A cry burst from her when she found him, bloodied and battered, slices and cuts crisscrossing his chest, his proud plaid in tatters. His left arm and right thigh bore significant wounds, the blood soaking his breeches alarming for how wide was the oval of red.

"We give up!" She shouted. "We surrender." She lifted her hands higher, wincing as her hair was pulled tighter. She twisted and glared at the filthy ghoul of a man holding her, stomping her foot near his. "I said we give up!"

She spotted Paedir, beyond Graeme, shaking off a MacHeth who had leapt most recently at him.

The chaotic scene trudged to a halt, several medieval thugs given pause by Megan's yelling.

"Bluidy hell, Megan!" Graeme cursed as he swiped his sword to defend against a late-coming though rather lackluster attack.

Possibly, the capture of Megan had eased some of the desperation on both sides. Otherwise, the man maybe simply didn't want to tangle too completely with Graeme. Though seriously wounded, Graeme still presented a formidable combatant, his teeth bared and his proficiency with the sword obvious. Only being hugely outnumbered and giving too much thought to Megan's safety had him in the position he was in.

"Don't you *bluidy hell* me, Graeme MacQuillan!" She shouted at him through fright and tears. Her voice wobbled then, "Please, just stop."

"I will nae—"

"MacQuillan?" Repeated one of the MacHeths, his English accent thicker than any she'd heard so far, though not enough that she hadn't understood that he'd recognized the name.

He said something else, garbled Gaelic that meant nothing to Megan save that she thought she heard *Graeme MacQuillan* in there.

Graeme snapped something back, the terseness of his reply filled with a hint of resignation, his gaze simmering as he considered Megan in their control. The man who held her lifted a dagger to her throat. Megan had all she could do not to wince or bust out sobbing any more.

A heated exchange followed, a frightening one in which Graeme and the man holding her began shouting at one another, Graeme's steed dancing forward with his own agitation. The MacHeth holding the dagger at her neck shouted back, he and Graeme yelling at the same time. When the knife broke her skin, Megan honestly thought it wasn't intentional, that in the heat of the moment as the MacHeth strained to roar louder than Graeme, that he'd only nicked her inadvertently.

She knew the skin was broken but knew also that it was not deep. Still, it must have bled immediately, and Graeme blanched and growled again his rage before he tossed his sword down. In her periphery, she saw that Paedir did as well.

Megan felt she was able to breathe again. She watched as a MacHeth youth cautiously approached Graeme, holding a rope out. Graeme's fierce mien darkened yet more, truly terrifying now. He glowered but did extend his hands to the kid, who was easily a foot shorter and a decade younger than Graeme, and allowed himself to be constrained by the rope, which the Ma-cHeth soldier tied around both Graeme's hands and then to the pommel. Paedir, likewise, had his hands bound to the saddle of his horse.

They were alive, that was all that mattered. The flush of anger in Graeme's cheeks abated quickly, leaving him nearly colorless to such a degree that Megan worried about how much blood he had lost.

The MacHeth who detained her said something, again in Gaelic that it was incomprehensible, save that the tone and the contorting of Graeme's lip in response suggested he'd been taunt-ed, perhaps with something similar to: *See? Now was that so hard?*

Megan was herded away, toward the man's horse. Apparent-ly, she would be forced to ride with him. She stared as long as she could at Graeme, measuring his condition only by sight, slight-ly difficult to do without seeing the wounds up close. Graeme's gaze rested like cold steel upon her.

She found neither admiration nor appreciation for what she'd done, for having brought the fighting to a halt.

Chapter Eighteen

Having nothing else durable enough to make a racket, Megan banged her phone repeatedly, frequently, against the bars of the cage into which they'd been thrown several hours ago. The screen had cracked about twenty-minutes ago—not that it mattered here in this century. Nothing mattered but that they weren't abandoned down here indefinitely. Or even a few hours more.

She'd done what she could for Graeme, but she was terrified that it wasn't enough. Within minutes of literally being thrown into the dungeon, before he might have let her have it for provoking their surrender, Graeme had passed out. Despite several days now spent in this time period, which now fantastically included that harrowing skirmish which she'd witnessed up close and personal, this present circumstance—*being thrown into a dungeon!*—seemed absurdly farfetched, so unreal.

But here they were, beneath the ground in the gloomy depths of a dank and musty cavern carved into the rocky mountain on which sat Hewgill House, the eerie looking fortress that was home to the MacHeths.

This isn't happening, played on repeat in her head, but hadn't changed anything.

Thankfully, she'd been tossed into the same cell as Graeme while Paedir had been confined in another. Megan could hear the young man but not see him, the few cells lined up in a straight row, and there being so little light, nothing but what was cast off from a torch or candle somewhere closer to the twisting stairs and creaking door by which they'd come.

She'd been visited by an odd sense of déjà vu—there should not have been anything familiar about having a three-inch thick leg iron clamped around her ankle. And then the fleeting impression of a dream wafted across her consciousness, one she'd had weeks ago after meeting Graeme, of the two of them trapped in a dungeon.

But she'd had no time to dwell on that strangeness.

As soon as the goons who'd delivered them had gone, slamming the door behind them, the sound of a thick wooden beam sliding into place on the opposite side of that door having a terrifying finality to it, Graeme had slumped to the hard earth against the wall, tipping over until he was laying on the ground on his left side. Megan had acted immediately, undressing him down to his boxers—not without difficulty; he was very large, his dead weight incredibly heavy, the space inside the cell barely large enough for the two of them. The clunky length of the curb chain was heavy and cumbersome but was long enough that it was more an annoyance than a hindrance, except that it meant she could not remove one of Graeme's boots or that pant leg.

It felt weird to be grateful for where the sword strike had landed, but she was relieved to discover that the thigh wound, which had bled profusely, soaking so much of the leg of his breeches, had not hit the femoral artery. It was deep, though, and long, and would require stitches, but she was unable to manage that, even in some medieval MacGyver style.

She'd had nothing to work with but hand sanitizer from her purse and her underclothes. Though certainly not sterile, her underskirt was the cleanest thing worn by either her or Graeme. His plaid was filthy and also coated with blood and she'd used that only as a soft pillow. She'd made pressure dressings out of strips torn from her underskirt on his right thigh and left arm, using the hand sanitizer there and over all of the stab wounds. It wasn't enough of course, and every few minutes when she pressed her hand to his forehead, she feared she would find his cool flesh on fire with a fever. Knowing even the smallest open cuts could become infected, she monitored all of those closely—hard to do in the dim lighting— having to peak under those dressed in tourniquets regularly for any signs of swelling, irritation, or pus.

"Cease, lass," Paedir called groggily from another cell now, referring to the noise she was making with her cell phone. "They'll nae come. Ye may nae want them to, dinna ken what they might do. The longer they leave us alone, the better our chances."

"That might be true under normal circumstances, Paedir," she allowed—whatever might qualify as normal in this situation, "but not presently. Graeme needs medical care, more than the hand sanitizer." She heaved a worried sigh and let her hand holding the phone fall limp outside the cell.

She'd tried to share the small plastic bottle of hand sanitizer with Paedir for his own injuries, but they'd been unable to determine if he were two cells apart or more. Paedir had insisted Graeme's need was greater, which was true then, but for how long, Megan had wondered.

She needed better light and wanted boiling water and clean cloths as well and whatever served as antibiotic here and now. She continued banging. She didn't care if she pissed them off, didn't care if she had to sell her soul, she meant to get those things. Graeme had obviously lost quite a bit of blood. He would not get any better, but only worse, unless she was given some basic medical supplies.

Earlier, Paedir had informed her that they—their captors, the MacHeths—were unlikely to care if Graeme died. They would die eventually, all three of them, he'd told her dispassionately. "Only waiting on the when and how," Paedir had concluded an hour ago.

Megan had refused to believe this.

"If they meant to kill us, then why didn't they already?" She'd asked Paedir. "They could have, easily, out there in that field," she'd argued. "They recognized Graeme's name back there, took us as prisoners for a reason." Of course this was only a guess, a hopefully drawn conclusion based only on reason and certainly not on any experience with this sort of thing. "If Duncan and Holly got away," she said, "Surely he will come for his cousin, right? Or Roari might have reached Newburn and Lucas Thain. He will come, right?"

"'Tis a big *if,* lass," was Paedir's reply. "Ye saw all those MacHeths out there. No better chances, either the laird and the mistress or Roari escaping that army."

Since that brief conversation with Paedir, Megan naturally had time to consider that she might die. Maybe people in this time faced the possibility with an unnerving regularity—though Paedir's seeming indifference gave her little ease— but Megan could not ever remember a time in her young life that she'd had to contemplate her possible death. With clenched teeth, she'd dissected her feelings over what was now, she supposed, a distinct possibility. Of course she was terrified. Terrified the method or pain would be excruciating, horrified by the very strong possibility that when it came down to it, she might enter the afterlife pissing herself with fright. Horrendous, all of it, and then easier to consider other aspects of her expected death, such as who would ever know? Maybe she would leave the world as she'd lived in it, with few people disturbed by her presence or disappearance.

Ignoring Paedir's continued pleas for her to stop, Megan continued to clang her battered cell phone against the rusty metal bars. She did this on and off for another hour or so, intermittently checking on Graeme, her heart breaking for his condition, her worry over him being more agonizing than the prospect of death.

Her banging was loud enough that she did not hear the brace being moved or the door being opened. Only a gruffly called shout from the stairwell alerted her of someone's coming.

Naturally, she feared what trouble she might have brought to them, as Paedir had repeatedly suggested, but greater than any dread such as this, she feared for Graeme's life.

"Remember, Paedir," she said, reminding the soldier of what they'd spoken of earlier, "repeat everything I say in Gaelic.

Not one but three different men showed themselves but she didn't recognize them as any of the ones who'd taken them prisoners. Megan's resolve wavered. Instinctively, she drew her hands inside the cell, away from the bars. These men were the monsters and her hands in this instance likened to her feet outside the blankets at night. Somehow, she managed to maintain her position though. Despite a desperate want to escape any one pair of malevolent eyes squinted into the cage, Megan did not retreat further into the dimness of the cell.

A low moan sounded from Graeme behind her, his still-booted foot laying between her own right now, and Megan recalled her most anxious need, and began shouting at them.

"Do you know who this is?" She hollered at the three men, pointing behind her. "This is Graeme MacQuillan! He is cousin to Duncan MacQuillan, beloved as a brother." She paused, waiting for Paedir to announce her opening in Gaelic but he did not. "Dammit, Paedir! Tell them!"

"Lass, that's Hugh MacHeth," Paedir informed her. "He dinna—"

"Say it!" She roared. She literally roared this, scratching her throat, widening the eyes of the nearest man—Hugh MacHeth or whoever, she didn't care.

After a mumbled curse, Paedir repeated her words.

The man in front of Megan, holding her gaze, lifted one hand and curled his fingers around the bar immediately in front of Megan while he cocked a brow in Paedir's direction, seeming to listen.

Megan swallowed but did not shrivel under the evil indifference of his gaze. He looked to be in his late fifties, with an incredibly wide and tall head that did not at all fit his body, he being only about as tall as Megan and just as narrow. He looked top heavy, in danger of tipping over.

When Paedir stopped speaking, Megan continued, her tone clipped, pretending at least that she knew no fear.

"If he dies, the laird of Thallane will not go easy on you," she promised the man in front of her, pointing her finger at him. "Assuming you didn't kill him to use him in some fashion—ransom or to make better terms for yourselves—you better make sure he stays alive." She paused while Paedir once more translated.

"If Duncan MacQuillan's closest kin is killed by the MacHeths, what trouble you thought you had previously with the MacQuillans will seem like child's play, I promise you."

When this, too, was translated, the man made a face to say he did not care and waved his hand impatiently, speaking swiftly and gruffly in his language.

Megan ignored him and Paedir's slow-coming translation into English. In her frustration, she lunged forward and banged her phone again on the bars, wanting his attention.

"I don't give a shit what you're saying, asshole! I need medicine and—" she stopped.

Because the man who was Hugh MacHeth had startled and jumped back, his arms bent at the elbows, his mouth opening swiftly and wide as he stared at Megan. The two minions behind him dropped their jaws as well, their gazes fixed in her direction. In the first split second of confusion, she thought for sure Graeme, in all his naked glory—boxers and lone boot notwithstanding—had risen up like an avenging angel behind her. Surely that was what had spooked the MacHeth trio.

Megan turned, finding Graeme still on the ground, unconscious. As she turned a small bit of light turned with her. It was coming from her hand. Inexplicably, her phone had turned on. Inexplicable because the battery had been dead for days. Having held it so rigidly, banging it so hard, she must have been squeezing the power button on the side. As stunned as Hugh MacHeth, though not for the same reason, she considered the fear she'd seen in his eyes and turned back around, facing him. She grinned, as wickedly as she could when she saw he maintained his stiff, guarded posture.

The screen had changed from the bright white light that came whenever it turned on, to the screen asking for her pin code. Assuming she might have seconds only before the stupid, unpredictable thing died again, she went directly to her music app and clicked on the first thing she found on the home page there, which were the same songs she'd listened to days ago while drying her hair, which happened to be not just audio but a video, a rousing Pink song, taken from one of her concerts.

Megan pushed the phone through the bars, knowing an evil satisfaction when Hugh and his minions backed up a bit more. She curled her lip as she'd seen Graeme do a hundred times by now.

"Paedir," she said levelly, "what I say next is extremely important. Translate it word for word, best you can. Give plenty of urgency to your tone. Do you understand me?"

"Aye," he said, a wee bit of hesitation heard.

"We have one chance here to save Graeme's life, Paedir. Repeat after me."

"Aye, lass."

"Tell him I can't step outside this cell, but my magic can." She continued to hold the wary gaze of the MacHeth while she spoke and Paedir interpreted. "Set us free before hellfire is rained down upon you," she invented, desperately wishing she watched more sci-fi or whatever genre of tv would have helped her to make up this crap. Hugh balked at this. Even as terrified as he was, he shook his head frantically. He would not release them. "Then you had better hope that Graeme MacQuillan does not die. If he does, then so shall you, Hugh MacHeth." Possibly having forgotten that she knew who he was because Paedir had only moments ago announced his name, Hugh MacHeth jerked his gaze from the video on the phone to Megan, as if he wondered where she'd come by this information. Anxious that her phone might quit any second, Megan waved it around dramatically and turned it off herself, with some tiny hope that the nitwit thought she was powerful. "Tell him," she instructed Paedir, "that I need either a healer, or a kettle of boiling water, clean rags—er, cloths— and whatever the word is for salve or an ointment to prevent fever. Tell him I need it now or that he, Hugh MacHeth, will die."

Paedir spoke fast, the words so rushed Megan hoped he didn't screw it up. He hadn't quite finished when Hugh MacHeth began to shake his head wildly and turned and fled from the dungeons. His companions bounded after him.

Just like that. No evil guy presenting his philosophy or purpose to the uninformed audience, no returned threat of greater harm or violence. He simply turned and ran.

"Get me some hot water, you bastard!" She screamed after him. "Send me a healer! Duncan MacQuillan will murder you slowly and...and gruesomely if his cousin dies! Or I will! Me and my magic!"

Megan's head drooped, slumping against the bars when only silence answered her.

"Lass," Paedir's voice came to her after a few moments, "what...what magic did ye threaten him with?"

"It's not exactly magic, Paedir," she said wearily, and was quick to assure him. "It can't harm you or us at all, I promise you. If we get out of here I'll happily show you." Provided her battery didn't go dead once more.

Having failed in her mission, assuming there would be no return visit where she might resort to begging, Megan dragged her chain backward and sat with Graeme, replacing the plaid pillow with her thighs, running her fingers through his hair in the darkness.

He was cool to the touch and so very still.

Quietly, Megan murmured a prayer to God. "Please, I'll do anything. I'll stay here. I'll go back. I'll reform or repent or...or start going to church, to confession, whatever You want me to do. Please let him live."

Supposing the chances of God listening to her when she hadn't spoken to Him in years might be slim, she pleaded instead with Graeme himself. "I hope you can hear me," she whispered in the stillness of their prison. "I'm not angry. Please don't die with my stupid anger the last thing you know of me. I can't lose you, Graeme. You're the only person I've ever....please don't die."

She realized that something was true now that never before had been with any other person. She feared losing Graeme as she never had another. Not that any of them had ever been close to dying in her arms, but had such an unlikely thing ever occurred, she was sure—absolutely positive—she'd have mourned only the loss of life and not the loss of love, of potential, of days and months and years denied them, of smiles she'd no longer see and a beloved deep voice she'd never hear again, of arms that could no longer hold her.

Her dawning understanding came slowly, but when it finally came, it crashed into her, filling her with an untimely, shaking light-heartedness. She was wracked by the joy of it and then knew a dreadful sorrow, for having realized this perhaps too late. She was seized by a want to tell him.

"I love you," she said, unable to recall if she'd ever spoken those words before to any other person. A giddy laugh erupted, and she said it again, filled with wonder. "I love you. I should have told you. I've never said that to anyone in my entire life. I've never...I've never felt that. I should have told you."

It was true.

Possibly, she loved her grandmother—as much as a young child could—but she didn't recall. Several times she'd convinced herself she'd been in love but had quickly discovered the truth about herself and her supposed condition—at the time, she thought she simply wasn't capable of it. She'd been in love with the idea of a certain guy or in love with the idea of having a relationship, a person of her own. The truth had fought for recognition pretty quickly in those few instances. She was, until Graeme, emotionally still a virgin. Certainly, what she felt now for Graeme shed more light on any previous relationship, any previous supposition that her emotions toward someone had been love. No, it had not. None of that, before Graeme, had been so raw, gripping with sharp talons at her chest. None of that had been so glorious, warming her from the inside, making her feel cherished as he had in those idyllic days before they'd gone back in time.

The orphan without a family had finally found her person. The fact that he happened to be from another century almost made sense, why she'd so often felt lost in her own time. Maybe it was never really hers anyway.

This was where she needed to be. With Graeme.

The most beautiful thing about this revelation was that it felt good. She was at peace with it, at peace with some heretofore unrealized knowledge that everything was going to be just fine. Graeme was going to be just fine.

It came with such decisiveness, with such clarity, that her anxiety was washed away nearly completely.

She told him so. "All is well, Graeme. Sleep now, get your strength back. We have our whole lives ahead of us." She wasn't sure where the knowledge came from—their circumstance did seem pretty dire right now.

But no, it was not. With knowledge came peace. With love came peace. And with peace came certainty.

She just knew.

Megan drew a deep breath and gently smoothed her fingertips over his temples, her eyes once more accustomed to the gloom of their prison cell. She traced her fingers down over lines on his face, those bracketing his mouth, the crow's feet at the corners of his eyes, the corded vein in his neck. She glanced at his chest and arms, zigzagged with fresh wounds, his arm wrapped in a linen strip from her shift. She would learn all these new scars, trace patterns across them as she had over his old ones.

War was this life, *his* life. His valor and sacrifice today, his want to protect her at all costs, colored in the picture of him for her. She was pretty sure that he must be in love with her, too. He was not without honor, would never have kidnapped her in time the way he had—that was an ugly way to describe what he'd done—if he hadn't feared letting her go, same as she did now. Possibly he'd been as desperate then as she felt now, willing to do anything to not lose him. And he would have died today for her, to save her.

She would give him serious grief for this. His death likely would not have saved her. He must never do that again. But he would, if warranted, she just knew. He was just made that way.

Still, she would yell at him. She didn't want a knight in shining armor to save her, to give up his life for hers. She wanted to love this knight for a long, long time.

Graeme lifted his dirtied and bloody hand from where it sat on his chest. His eyes were closed. His hand moved slowly, his fingers twitching as if he were searching for something. Megan twined her fingers with his. Graeme closed his hand around hers and it moved no more, just held hers.

At length, his lashes fluttered though he did not open his eyes.

"If I dinna die, will ye tell me again?" He asked in a low, raspy voice. "Or will ye rescind the declaration?"

Another quiet, happy laugh burst from her. "I will tell you every day, all my life. I am in love with you."

He was very weak, groggy yet, his words sluggish. "Most convenient, lass. I dinna want to be the only one in love."

Megan closed her eyes and wept, her joy unbound. The feeling was warm and wonderful, gushing upward from her belly, settling serenely inside her chest.

So this is love.

He slept again, weak yet. She felt confident he hadn't lost consciousness. Graeme's pulse was steady, his flesh was warm though not dangerously so. Occasionally his fingers tightened around her hand.

She called out to Paedir when she'd heard nothing for a while.

"Aye, lass," came his voice, strong but weary. "Aul guid here."

Sometime later, Megan could not say how long, not how long since she'd told Graeme she loved him or even how many hours they'd been locked in this cell, there arose above their heads a muffled rumbling of noise. She thought it sounded like people running. Someone screamed. There was a loud crash. The sounds came slowly, not all packed one on top of another.

Assuming they might be under Hewgill House's great hall, she wondered if it were simply the MacHeths gathering for supper. Surely enough hours had passed from when they'd been taken around noon that it might be the dinner hour.

Another booming thud was heard, and then felt as bits of dirt and brittle rock pieces were shaken and dropped from the ceiling over her head and from the walls around them.

A thunderous voice roared overhead, widening Megan's eyes. Graeme did not open his.

"Paedir?"

"Come the MacQuillans or come the Thains," Paedir predicted, his tone risen with some excitement.

A chain rattled nearby. Megan pictured Paedir darting toward the front of his cell, squeezing his face anxiously between the iron bars.

"Aye, they come," he said. "Victory is nigh. They canna lose now, nae if they've gotten as far as the keep."

More crashes, screams, and thuds were heard overhead, Megan's eyes glued to the dirt crusted ceiling except for when she had to lower them, blinking away falling debris.

It felt like an eternity but possibly wasn't more than five minutes from that first unerring sound until the barred door to the dungeons was opened.

"Graeme!" Was shouted down the stairs before any person showed himself.

Megan thought for sure the powerful, resonating voice belonged to Lucas Thain.

"Here!" She called out at the same time Paedir cried, "Aye, aye!"

Graeme was woken by the disturbance, as several men crowded into the open space in front of the cells. One of them carried a torch, the light blinding. Megan lifted her free hand in front of her eyes.

"Christ Almighty," someone cursed.

Lucas Thain, indeed.

"Where's the bluidy key?" He barked.

Metal rattled.

"Duncan? Holly?" Megan asked, as relief for their own circumstance flooded her.

"Looks like Graeme here, his laird," Lucas Thain said as one of his soldiers hastily attempted to unlock the cell, one key at a time, the large ring containing many keys. "Nae worse, nae better, though they had made it nearly to Thallane. The lass was unharmed."

"Oh, thank God."

"Took ye long enough," Graeme remarked sleepily, not so much enlivened, as if this, his rescue, were an everyday occurrence.

"*Jesu*, mate, but I wanted to finish the noon meal ere I took off to rescue your sorry arse," Lucas Thain quipped.

"Aye," retorted Graeme. "I ken Cora bid ye to digest first, avenge later."

Lucas Thain chuckled at this just as the key was finally located, the lock mechanism turning, the gate opened.

"She was, ye ken, running along beside me from the door, thrusting my sword at me," the Thain said as he entered the cell, "persuading me to hasten."

Megan smiled at this, relief coming in a burst then. Tears fell abundantly, making fresh tracks down her cheeks.

Even as Graeme was carefully lifted from her lap by Lucas Thain and his soldiers, he did not let go of her hand.

"Ye canna take it back, lass," he said, his drowsy eyes capturing her watery gaze, "just because we're saved."

"I don't want to," Megan told him confidently. "I like the way it feels."

Epilogue

Thallane
Three months later

He sat upon his destrier under a cloudy gray sky at the peak of the hillock that separated the keep from the village.

Rain would come, he thought, and soon. The light breeze that had stirred the dry grass and shaken brittle autumn leaves from trees all morning was more unruly now, swirling bits of dust from the barren, harvested field into cyclones not far from where he'd paused.

He stared down into the glen where sat the village, his gaze arrested by the sight of Megan making her way back from the loch, where in the fringe edible roots and nuts were regularly found. Holly walked beside her, each with a basket hung and swaying from their arm. They turned around the last cottage and made for the third one upon that lane, which he'd shared with Megan for the last several months, knowing more joy in that small amount of time than he had at any other time in his life, he was sure. As captain of the MacQuillan army, he'd spent the last dozen years living inside the barracks attached to the gatehouse, not unhappily, but those days were now done. As immediate kin to the laird of Thallane and now wed, he'd been invited to take a chamber inside the keep but he'd been persuaded otherwise by Megan, who'd reasoned that she rather liked the idea of her own home with him. He did, too.

With Hugh MacHeth killed by Lucas Thain in the skirmish to see Graeme and Megan freed, Duncan had offered Graeme Hewgill House as a residence. Graeme wanted nothing to do with the fortress built into the mountain. Too long had the MacHeths spewed from that stone stronghold to confound the MacQuillans. He didn't want to breathe the same air as any MacHeth ever had. Duncan had instead garrisoned half the McQuillan soldiers there, merging that fortress under the MacQuillan banner. It was done now, the MacHeths were no more.

Graeme was not close enough now to see much detail, but he needn't be; he knew Megan's shape and her face and every inch of her beautiful body by heart.

Megan and Holly stood for some time just outside their cottage door, long enough that each of them eventually moved the baskets off their arms, settling them on their hips. *Girl talk* is what they were about, he guessed, as Megan had recently advised when he'd asked what she and Holly talked about, so much time spent together, so little of that with their mouths unmoving. Most of his conversations began and ended with only a few succinct phrases, all the necessary elements conveyed or received. He could find no fault with it, pleased to see that once she'd accepted what Fate had in mind for her, how enthusiastically she'd embraced life here at Thallane.

More than once, from both Megan and Holly, he'd been told that they were pleased to have another to go about with, learning the same things at the same time, since Holly hadn't been here so much longer than Megan to have absorbed everything a mistress needed to know about running so large a keep. They were found together often throughout the day, in the kitchens, in the yard with the washerwomen, in the village at the brewer's hut, in the herb garden behind the keep. Last week, Duncan and Graeme had led an excursion to the market town, which Graeme had realized was the twenty-first century Fort William.

He couldn't recall the last time he'd known pleasure over something seemingly so trivial as a lass finding delight in so many sights and sounds as Megan had at the market. He had that day, his chest expanding each time Megan thrilled vocally over a vendor's wares or when she'd cooed expressively over the sweetmeats they'd shared. She'd been animated and so vibrant, her smile nearly a constant thing. She'd walked shoulder to shoulder with Holly for part of the day and for a while had walked beside Graeme, threading her arm through his. "I'm so happy to share this with you."

At Thallane days later, when Red Moll in the kitchen had burned her hand so severely that blisters rose more than an inch high on her palm, and Kennera could not be found, Graeme had summoned Megan. She'd tended and treated both Red Moll and her wound with startling efficiency, having returned every day for more than a week about some business to keep Moll from losing any mobility in her hand. At Graeme's questioning of this extended care, she explained it further to him. "If you're hand was injured, Graeme—the one that handles your sword—and it didn't heal right and was tight and painful, that would effect how well you wielded your sword, wouldn't it? Same for Moll, she uses her hands all day long, constantly stirring and chopping and whatever. She would know increasing pain with any little task if it's not treated properly now."

She'd since been summoned often as a healer, cleaning and treating small scrapes and cuts, setting a stable lad's broken arm, plucking slivers from the thumb of the wee lad, Dawy. She didn't believe it a curse, but Graeme was a wee miffed at times for people banging at all hours upon their door, seeking Megan's restoring expertise.

Acclimating well, he'd proudly determined, save for in one area.

She would never, he would be the first to admit, be a fine horsewoman. Capable was the most she might ever attain. Graceful might be her walk and delicately elegant might be some of their lovemaking, but her riding was another matter altogether, one that frustrated her almost to the point of madness. Telling her it didn't matter, she hadn't so many places to go, had not appeased her in any way but had reinvigorated her want to find success in the saddle.

"If it's expected that I will spend all the rest of my days right here in this place, on this ground, and in this cottage, Graeme," she'd said to him weeks ago, "I will tell you you've got another thing coming. You still owe me a tour of Scotland, which you robbed from me by hi-jacking my vacation. So I'm going to learn to ride if it kills me, and then you'll have no excuse not to take me places. I want to see everything there is."

He didn't understand Megan at all times, though language was rarely a barrier. Things that shouldn't have upset her did, such as her first attempt at a meal inside the kitchen of their cottage. The venison procured from the keep's kitchens had been tough, and Graeme had been forced to twist his face and mouth, attempting to break the small chunk with his teeth. His wee chuckling over this had made her smack down her kitchen cloth, which was regularly found over her shoulder while she labored, telling him she'd tried, and he could make his own supper.

Quickly turned around she'd been then, Graeme chasing away her wee distress with a warm embrace and profuse apologies.

And then one day she'd tumbled off the mare she was learning on, tumbled hard, feet thrown over her head—hard enough to stop Graeme's heart for the space of a second. She should have cried then, should have been wary of returning to the saddle. Nae, Megan had brushed off Graeme's help, had brushed off her bottom as well, and had scolded the mare for her rudeness, climbing right back on.

"If I can ride a bike and dissect a pig without a lab partner," she'd grumbled, "and hop up on a gurney to stop a GSW victim from bleeding out, I can damn well ride a horse."

She couldn't, of course. Not well, but she would get there, he had no doubt.

Holly finally ambled away, leaving Megan alone at their doorstep. She retrieved the basket she'd eventually set down on the ground and made to turn toward the door, pausing then, seeming to glance his way. He suspected he was silhouetted up on the hill, with naught but gray sky beyond him, and wondered if she would recognize him from this distance—wondering if she would acknowledge him at all after their little spat this morn, when he'd informed her he'd be gone for a few days down to Glasgow and no, she couldn't go with him.

Apparently she was over that vexation. Presently, she lifted her free hand to her lips and made a show of kissing her fingers and letting her hand fly away. She did this several times, throwing him kisses, her motions subsequently becoming more enthusiastic until she was fair bouncing on her feet, sending love his way.

Graeme chuckled at her antics and knew a pleasant warmth in the middle of his chest.

Nae, little did he understand her, but aye, there was joy to be had in the learning.

He clucked at his horse and kicked gently at his flanks, making his way toward Megan.

***

Lodge of the Loch
September, 2022

Autumn Winters sat in the chair near the window and balcony of Room 203, her elbows resting on the arm of the chair, her perfectly manicured fingers tapping a steady beat on the edge. She'd been here, in this spot, for more than twenty minutes, having only just checked in this morning.

The hotel room was non-descript, a worn commercial Berber carpet covered all the floor but the entry and bathroom. A pair of uninspired solid blue quilts covered the two queen beds. The furniture, this table and chair included, was dated but not attractive enough to have been considered vintage. The artwork on the walls was rather pedestrian, some wannabe photographer's prints of local scenery, hung poorly—crookedly in one instance—in cheap frames with no mats, small pictures lost on large walls.

And the police had, according to Janet McLaren, the middle-aged, thin lipped woman in the hotel's office, combed over every inch of this 300 square foot space for more than three weeks, leaving Autumn with little which to investigate. The room had only been released as a crime scene ten days ago. Autumn had been calling for three months trying to book this very room.

Megan West might have sat in this very chair, she thought.

And now I am. A prickling sensation raised the hair on the back of her neck.

Autumn ignored this. She was a reporter for the WGRN news station in Des Plaines, Il, the junior-most member and rising star of the investigative team. She dealt with facts and evidence, not prickling sensations.

It was only a lucky break that had landed her this sensational story—an opportunity—having met with Jasmine Lane, who for some time had been enjoying her fifteen minutes of fame. Had been, that is, until it was discovered that she was not merely the friend-in-mourning of the most recent missing American woman in Scotland, but instead was the shitty friend who'd made plans with Megan to vacation in Scotland, only to invite her boyfriend along once they'd landed. By all accounts—interviews with the glaring Janet McLaren, the driver Jasmine and her boyfriend had hired, and then the (now ex-)boyfriend himself, currently known around the world as McSteamy 2.0—Jasmine had dumped Megan, had gone down to Edinburgh with McSteamy 2.0 and had left Megan alone here. Alone, that is, save for the 'weird hot guy' that the entire English speaking world was looking for, an e-fit of him seen almost every hour on any channel in any country, he being the very first solid tip authorities had as a lead to follow after all these years of women going missing. But Graeme—MacSomething, according to Jasmine—was a phantom.

Autumn had interviewed Jasmine for the local news shortly after her arrival in Chicago. That had been before the truth had been made known, about how she'd ditched her friend. Jasmine's fleeting love of the camera had crumbled. She'd barely spoken to a soul since, hadn't worked, hadn't gone out, had changed her phone number. Having met her, having built a fairly basic rapport with her, Autumn had written her a letter, asking her if she'd like to tell her story once more. She invited her to take the opportunity to explain what had really happened with her separating from Megan in Scotland, and not let the public at large fill in the blanks so uncharitably on social media, where Jasmine Lane was daily fodder for even those who weren't fanatics about the cases. Honestly, Autumn had been surprised when Jasmine had called her. In tears, she asked for Autumn to help her.

Autumn glanced down at the journal in her lap.

Megan West's journal. Which Jasmine had hidden from the police.

To her credit, Jasmine Lane *had been* concerned for her friend when she'd not arrived at the airport on the date and at the hour of their scheduled flight. Belatedly bit by the guilty conscience bug, Jasmine had missed her own flight to return to this inn to locate Megan, she being the first and for a while, the only person to see Megan's small notebook.

"I didn't want them to think she was crazy," Jasmine had said when she'd shown Autumn the small greeting card size notebook.

Autumn didn't blame her.

"I didn't want them *not* to look for her," Jasmine had cried—earnestly and unattractively cried; she'd probably been thankful she'd only agreed to meet with Autumn off camera.

It had been the right call to make.

Autumn still didn't know what to make of the words on the first page, the only page that had been used.

Reasons To Go back in Time with Graeme and *Just do it. Be brave. Take a chance. Go to the ruins of the broch with him and go back to the fourteenth century!* did not inspire confidence that the person they were looking for wasn't simply in need of meds, that she wasn't strung out somewhere, needing not only to be found but in greater need of medical attention.

Of course, it was as puzzling as it was fantastic, and there was no way Autumn wouldn't be using it in her story, once she was ready to unveil the bombshell. But for now, she wanted to dig around a bit, maybe discover if the words could possibly mean anything else but what they appeared to fantastically imply.

Having learned little from the sterilized hotel room, Autumn stood and collected her shiny gold rolling suitcase. It was tiresome, always lugging it around, but she needed it. Inside was her small digital camcorder, her regular digital camera, her laptop, several steno books and an entire pouch of her favorite ergonomic roller-ball pens. She smoothed down her taupe pencil skirt and yanked on the hem of the matching jacket—not navy, she wasn't a politician; not gray, she wasn't an attorney—and paused at the bathroom mirror to freshen her Yves Saint Laurent lipstick—Conflicting Crimson, which was best suited to her coloring and showed well on camera. She examined the rest of her face and hair, giving a quick spray to her blonde hair, hoping it wasn't too windy outside.

The three-inch heels of her designer shoes tapped along the tiled floor and then were muffled on the short-pile carpet of the hallway as she made her way downstairs, taking the tiny and dubious elevator.

Janet McLaren was no more pleased to see her now than she had been an hour ago—"the inn is nae a tourist attraction, Ms. Winters" had been her reply when Autumn had asked if she might be shown around, to places Megan West had visited.

Presently, pretending she had no agenda at all, Autumn asked if there were any ruins of brochs nearby that she might visit. Twenty minutes later, having wasted much of that time explaining to Janet McLaren all the reasons she was not prepared to "find my way on a bicycle", Autumn had a semi-detailed hand-drawn map from the grumbling woman, illustrating how she could get there by car.

She tossed her rolling luggage into the backseat and set out in her rental car, having quickly grown accustomed to driving on the left side of the road, as the drive from the airport to this inn had taken several hours. After thirty minutes, a few wrong turns, and nearly getting stuck while backing out of a muddy trail that was not a road, Autumn finally found the ruins.

She pulled off to the side of the road, hoping the car didn't get swiped or smashed by someone speeding around that last bend on this very narrow road and stared out her window, up the hill at the ruins. Brochs, she'd since learned after a bit of internet searching, were found only in Scotland and were thought to be from the Iron Age, roundhouse totems to Scotland's prehistory. Having no idea how much daylight she might have, she exited the car, retrieved her luggage, and wheeled that up the hill, having to walk on her toes to prevent her heels from sinking into the marshy ground.

As far as tourist-y things went, she considered this one unimpressive. Of course the age of it was remarkable for having stood for so long, minus the collapsing front half, but it was rather bleak, gray and overgrown, no care taken with the vegetation surrounding it.

And yet as she neared it, she...felt it. Or felt something. She was not a history buff, didn't get excited over ancient things, was more apt to be wowed by the performance of a fine orchestra or the display at an art gallery, or perhaps be impressed by a more modern castle or mansion, so she wasn't sure what she felt was any reaction to the site, to its mysterious history.

Still, there was a current, some altering of the air or the way she perceived it. Suddenly and just here within only a few feet of the broch, the air had a distinct richness and depth. Or maybe she had simply failed to notice the air in Scotland until now, she could not be sure, but then could not discount that this present awareness left her a little rattled.

She turned away from the ruins, meaning to grab her camera and take a few pictures before she scoured the area, looking for anything that might clarify Megan's cryptic words in her journal.

As Autumn turned her back to the ruins, she felt a greater, inexplicable, creeping consciousness, this one larger and more urgent, lifting not only the hair at her nape but also the ones on her arms.

"Hello...?" She called out weakly, her hand clutched on the handle of her luggage.

She was alone. There was no one around here.

No one spoke.

And yet she clearly heard—felt, actually—someone say, "Dinna go, lass. He's coming for ye."

***

September 1303
Near Inverness, Scotland

Clumps of peat were furiously kicked up and just as swiftly flopped back down, the ground disturbed by the bruising pace set by Magnus McInnes. No sooner had bits settled than they were agitated just as violently by the thundering army that followed in his wake.

"There!" Called out Inan, riding closest to Magnus. "The glint in the trees!"

Aye, Magnus saw it, and supposed as Inan did that it might well be a reflection of the bright sunlight off the sword of any one of the callous marauders who'd just visited an unholiness upon the wretched souls of the Darrie village, the attack carried out while the Nicholson army was away.

Magnus' lip curled as he spurred his destrier on. He would show no mercy, would grant no quarter, just as they'd done inside Darrie. He'd leave their bodies to rot in the autumn sun, would mark them with black soot as traitors to humanity—making war on their own bloody people!—would incite the devil to collect their souls before any feeble-minded angel might take pity on their faithless carcasses.

Inan cursed something unintelligible and then exhorted the army behind them, "By my oath and my order, lads! No mercy! Naught but death!"

The victors would now become the vanquished.

Compelled to larger urgency by these words, several of the McInnes archers let loose as they rode, wild volleys meant not as warning—they would not be allowed to escape—but as a hint of the might and power of the McInnes army. They would bring hell to those raiders, who would find no place to disappear, no escape inside the forest of pines into which they'd apparently gone. Another arced stream of missiles flew overhead while they were still a hundred yards out.

Magnus narrowed his eyes, a wee surprised that even through the dense boughs of greenery he detected no scattered movement, saw not one more glint of sun off steel, could discern no figures scrambling for cover or incited to flight.

Damn, but they might be further behind them than they'd guessed.

Straightening in the saddle, slowing his mount to be able to navigate the trees without mishap or misstep, Magnus was the first to enter the forest, and had progressed not more than fifty more yards when he was brought to a crashing halt by the sight before him.

So vigorously did Magnus jerk on the reins that the destrier's front hooves were lifted off the ground. The steed shook his head with displeasure, but Magnus paid him no mind, unable to lend consideration to anything but the apparition that stood directly in front of him.

A woman....

Or a ghostly specter of one. Oddly garbed and seemingly unruffled by the coming of his army though already she was apparently a victim of its furious reprisal for the harm done at Darrie.

While his army came to a crashing halt all around him, he met and held the bright but stricken gray eyes of the woman. Her peculiar fawn-colored garb, indecently bared legs, and the unusual gold box attached to her white-knuckled hand by way of a black metal rod were of little significance presently.

Nae, the arrow protruding from her left shoulder and the circle of vivid red blood growing larger around it, darkening her fawn surcote, was what held so much of his attention.

"Blessed Màthair of God," Inan breathed at his side.

Magnus grunted. "Whatever she is or nae, she is nae that, mate."

The End

Read Magnus and Autumn's story in *When & Where*,
Coming Soon.

Far From Home: A Scottish Time-Travel Romance
And Be My Love
Eternal Summer
Crazy In Love
Beyond Dreams
Only The Brave
When & Where
Get the Free Novella (Nicol and Eloise's story) by signing up to my Newsletter
A Year of Days

Other Books by Rebecca Ruger

Highlander: The Legends
The Beast of Lismore Abbey
The Lion of Blacklaw Tower
The Scoundrel of Beauly Glen
The Wolf of Carnoch Cross
The Blackguard of Windless Woods
The Devil of Helburn by the Sea
The Knave of Elmwood Keep
The Dragon of Lochlan Hall
The Maverick of Leslie House

The Brute of Mearley Hold
The Rebel of Lochaber Forest
The Avenger of Castle Wick

Heart of a Highlander Series
Heart of Shadows
Heart of Stone
Heart of Fire
Heart of Iron
Heart of Winter
Heart of Ice
The Highlander Heroes Series
The Touch of Her Hand
The Memory of Her Kiss
The Shadow of Her Smile
The Depths of Her Soul
The Truth of Her Heart
The Love of Her Life

Sign-Up for My Newsletter and hear about all the upcoming books.
www.rebeccaruger.com

.

Made in the USA
Columbia, SC
05 June 2023

17672759R00193